A Hint of Witchcraft

Also by Anna Gilbert

A Hint of
Witchcraft

ANNA GILBERT

www.stmartins.com

ISBN 0-312-19984-8

First published in Great Britain by Robert Hale Limited

First U.S. Edition: August 2000

10 9 8 7 6 5 4 3 2 1

CHAPTER I

Blinds were drawn at all the windows. The shrouded panes – always ruddy with firelight when she came home from school in the winter dusk – were a reminder that the house was empty: she was free to linger in the shade by the side door, remembering those others who had gone in and out.

Skirting a damp patch by the water butt, she came round into the sunshine and walked slowly down to the front gate. The low-leaning pear tree had shed its petals on the path. Soon wild roses, intruders from the lane, would mantle the high garden wall. The old gate with its rustic arch had gone.

The arch had been a rickety affair: a ridiculous thing to have over a gate, her father said, without ever bringing himself to get rid of it. As a child she could look up and see within its curve segments of sky wreathed in a tangle of clematis. The side pieces enclosed a view of the Dene and central to the view, between the trees, the War Memorial.

As she grew taller, the memorial had grown too but with much less ease, its growth impeded by disputes and lack of funds. And yet the long-delayed day of its dedication had marked not only an end but a beginning: it was the day when they all came together for the first time. Margot's smile was wistful. Could it have stolen in already on that first day, the threat of change, bringing an altered mood, a shift of influence imperceptible at first as a hair-line crack in porcelain? So soon?

It was a morning in April 1923: early sunshine promising a bright day; trees turning green; wall-flowers opening; birds singing; every omen favourable.

True, Margot herself had been bothered by a possible awkwardness.

'Suppose they arrive while we're still at the ceremony. There won't be anyone here, not even in the kitchen.'

It would be over in less than an hour, she was told, and the Greys would not arrive before twelve. In any case they would find the front door unlocked and lunch – cold tongue, ham and salads – all ready laid in the dining-room.

'Like that ship. The *Marie Celeste*. They'll think we're all dead.'

'Your friends are not blind, I presume.' Alex swallowed the last of a purloined hard-boiled egg. 'Or too short-sighted to see the entire population of Ashlaw, Hope Carr and Fellside assembled at the monument directly opposite our gate.'

'Of course not.'

It was the second time she had come downstairs to join the others in the hall. The first time she had been wearing her white dress. Practically every girl in England had a white dress for special occasions. Even the poorest families had one to be shared among sisters. She had been sent back to change.

'Your navy kilt and blouse.' Her mother was firm. 'It isn't summer or a party.'

It was no use trying to explain; they didn't know Linden. When they saw her, they would realize that her first visit ranked as an experience every bit as special as a party, though in a different way: a more refined and elegant way.

'This is an occasion for solemnity.' Her brother flicked a yellow speck of yolk from his tie. 'Strictly speaking, we should all be in mourning for the Fallen.' He was wearing grey flannels and his dark-green school blazer with the Ist XI cricket badge on the pocket.

'We'll stand on the east side,' Lance Pelman said. 'Then if they do come early, you'll be able to see the taxi turning into Church Lane – and slip away. I reckon it would take less than sixty seconds to scoot back and be waiting at the gate to meet them.'

'They won't arrive before twelve.' Mrs Humbert buttoned her gloves and led the way.

'There's just one thing.' Margot reached the door first and faced them desperately. 'Please, don't anyone call me Meg, not in front of Linden. That's all I ask. Promise.'

All promised.

'We will use only your baptismal name,' her father said.

'Though it occurs to me,' Alex said, 'that I might not much care for a girl in whose presence I must not call my sister by her familiar name.'

'Oh, you'll like her. Honestly. She's marvellous. Phyllis and Freda think so too. We all do.'

There was no more to be said. The authority of the girls at the Elmdon High School was known to be incontrovertible.

In predicting the size of the crowd, Alex had exaggerated. Disputes as to where the memorial should be placed had been heated and long drawn out. Eventually Fellside and Hope Carr had conceded Ashlaw's claim that fourteen names out of the twenty-six on the roll of honour entitled them to choose the site. So far as Fellside and Hope Carr were concerned it also entitled Ashlaw to the most active share in the work and expense involved.

So that it was chiefly Ashlaw folk who stood in a jagged half-circle facing the memorial: a plain column surmounted by a cross, approached by three shallow steps and flanked by two rows of chairs for the official party. The chosen spot was picturesque: level ground at the foot of a green slope with gorse and wild cherry in bloom in the uncultivated stretch of land known as the Dene. Long ago the monks of Langland Priory had hunted deer there: an historic spot, Mr Ashton, the schoolmaster, had said, giving it his vote, though there were dark hints that the Dene was prone to subsidence. Look what happened to the Quaker school-room and the old Rectory.

There had been time for the post-war tide of grief and thanksgiving to ebb a little; yet now that the moment had come there arose in the quiet gathering of shabby folk a mood to match the hour. Most of them were women. Men coming off work at Hope Carr had a mile and a half to walk and could hardly come in their pit dirt. But others on night shift had turned up, as well as farmworkers and some of the unemployed.

Standing between her brother and Lance and facing west, Margot was thankful for the correctness of her kilt. The white dress would have stood out like a sore thumb. Besides there might just be time to change before the Greys came. For a few minutes she contrived to forget them. Every day, for ages it seemed, she had seen the memorial taking shape but she had never been interested in whatever it was the thing stood for or shared the thoughts she now vaguely imagined the other people were thinking. And how ignorant she had been, not knowing east from west!

Heads turned as between the trees bordering Church Lane gleamed the black and silver of a motor car. Her heart sank; the worst had happened: the Greys had come too soon.

'Keep calm,' Lance said. 'It isn't a taxi.'

It was the Daimler from Bainrigg House. She breathed again. The Rilstons and their grandson descended and approached. Amid a general hush, attentive rather than respectful, they shook hands with the rector, several councillors, Father (representing the Coal Company) and Mother (wearing the clerical grey coat and skirt she had worn when opening the hospital bazaar).

'O God our help in ages past. . . .'

Overpowered by the Hope Brass Band, voices were thin in the open air. Margot's attention wandered from the white cherry blossom on the green slope to the smaller schoolchildren pretending to read from their hymn books; to Mrs Dobie, black-clad and red-faced and, as Alex said, seeming to breathe fire; to Rob and Emily Judd, dark-browed and scowling; to Katie Judd. With disapproval she saw that Katie's stockings were coming down. Really it was too bad. People had tried to do something with, as well as for, Katie. She stood in her usual attitude, sideways with one foot turned in, shoulders hunched, eyes staring as if from fear. The fear was genuine; Katie was always afraid. But the stockings! Something must be done. Suspenders? It would probably have to be garters, though according to Miss Peters they caused varicose veins.

But wait. The rector was reading out the names inscribed on the column. Joseph Judd. That was Katie's father. Poor Katie!

Stony-faced at Katie's side, Mrs Judd heard without a tear. She was past weeping. The bitter years since the Battle of the Somme had drained her of tears. From under the dark brim of her sateen-trimmed hat she stared sombrely into space, no longer able to see in it a vision of Jo, his face crumpled in his derisive smile; no longer caring about anything except how to feed and clothe her family, all now at ages when they ate like wolves. They were all present, she had seen to that, although Ewan had arrived, hot and panting, and had to be nudged to take his cap off. His face above his white muffler was sullen.

'"He maketh wars to cease in all the world".' The rector read with exasperating slowness. '"He breaketh the bow and knappeth the spear in sunder and burneth the chariots in the fire. Be thou faithful unto death and I will give thee a crown of life. . .".'

And suddenly, as at the crack of doom, the mild morning exploded in disarray.

'Crowns?' Mrs Dobie elbowed her way to the front, ignored the rector, glared at the memorial. 'We don't none of us want crowns.' Her voice was rough and loud, her face redder than ever before. Like a fiery prophet she raised her bare right fist. 'We want them lads back, that's what we want. Every one of them lads should be here now, I'm telling you.'

They listened, appalled. The rector lost his place on the page. She stood upright, a solid black shape, in the deep-crowned hat and long coat she had worn since the day of Queen Victoria's funeral and would wear until a few days before her own; her black buttoned boots firm on the ground, her feet firm inside them.

'I'm telling you, they've all been cast away for nothing, them lads have. It's been a wicked waste of living flesh and blood. And now you're trying to bring God into it. It's too late to bring God into it. He had nought to do with it, hadn't God. And He's got nought to do with yon monument either.'

Her outburst ended in a few muttered words. She pushed through the people behind her and walked heavily away, not to the village but towards the river, along a path between ancient oaks that had not even been acorns when the monks hunted deer there. Somehow she seemed to belong to their long past; somehow it was she, Mrs Dobie, who had brought God into it as she raised her eyes – and her fist – to the sky.

Not one of those present ever forgot her. In the unwritten annals of Ashlaw she had achieved as lasting a place as if her name, too, had been inscribed in stone. To look at the memorial was to remember her – with discomfort – and only after that to remember the men who had died. Indeed the memory of Mrs Dobie outlasted the memorial. Threatened as it was from the outset by subsidence owing to mine workings below, it was already obsolescent, a trifle forlorn. Lifeless, it could not compete with so formidable an embodiment of active wrath as Mrs Dobie.

They watched her, all the blacker for the sunlight between branches, until she had trudged out of sight. Only then, as with a communal sigh, did they begin to recover.

'She's right,' Lance muttered.

'Yes. Bows and spears would have been pretty useless in the trenches, never mind crowns. Still, she was a bit illogical about the Fallen. It's because they aren't here that we are.'

It may not have been the last clever-sounding thing that Alex said purely for its effect, but it could have been among the last. Mrs Dobie had not taken him by the shoulders and shaken him until his teeth rattled, but she had shaken some of the nonsense out of him and shoved him in a new direction. Alex had already undergone several changes of direction and there would be more, but he had recognized in her protest the ring of fearless sincerity. A new-found directness, while it lasted, was to cost him several friends.

Chaos had threatened but had not quite come. In response to an unseen signal a bugler from the Elmdon Barracks stepped smartly forward to sound The Last Post. The brazen notes cleft the April air, raising grief to a pitch beyond speech, beyond comfort. Those lost, they proclaimed, could never come back. For those who were left there was no hope, only endurance. Having condensed in their merciless message the totality of human suffering, the bugle notes ceased.

As the last of them died into silence, Margot felt her flesh creep, her scalp tingle. She seemed at last almost to understand why they were there; why they had bothered to build the memorial. It was because there was nothing else they could do. That was why Mrs Dobie had shaken her fist at the Cross and been rude to the rector – because there was nothing else she could do to make up for. . . .

For what? Margot was aware of a huge unanswered question, as unanswerable as it was huge; and as the bandmaster raised his baton for 'All people that on earth do dwell', she began to cry and felt in vain for her handkerchief, unwisely secreted in an inaccessible part of her clothing instead of up her sleeve where it would have been easier to get at but might have fallen out, which was why she had preferred to rely on elastic. Conscious of having made a wrong decision, she had to let the tears fall.

Alex looked down sternly.

'People,' he had more than once decreed, 'don't cry in public.'

'But if they can't help it?' she had once asked, snivelling.

'They can always help it.'

The remedy, it seemed, was to think of something else. Presumably it worked for him. He was not immune to tears. Once when he was donkey in the card game, he had rushed away, red-eared and blowing his nose, for a quite unnecessary drink of water; and when his rabbit, gorged by over-feeding, then starved by neglect, had patiently died, Alex had gone into the garden shed and wept in remorse.

But not in public. One thought of something else. Pressed for an example, he had recommended the French Foreign Legion in which at that time he was intending as soon as possible to enlist. Margot closed her wet eyes and fixed her mind on the cover of *The Gallant Legionnaire*, on horsemen in head-dresses with flaps galloping wildly over a hill of sand. . . .

The band was playing 'God Save the King': the ceremony was over.

'Let's go,' Alex said. 'I'm famished.'

'Me too.' Lance handed Margot a handkerchief.

'But I don't suppose we'll be eating yet, not for a good half-hour.'

'Then what about getting on with the job? There'd be time to put a thin layer of shellac on the cardboard. Then we can wind the coil on to the formers this afternoon.'

'It looks as if the Rilstons are being asked in for sherry or something. I'd better hang about here but you can go. See you at lunch.'

Lance looked at his watch and disappeared. It would take him exactly three minutes to get home, a further thirty seconds to reach his bedroom. Assuming the same length of time for getting back to Monk's Dene and adding another minute for hand-washing etc., that would leave just under twenty-three minutes for coating the cardboard formers and possibly, though it would be a rush, drilling holes in the fibre ready for the terminals. No time need be wasted on popping in to the surgery: his father would still be out on his rounds. They hadn't seen each other for a couple of days owing to a difficult confinement and a nasty accident with a chain-saw.

Absorbed though he was in these calculations as he turned into the main street at top speed, Lance noticed two people standing on the pavement to his right opposite Burdons' shop: females; strangers. It was no time to be standing at the bus-stop. If they were waiting for the 11.55, they had missed it. In that case they might as well settle down to wait two hours and eight minutes for the next. If, on the other hand, they had got off the 11.55, why were they still there seven minutes later, assuming that the bus had been on time? Putting on a spurt, he reached his own front door with two seconds in hand.

They had alighted from the bus to the sound of music. Somewhere close at hand a band was playing.

'A service of some sort. I wonder.' Mrs Grey looked round anxiously as the bus lumbered off. 'It can't be far to walk. On Church Lane to the left of the main street, Sarah said in her letter.'

'There.'

'Then that must be Monk's Dene. It's the only house.'

It was half hidden by a high wall, but its size and the tops of orchard trees were enough to confirm the impression that Sarah Humbert had done well for herself. Marian Grey had sensed that at once when, after a separation of twenty-one years, they had met by chance in town. She had felt the contrast with her own situation; had felt too the absolute necessity of concealing it. Years of war and its aftermath had been less than kind to her, but it was one's duty to hide the scars, especially from an old school-friend who had so obviously prospered. But the humiliation of having to walk to her front door with the dirt of the lane on their shoes!

She was already tired. So far the day had not gone well. There had been rather an unpleasant incident as they waited for the bus in Elmdon, standing on the pavement like working people. It was a cool, sunless spot, shaded by a warehouse wall and still damp from overnight rain. The only other would-be passenger was an insolent-looking youth wearing a cloth cap and a white muffler, no doubt to conceal his lack of shirt collar.

The bus – a wretched little local affair – came at last, drew up with a lurch and almost splashed them with muddy water from a puddle. They had both been obliged to step back smartly. Her own stockings were spattered; the marks still showed though she had done what she could with a handkerchief. Fortunately Linden had got out of the way in time, but in stepping back she had bumped into someone standing against the warehouse wall: a gypsy-looking woman with a pedlar's tray of goods slung round her neck. The woman lost her balance, the tray tilted and her things were spilled on the pavement: laces, packets of tape and so on.

She had been extremely offensive, out of all proportion to so small an accident. She had actually sworn at Linden and muttered some kind of threat. Fortunately a policeman was passing, otherwise there might have been more unpleasantness. Of course, there was nothing they could do but get into the bus quickly – the conductor was impatient – and pay no attention. The youth in the cap kept them waiting while he picked up some of the things and put them back on the tray, until the conductor threatened to leave without him.

The three of them were the only passengers. At the top of Ashlaw's steep main street the bus slowed down for him, he jumped off and made a rude sign to them from the roadside. Linden had simply turned away: she was always cool-headed and never out of temper. But she herself suffered from sensitive nerves and the incident had upset her.

And now they waited until the hymn ended and was followed by the National Anthem.

'It's over, whatever it was.'

On the other side of the wall there were no houses, only open land sloping to a hollow with trees and clumps of primroses.

'It's quite pretty really. I thought when you said Mr Humbert was a colliery agent, there'd be. . . .'

'An agent has a very good position and doesn't have to live near a colliery. Actually there isn't one at Ashlaw.'

'There are a lot of people down there and a motor car.'

To have to manoeuvre one's way through a crowd was an added inconvenience. Fortunately people were dispersing, though in no particular hurry, except for an athletic-looking, russet-haired boy who came up the hill at an astonishing speed and made for the house with a brass plate, set back a little from the street. The doctor's? An emergency?

'It's a big car.' They had drifted to the turning and could look down the lane. 'If we had come in a taxi, we wouldn't have been able to get to the gate.'

'Exactly.' Mrs Grey's manner had changed. 'Come along.'

They exchanged smiles of understanding and hesitated no longer.

CHAPTER II

By one o'clock those who had been famished at twelve were ravenous. According to Alex, who had charge of the decanter, they had remained steadfast to the call of duty, hoping eventually to be rewarded for gallantry.

'We really must be going,' Mrs Rilston said for the third time. 'It has been delightful. I envy you, Mrs Humbert, living in the centre of things. I'm afraid we're out of touch up at Bainrigg.' She lowered her voice. 'It was good of you to ask Miles to stay for lunch. He's away at school most of the time and has no friends here. We know so very few young people.' She looked round. The presence at such close quarters of even so very few young people had already given her a headache. 'Margot is a charming little hostess. So natural and unspoiled.' More thoughtfully her eye turned to the other girl. She was standing just inside the drawing-room door with her mother, Mr Rilston, Mr Humbert and Alex.

'Linden is a little older.' Mrs Humbert's gaze had taken the same direction. 'She's nearer Alex's age. Margot had told us about the new girl at school. She was thrilled, and so was I when I realized who it must be. Linden's mother and I were at the Elmdon High School together as girls.'

'You hadn't kept in touch?'

'Army people move about a good deal, don't they? We heard of Captain Grey's death, but it wasn't until Margot mentioned Linden's name that I knew Marian had come back to Elmdon. She hopes to give Linden a more settled background and make suitable friends.'

'That should not be difficult.'

Linden was apparently a good listener. She seemed at ease, a slim, graceful girl. She had not yet taken off her hat, a brown velour with the broad brim turned up all round to show dark hair framing a face of pale, clear complexion.

'She must miss her father. It can't have been easy for Marian. But you know what it is.' Sarah Humbert hesitated. 'This morning must have been an ordeal for you and your husband – and for Miles too.'

The Rilstons' only son, Miles's father, had been killed at Ypres. The discovery that he and Captain Grey had been in the same regiment had been made just as the Rilstons were on the point of leaving – twenty minutes ago.

'And the auburn-haired boy? Not one of the family?'

'Dr Pelman's son. His mother died when he was very young and he spends a good deal of time with us.'

'I see now. The resemblance. The same intensely blue eyes as his father.'

Lance stood with his back to the hall clock. He was forcing himself not to look at it. His obsession with time and not wasting any of it was getting out of hand. It was important not to let anything get out of hand, always to be in control. Self-control was essential in every walk of life.

Margot, having met the Greys at the gate, ushered them in and made the breathless introductions, had later found Miles stranded at the foot of the stairs and felt sorry for him. He had not yet been introduced to Linden and she must see to it that the privilege was not too long delayed. Meanwhile—

'Lunch won't be long,' she said encouragingly. 'In fact it's been ready for ages. I'm glad you're staying.'

'Thank you.'

Like the others, he was older than Margot who thought him delicate-looking. Perhaps he was outgrowing his strength. She racked her brains for a topic that might interest him.

'Alex and Lance are making a crystal set. Wireless, you know. They've taken a vow to make it as cheaply as possible. Well, they would have to anyway but it makes it more interesting when you take a vow.' To her the vow was certainly more interesting than the crystal set.

'I see. I suppose it does.'

'It's the second one. The first one almost worked but. . . .' Why hadn't it worked? 'It was something to do with the aerial. Actually I'm not sure that it's worth all the bother. All I could hear was a sort of whistling and wailing.'

'I expect that's why they're trying again. When it works properly there are interesting things to listen to. It's better if you have a set with valves but more expensive, I'm afraid.'

'You mean – the vow?'

He smiled. She was a friendly little thing with light-brown hair and dark eyes. They were soft, like velvet, the whites faintly tinted with blue. Usually he felt awkward with strangers, especially girls. For that matter he hardly knew any. To have to stay to lunch had promised to be sheer torture.

'Sometimes there's music.' The smile had changed his thin face, his whole self. It gave to the remark a special charm. She was to remember it as one remembers a line of poetry.

'You like music?' And when he nodded, 'So do I. I'm. . . .' She stopped, remembering Alex's rule about not bragging.

'Yes?'

'I was going to say that I'm in the school choir but it sounds like boasting.'

'What sort of thing do you sing?'

'"Nymphs-and shepherds-come-away".' She looked at him doubtfully, wondering for the first time what it actually meant. Quick and bright, the five words came again and again and nothing seemed to happen until the desperate '. . .come come co-o-ome away' at the end. 'That's what we're working on now.'

The clock struck one. Lance relaxed as after an ordeal. Mrs Rilston moved purposefully towards the drawing-room door.

'Frederick dear, we've been forgetting the time.'

'I hope you'll come again. Your husband and I seldom have an opportunity to talk.' If Edward Humbert silently added the word 'alone', there was some excuse for him. The presence of Marian Grey and her pale-faced silent girl had been a confounded nuisance. There were several topics he would have liked to discuss with Mr Rilston who had considerable influence in the district, where his family had been the principal land-owners for more than 200 years.

'I was meaning to ask you' – he steered his parting guest to the hall – 'could you by any chance find a job for one of our Ashlaw lads? Ewan Judd. His father was killed on the Somme and the family are in a bad way. Ewan has never worked since he left school. We haven't been able to take on more boys of his age at any of our pits. First chance had to be given to family men coming home from the front – not even all of them. Once the Germans are back in the Ruhr, we're going to feel the difference here. By next year there could be over three hundred thousand miners out of work, taking the country as a whole.'

In full daylight, Rilston, still in his sixties, looked older, his blue eyes faded, his cheeks sunken. Humbert's conscience smote him. He was used to arguing with hard-headed directors of the Fellside and District Coal Company and felt the contrast between them and this gentle, courteous man.

'I'm sorry, Humbert. I'd be glad to find him something to do. Certainly I'll bear him in mind. His father and my son down there together.' He nodded towards the Dene. The homely little ceremony had touched him. Mrs Dobie's protest had not been mentioned but watching her trudge away, he had felt his personal grief as part of a catastrophe too vast and irremediable to be borne except in being shared. 'I'd like to help but I've had to turn men away. Can't afford the staff we once had, indoor or out. To tell you the truth, money is tight: all we've got is land. The day may come when we shall have to sell. I dread it. And there's Langland Hall standing empty; haven't been able to keep it in repair. All the same – Judd. I'll remember the name. Thank you, my boy.' Alex had brought him his stick. 'You've a daughter, too, I see.'

The silent listener at his elbow was not Margot. Her father, his mind on more important issues, answered vaguely.

The old gentleman stepped out into a garden alive with nesting birds as into a world he no longer recognized, empty as it was of so much that had been familiar, of clearly marked obligations and expectations and people he had known and trusted.

'I must apologize, Mrs Grey,' his wife was saying, 'for taking up so much of the lane with our car. You must have come by taxi. There wouldn't be room for it to bring you to the gate.'

'There is no need to apologize. It only meant stopping a little further up the lane. We didn't mind that at all, did we, Linden?'

Linden smiled. Her smile was charming.

'Perhaps we could make amends. I wonder – how are you getting back to town? We could send the car. It will be coming for Miles in any case. Chapman could take you home.'

'How very kind.'

Lance heard these exchanges with interest. He wondered what arrangement the Greys would have made if Mrs Rilston had not solved their problem. Mr Humbert had the use of a company car and chauffeur and had kept on his horse and gig. The family commonly used buses, a recent innovation and infrequent but cheap, and occasionally taxis. The station was a quarter of a mile away.

Later, from his place on the opposite side of the table he was able to take a closer look at the visitors. Mrs Grey must be about the same age as Mrs Humbert, but looked older as if always bothered by some worry or other. It was thus that Lance reacted to the fretful expression on a prematurely lined face and to Mrs Grey's tendency to fidget – with a gold chain round her neck, with a cuff, with her hair (disarranged when her hat had been snatched at by a briar dangling from that tiresome arch over the gate and coolly disentangled by Linden).

Linden? What did poor old Alex see in her? She wasn't bad-looking. Not exactly in the film-star class. Nothing like as pretty as Margot. But Lance could see that there was something about her: a difference from other girls. This time, he thought, without undue concern, Alex had better watch out. He transferred his attention to his plate and dealt with an ample helping of raised pie and cold meats in roughly – he refrained from looking at his watch – three minutes.

Seated on the same side of the table as the Greys, Margot could not see her friend without leaning forward, nor could she help doing so as inconspicuously as possible. Otherwise everything had gone well. Perfect! The word floated to the surface of her mind and lay there, pure white and shining like a water-lily. Her eyes sought her mother's. 'You see what I mean?' they ardently asked, turning in Linden's direction.

Mrs Humbert would have described herself as weary of the very sound of Linden's name but she rose to the appeal, nodded and smiled significantly. The infatuation could do no harm and it couldn't possibly last: neither worshipper nor idol could sustain it for long. And the same applied to Alex who could be counted on to fall in love with every presentable girl he met.

The Greys were lonely, she thought. They must be looked after a little until they found their feet. A weekend visit perhaps. The extra leaves were rarely taken out of the Humberts' hospitable dining-table. When they were alone, they ate in the morning-room. The round table there seated five comfortably, themselves and Lance who had become one of the family.

Even to think the word 'perfect' is to take a risk: there is always a snag. In this case, for Margot, it was that she couldn't quite see Linden properly: not fully, not then – or later – or ever.

CHAPTER III

As soon after lunch as politeness allowed, Miles made his excuses: he would not wait for Chapman but would walk home. With their crystal set in mind, Alex and Lance took the opportunity of leaving with him. They had got as far as the gate when Mrs Grey and the girls came out on the front steps.

'Such a lovely day.' Mrs Grey's glance moved from the three youths to her daughter. 'A walk would do you good, dear,' and to Margot, 'Linden doesn't often have a day in the country.'

'We could have gone with the boys,' Margot said, 'only Chapman will be coming for you. There wouldn't be time. But Linden and I could have a walk on our own, just to the river and back. It's pretty down by the bridge.'

'A pity.' Mrs Grey might not have heard. 'Of course, I must wait here but perhaps we could pick up Linden somewhere on the way home.'

'Not if we go with Miles. Bainrigg isn't on the way to town. But – oh yes – there's Clint Lane.' Margot explained. There was a short cut from the Rilstons' land to the Elmdon road. 'We could come back that way and you could pick up Linden at the end of the lane.'

While Linden was saying everything that was proper to her hosts, Margot dawdled to the gate and found Katie Judd crouching by the hedge just outside, beside her a basket of the Humberts' freshly laundered linen. No need to ask why she was hiding there instead of delivering the laundry as usual: she had seen strangers in the garden and had taken fright.

'There's nobody about, Katie. You can go up through the orchard and round to the back door.'

21

Cautiously Katie uncurled herself, nodded and almost smiled: with Margot she was safe. Unfortunately, before she reached the point where garden merged into orchard, Linden came down from the house. They met midway down the path under a low-hanging bough of a pear tree. Both stopped – Linden composed, hatless, her thick dark hair shining, her dress and jacket of fine worsted without a crease: Katie instantly distraught, in cast-off navy-blue serge too big for her, draggled stockings and scuffed shoes, with a handkerchief pinned by one corner to the front of her dress as if she were still a little girl. When she was afraid, as now, her pale eyes grew prominent as if they would start from her head.

Momentarily, Margot's admiration for Linden gave way to sympathy for Katie. She had always known but never fully realized that Katie's impoverishment was not just a matter of awful clothes: she had also been given faulty equipment with which to do battle against the bombardment of terrors that life inflicted on her. It wasn't fair. The worst of it was that Katie was excelling herself. She gaped, clutching the handle of the basket, her knuckles white, her knees bent. She might have been expecting the lash of a whip or a sentence of death. Whatever would Linden think?

'Give me the basket, Katie, and you run home.'

By the time Margot came back, Katie had gone.

'You mustn't mind Katie. She can't help being like that.'

'I suppose she's what's called the village idiot.'

'Well, no. Oh, no.'

Katie needed to be explained. She was simple-minded and, according to Dr Pelman, her development had been retarded by the ill effects of measles and under-nourishment. What she needed was good food, care and understanding. The Judds and their neighbours took a less rational view. If there was such a thing as a changeling, that was what their Katie was. Margot had not yet come across the word but anyone could see that Katie was different from her two older brothers and her sister. She was fair-skinned and almost thin enough to be seen through. Her fine light hair radiated from her head like the gossamer of a seeding dandelion and with a similar suggestion of being at the mercy of the wind.

The other Judds were broad-shouldered, big-boned, strong-jawed and dangerous when roused, like crocodiles. Whereas Katie existed in a state of anxiety bordering on panic, they were fearless. It was possible that, unintentionally, they were responsible for her nervousness. Any creature of the least sensitivity must, even in the cradle, have quailed from a domestic atmosphere that smouldered and could, on occasion, ignite.

On the other hand, the fiercest of their outbursts would most likely be on Katie's behalf. Let anyone lay a finger on her and the Judds would rise up and smite the offender as Judah and Simeon smote the Canaanites. So far no one had risked – or wanted – so to offend; the girl was harmless. As Mrs Judd said, Katie had never needed to be smacked. Whatever she was told to do, she did, not only from fear of the consequences if she did not, but because she didn't know what else to do. Her forté was running errands: she never forgot a message. Once a thing got into her head it remained and could not be dislodged. Her dim wits were remarkably retentive.

When crisis arose, her remedy was to hide. She was continually vanishing and being sought for. 'Have you seen our Katie?' had become a village byword. What she loved best – it was Margot who had found this out – was quietness with nobody there. Once when they were both very young, Margot had taken two of her dolls, Anabel and Rosaline, into the garden. In a sunny spot behind the tool-shed, curtained by honeysuckle, Katie was sitting on a log, quite still. Margot, too young to wonder at her quick shrinking like a furtive animal cornered, gave her Anabel to nurse. They sat together in silence until, still without a word, she retrieved Anabel and ran back to the house.

And now the sight of the two girls face to face yet worlds apart may have been responsible for Margot's sudden feeling of concern: the concentration of numberless glimpses of Katie's plight into a steadier view. She remembered the incident of the doll and was sorry to have snatched it away: Katie liked pretty things. Margot had once given her two tatting-edged handkerchiefs and she knew – Katie's sister had told her – that Katie kept them in a paper bag in her share of a bedroom drawer. They were too white and beautiful to be put at risk when there were so many risks to be dodged and fled from.

Good gracious, it wasn't a crime if a person's stockings came down. One of her own liberty bodices with suspenders attached would fit Katie, even be too big. Well, it would have to be two, for washing.

Some or all of this she might have confided to Linden, only—

'I suppose she's what's called the village idiot.'

Linden's voice was low-pitched, soft and all the more pleasing for never being over-used. The words had not matched the voice, not just because they weren't true, they were wrong in another way. Margot no longer wanted to talk about Katie. Besides, Linden hadn't minded the girl's behaviour; it hadn't upset her. In fact – it was an odd conclusion to have reached considering the two had stood within touching distance of each other – Linden hadn't paid any attention to Katie. Odder still to be almost sure that Katie had felt in every nerve of her defenceless being the impact of Linden. Had she also received from her the most frightening of all messages, that of being as if she wasn't there? It wouldn't matter if she didn't exist?

'That boy.' Linden was looking up the lane. 'I suppose he's a relation of hers.'

'Yes, that's Ewan.' Hand in hand, brother and sister were turning into the village street.

He had been passing the gate when Katie rushed out as if escaping. Linden, following sedately, had been confronted by an individual whom she would have described as a rough lout. He had scowled at her entirely without respect. She recognized him as the fellow-traveller on the bus. He had shed his white muffler and slouched moodily, hands in pockets, cap on the back of his head. Recognition was mutual.

'What's up, Katie? What's she been doing to you?' His manner was almost threatening. 'Come on home.'

Linden had glanced at him with distaste. A moistening of her lips with the tip of her tongue like a fastidious cat was the only response she allowed herself to a ferocity of resentment that might have startled a girl less self-assured. She made no reference to the incident: it was not the sort of thing one talked about.

Alex and Lance did not devote the afternoon to their crystal set. When the girls caught up with them at the Pelmans' door it was not mentioned.

Miles found himself with an escort of four on one of those loose-knit rambling walks familiar to young people brought up in the country. Whenever Alex made such a foray, a random assortment of village children materialized in confident expectation of some spectacular feat of hedge-leaping, gate-vaulting or tree-climbing. There had been the hair-raising Tarzan episode when Alex had hung upside down from a tree, his knees crooked over a branch. Margot had closed her eyes and kept them closed in silent prayer until somehow with Lance's help he had got down. 'Just stop it, will you?' Lance had growled.

Alex's prowess in ball-throwing was particularly admired and was on the whole safer. Anyone could throw a ball horizontally but Alex would produce one from his pocket and throw it upward to an incredible height. Heads back, chins upturned, his devotees followed its upward flight: the earth fell away; they gazed, dazzled, into the sky.

For Margot, too, there was magic in it. The ball was no longer solid. It was bodiless yet alive. It became ethereal, escaping heavenward through bird-inhabited air and even, it seemed, into the clouds. Then came the turning point, the utmost moment before the speck reversed its direction and fell with lightning speed, and there once more were the fields, the trees, the cows still munching.

At the old Toll House Lance left them and went home to fix the terminals. The others turned into the cart-road leading to Larsons' farm, Linden walking between Alex and Miles, Margot hurrying ahead in the hope of seeing the Larsons' new baby. And there it was in its pram, shaded from the dazzle of sunlight on the whitewashed wall of the house; and there, too, was Mrs Larson on the bench outside the door. She was a fair-haired, delicate young woman, still pale and limp after her first confinement. A red-combed cock strutted; hens humbly pecked; pigeons cooed; a dog crouched low and came creeping to sniff at Margot's ankles.

'Now then, Miss Margot, what do you think of our little girl?'

'Oh Mrs Larson.' Margot's awestruck whisper as she bent

25

cautiously over the pram would have gladdened any mother's heart. 'Look, she can yawn already.' Then, as the others caught up and lingered on the path at the edge of the farmyard, 'Come and see. It's a new baby.'

Linden nodded and smiled and remained on the path. Alex called out a greeting to Mrs Larson and the two moved on. It was Miles who came to inspect the newcomer to the Bainrigg estate. As it happened she was the youngest human being he had ever seen at close quarters.

'What are you going to call her, Mrs Larson?'

'Well, sir, since you've asked, I'll tell you – we're not sure. Albert and me, we've got different ideas. Albert wants to call her after his mother – that's Mary – and I don't want to go against what he wants. But I want her to have a name she'll like. I've never liked mine. Nancy. Albert thinks I'm foolish, but I want to call her Lilac.' In the brief silence that followed she looked anxiously from one to the other and Margot was quick to say, 'Of course you want her to have a pretty name.'

'We'd be calling her after the lilac bush over there. In another month it'll come in flower and it'll be the first thing she sees and smells when I bring her out of a morning.'

'And then in another month,' Miles said after a thoughtful pause, 'there'll be roses. . . .'

'Rose is a lovely name. I wish I'd been called Rose,' Margot said. 'The heroines in stories are sometimes called Rose.'

'And if you called her Mary Rose, you'd both be satisfied.'

'I do think Mary Rose sounds more . . . smooth . . . than Mary Lilac. Mary Rose Larson would be a graceful name.'

'There now, you're right.' Nancy had flushed and brightened. 'And it's only fair for Albert to have his say. He'd likely be satisfied if Mary came in the christening.'

'And you could *call* her Rose.'

'If you would like it,' Miles said, 'I'll send down a rose bush when she's christened. Henderson will plant it for you.'

As she told Albert, they really bucked her up. The naming had been a worry and they made it all so simple. It was very quiet at the farm. She could spend a whole day without seeing a passer-by and she missed having somebody to talk things over with.

'The rose bush was a good idea,' Margot said, as they left. 'She was delighted, I could tell.'

'Do you think we saved the baby from being Lilac?'

'I think so. I don't know why but Lilac doesn't sound right for a person's name.'

The cart track veered to the right between hawthorn hedges. Linden and Alex were still ahead, Alex talking, Linden presumably listening. On their way to Bainrigg they must pass the Lucknow chimney where something rather interesting had once occurred. It was just coming into view, a sombre intrusion on the green countryside, rising apparently from the bowels of the earth on the ridge above the village. Not that there was much of it left. Although it looked like a squat chimney it was in fact an updraught ventilating shaft, all that remained of the old Lucknow Drift.

Originally it had been encircled by a high wall but time and weather had weakened the structure. Brickwork had crumbled and been carted away for more homely use. On the north side the wall was more than half gone and the cavity had become an unofficial dump for items not otherwise disposable. Elder and ivy had encroached to within a few feet of the square stone base.

It was here that one of Alex's ball-throwing exploits had literally taken an unexpected turn. The descending ball had ricocheted from the ash tree on the other side of the path and by some freak of dynamics had fallen – plonk – into the chimney as if with all the countryside to choose from it had deliberately chosen to go there. The faint distant ghost of a sound and it was gone. A chorus of gasps from the audience as Alex sauntered to the chimney and stood on the base. Few would have ventured close to it, not while they were still at school; boys had been caned for just playing near it.

But Alex had leaned over the crumbling brickwork and intoned into the cavity, 'Gone but not forgotten. Rest in peace.' His voice raised a weird sepulchral echo as from infernal regions. As he released his hand from the edge a loose fragment of brick fell into the void. Perhaps its sudden vanishing had a sobering effect. When Alex turned to face his juvenile admirers, he had the grace to improve on the occasion.

'See what happens if you go near that shaft? If anything falls down there, you'll never see it again. Skedaddle off, the lot of you. A penny for the first one to Larsons' gate.'

The message went home. Threats from the schoolmaster could not compete with so striking an object lesson. With characteristic panache decently modified, Alex claimed to be a public benefactor. Toddlers had it drummed into them by older brothers and sisters, 'If you fall in there you'll never get out and nobody'll know where you are.' An invisible circle round the base of the chimney remained untrodden like one of the forbidden areas on which a tribal wise-man has laid a taboo.

In the course of history, such places, once sinister, have become sacred, as Alex enjoyed pointing out, but as yet the chimney had taken on no odour of sanctity and served only as a melancholy reminder of the tragic variations in the history of mining.

Today nothing happened. The children drifted off to watch rats being clubbed to death in Larsons' stackyard; the others sauntered on. Margot was hurrying to catch up after taking a stone from her shoe when Miles turned to wait for her.

'Do you often come this way?'

'Oh yes. As far as that tree.' The ash tree at the corner of the field marked the beginning of Clint Lane. 'And I've sometimes. . . .' She hesitated. 'We shouldn't really but we've sometimes come to gather bluebells – on your private land.'

'I wish I'd known.'

'Through the gate, then turn left along the hedge and you come to a sort of hollow. It's a lovely little place. But of course you know it.'

'It used to be a stone pit. The path is marked on the map as Beggars' Way. It leads all the way to Langland Priory.'

'Through the wood? That's where the bluebells are.'

'I hope you'll come and pick them every year. If I'm at home I'll come and help you.'

'But boys don't. . . .'

'I could hold the basket and you could tell me all the news.'

They had come to the parting of the ways. To the right, close at hand, rose the chimney, bringing a touch of desolation to the

sunny afternoon. To the left, the ash tree overhung a gate opening on the fields surrounding Bainrigg House. Ahead lay Clint
Lane.

Three of them, unversed in the art of leavetaking, could only
ward off the final moment by repeating things already said,
until. . . .

'Goodbye, Miles. It's been so nice meeting you.' Linden held
out her hand. This time there was no discrepancy between the
charming voice and the words spoken. Released from awkwardness, the others followed suit.

'Goodbye, Miles. You'll come again, won't you? Promise.'

'So long. See you in the summer holidays.'

'Well, I'll be off then, and thank you,' Miles brought himself
to say, wishing he could say more. The summer holidays seemed
years away. A whole term yawned ahead.

Margot liked him, especially when he smiled. He was shy but
kind. She was aware of a quiet grace in his farewell gesture as he
closed the gate behind him. His way lay uphill where ewes with
their lambs speckled the green slope.

'He's a thoughtful person,' Margot said.

'A good chap,' Alex said, his eyes on Linden.

Hers, heavy-lidded and long-lashed, followed Miles's receding
figure. They lost sight of him as they turned into Clint Lane. It
was to be more than one summer before they saw him again.

Meanwhile Margot had the safety of her guest in mind.

'By the way, Linden, don't ever go near that chimney.' She
delivered the caution with some importance. 'Those bricks
aren't safe. Alex once—'

'Don't be such an ass, Meg. Why on earth should Linden go
near the chimney?'

'Why indeed? But thank you for the warning, Margot. I won't
forget.'

Margot was abashed: she had been silly and officious. 'Ass'
didn't matter. But 'Meg'! She lagged behind and walked slowly
past the row of workmen's cottages on the right. They were
always interesting. High on the ridge, exposed to all the winds of
heaven, Clint Lane was the best place in Ashlaw for drying
clothes. Moreover the tenants had splendid views over the

rooftops of the village below to the distant blue fells in the west.

But that was from the front windows, or from front doors rarely opened. The active life of the Judds and their neighbours throbbed in the narrow backyards with their ash-pits and privies, pigeon lofts and dog kennels, bicycles and pushchairs, but from the purposeful squalor of such scenes one had only to cross the lane to pick cowslips on the grassy bank and sit for a few blessed minutes in the shade of the hawthorn hedge.

There was a homeliness here that Margot liked. She recognized some of their own towels from Monk's Dene on Mrs Judd's line – then turned. On the opposite side of the lane where a gap in the hedge gave access to the fields beyond, something had moved.

'Katie,' she called softly. 'Have you been hiding?'

Katie didn't answer but she didn't shrink away either. It seemed to Margot that she was at home there among green leaves and budding may-blossom with her own back door close at hand. She was no intruder on the natural scene as she sometimes seemed elsewhere. Only her face was visible: pale-skinned, fine-boned, her features indeterminate below the fluff of fair hair rising like a halo, as if she had just alighted. Against her will?

It was a glimpse of Katie that she was to remember. She had never seen her like that before – disembodied – so that one forgot the dismal clothes and the awkward foot and the sidling walk that made her seem – as she so often did – unwillingly earth-bound.

Katie's hair stirred in the light breeze. Boughs and leaves glimmered in the fitful play of sunlight so that the face, half turned away, lost definition and became unfamiliar.

'Katie!'

A gentle movement and the face was gone: she was alone and ran to join the others. Chapman and Mrs Grey were waiting in the car. The visit was over.

CHAPTER IV

There were to be many similar days. The Greys came several times in their first year in Elmdon, sometimes the only guests, sometimes to meet other friends of the Humberts. There were picnics on the fells, tea in the garden, misty autumn walks, sledging in snowy fields, and afterwards card games in firelit rooms and songs at the piano: a pageant of family scenes varying only with the seasons; a life untroubled and safe and, in retrospect, seeming safer still.

But it was changing. Even on that first spring day there had been prophetic signs, slight and untimely as the rustle of an early-fallen leaf presaging winter. It was after that first visit that Edward Humbert took to emphasizing a topic he had touched on before: the need for girls to be equipped to earn their own living. The argument that most of them would find husbands to support them was hopelessly out of date. A million spinsters and widows had been left to fend for themselves, unprepared and untrained. What was to become of them?

'Miss Bondless fends for herself,' Margot reminded him. They had, as it happened, just said goodbye to her. She had been staying with the Pelmans and was leaving that morning to take up a new post as companion to a lady in Cannes. She was a distant connection of Dr Pelman and came from time to time to restore order in a masculine household where disorder sometimes came close to chaos.

'Miss Bondless is an exception,' her father conceded. 'She has wide interests.'

'And courage,' Sarah said. 'Not that she says much about all she's gone through.'

Even Alex was a little in awe of a woman who had been within earshot of German howitzers, endured air-raids when she nursed as a VAD in a casualty dressing station on the Western Front and survived the sinking of the *Britannic* when it was torpedoed on the way to Malta. Since then she had managed a home for war orphans in London, had been a prison visitor, secretary to more than one charitable organization, and had shown no sign whatever of needing the support of a husband.

'A remarkable woman,' Edward repeated. 'But look at Miss Burdon, left to run a successful family business and making a hash of it. Look at Mrs Judd. Look at Mrs Grey.'

Margot looked at each of the three as bidden. Any similarity between them, especially between Mrs Judd and Mrs Grey had not occurred to her.

'You're thinking of our generation, Edward,' her mother pointed out. 'Girls growing up now will find a husband, surely.'

Husbands, it seemed, had to be found; they did not materialize of their own accord. Doubts as to her own ability to search successfully inclined Margot to take her father's advice. She must somehow, albeit in the remote future, be able to earn her own living. Miss Burdon did, if only just; Mrs Judd did by taking in washing; on the other hand, Mrs Grey did not.

'No,' her father said when she mentioned Mrs Grey's abstention from work. 'That's just the point.'

'I wonder if Linden will be able to earn her own living.'

'We must hope so. Otherwise. . . .' From Sarah's glance at her husband Margot understood that otherwise Linden would be faced with the ordeal of searching for a husband, an ordeal which she herself hoped to escape.

'What shall I do? About earning my living?'

'Well,' – his daughter's brisk acceptance of her lot found Edward unprepared – 'you must work hard at school and pass your exams and then we'll see.'

Margot relaxed. The path ahead if not smooth was less stony than she had feared. She worked quite hard already: not being clever like Alex, she had to. Unfortunately the topic prompted her father also to think of Alex.

'It's time he settled down.'

The French Foreign Legion as a choice of career had lost its appeal, as had medicine (like poor old Pelman), mining engineering (like poor old Dad), the stage (he hadn't dared to mention it). At present he favoured the law. As a barrister he would confound the judiciary, the public, the innocent and the guilty with the eloquence of his pleas.

'If he fails his matric this term,' Edward said, 'he'll have to leave Bishop Cosin's and go somewhere else for a year's cramming. He can't go on picking and choosing.'

The Humberts were comfortably off. Edward would inherit his father's share in a family shipping company, importers of timber from Scandinavia mainly for pit props. In his early twenties, he had reacted from trade and commerce in favour of the ministry, but had soon found himself unable to accept its orthodoxy. He abandoned theology and trained as a mining engineer. Spiritual guidance was questionable as to the form it should take: the need for coal was indisputable, its quality easier to assess.

But the imagination and compassion that had drawn him to a pastoral vocation remained unchanged. He was efficient and practical in his present position as agent to the Fellside and District Coal Company but he found it hard to reconcile the aims of his employers with the needs of their employees, was often troubled by the ambiguities of his situation and tempted to change course again and put up for Parliament as a Liberal candidate.

'When the children are settled,' Sarah said with her heart in her mouth, 'we can think again.'

Meanwhile they were more active in the community than other agents had been and Edward enjoyed his position as consultant to the whole Fellside coal-field. In accepting it he had been influenced by the house that went with it. As Linden had been quick to see, Ashlaw had remained mainly a rural village. The coal under its fields was got out elsewhere. Certainly the waters of its leaf-shaded river were polluted by the Fellside colliery upstream but Ashlaw itself had no slag-heap, pit pond nor head-stock to disfigure it.

Various dwellings had occupied the site of Monk's Dene since the Middle Ages but the present house was a substantial Victorian residence with a look of age and none of its inconveniences. It faced away from the village but its back door was accessible from the main street to callers who had problems to unburden, forms to be filled in, letters to be explained – without the toil of having to get into their good clothes.

As for front-door visitors, Sarah did not flag in her intention to look after the Greys a little; that is to say, she did not flag for some time. It was a one-sided relationship. Once during the summer term, Margot was invited to 5 Gordon Street where the Greys occupied the first-floor rooms.

'You enjoyed it?' Her mother's question invited a more generous response than Margot seemed able to make. Her hesitation was just as illuminating. The dinginess of the sitting-room, the flimsiness of the refreshments – thin bread and butter and a slice of fruit cake – could not be described with enthusiasm. The dinginess didn't matter. The flimsiness could be rectified by the cramming down of a milk chocolate bar in the bathroom. It wasn't so much the absence of cosiness and fun as the presence of a sort of stiffness that caused Margot to ponder. Linden had been as sweet as ever but had been even less talkative than usual. The room was cold. Mrs Grey, wearing a thick tweed costume and amber beads and pouring tea from a silver tea-pot into wide shallow cups, had mentioned that 'the rest of the silver' was in store 'until we are settled in a permanent home.'

'Oh yes,' Margot had said brightly, the brightness a substitute for any sensible answer she could think of to such a remark.

'I like it best when they come here,' she told her mother.

Certainly at Monk's Dene there was less constraint and more food, but seeds of doubt had been sown. Were their own meals too hearty? Too unrefined? Common sense came up with a negative reply: people needed food especially after a long day at school with a load of homework ahead. On the other hand Linden's superior sophistication could not be overlooked; she knew how things should be done.

'They're snobs,' Lance said. 'They're trying to keep up appearances.'

'Why?' Margot demanded, aghast.

'Don't ask me why. It's a form of cheating.'

Nevertheless Margot became an enthusiast for refinement. It made little difference to her life-style which was too firmly geared to fit in with other people's to offer scope for change, but her manner did alter. Linden never talked about herself, never exchanged confidences. Perhaps that was why she was so interesting – intriguing, like an unopened book whose contents may be dull but will not be found to be so as long as they remain unread.

'Margot hasn't said a word for at least two minutes.' Her father paused in carving the Sunday joint. 'Is anything wrong?'

'She's stopped gushing,' Alex said, 'and that can only be an improvement.'

'I rather liked the gushing.'

Her father's regretful smile brought tears to Margot's eyes, but she was suddenly happy. For some reason she was constantly lurching from one mood to another these days. In the natural process of growing up her artless sincerity would doubtless have been modified as it was being already by exposure to Linden's adult manner. Linden never put her foot in it, was never impulsive. All the same, Sarah was not sorry when, at the end of term, Margot came home with the dramatic news that something terrible had happened: Linden had left school without even taking her exams and would not be returning to the Sixth Form.

'I was stunned. So were Phyllis and Freda. It was the most awful shock. Did you know it was going to happen?'

'Marian didn't mention it. What is she going to do?'

'I don't know but it has certainly cast a cloud over the holidays.'

'Seven weeks of official mourning and then a slow lightening of the gloom.' But Alex was less patronizing than usual: he had problems of his own and became visibly on edge as August drew to a close, bringing ever nearer the date of the examination results, bringing at last the fateful day.

'I'm sorry, Dad.' He was white-faced and miserable. 'I didn't think it would be as bad as this. I should have scraped through in maths. . . .'

'Scraped!' The eloquence of the future barrister had been inherited from his father. Edward Humbert did not mince his words. Things were so bad that Margot crept to her room and closed the door, to writhe in sympathy. Presently her brother's

35

slow footsteps on the stairs and the uncharacteristically quiet closing of his door told her that the storm had been terrible indeed.
It was worse for Alex because he was so clever. Nobody would have
minded, or at least not so much, if she had been the one to fail, a
calamity which she prayed every night to avoid.

It had been rather a shock to learn that Linden never prayed.
'Never?'

'Perhaps I might' – Linden had shrugged – 'for something very
important if there was no other way. But I don't suppose it would
do any good.'

Though shaken, Margot felt bound to go on praying. To stop
now and risk failure in her exams would be foolhardy and of
course there were all the other reasons for praying. All the same,
now that Alex had failed, it seemed mean to pray more earnestly
than ever that she would pass, especially as there were more than
three years to go.

Meanwhile Alex was granted a reprieve. After a consultation
with his headmaster, the threat of sending him to a crammer was
withdrawn – provisionally. Instead he was enrolled as a boarder at
Bishop Cosin's on the understanding that his nose was kept firmly
to the grindstone; exeats and even games were to be strictly
limited.

Alex accepted banishment gracefully, even cheerfully and with
a determination that astonished his parents, applied himself so
steadily to his studies that in one year he had matriculated with
honours and two years later enrolled as a student at London
University.

'I should have put my foot down earlier,' his father said. 'A
disciplined life with no distractions was what he needed.'

'He came to his senses just in time,' Sarah agreed. 'We have a
great deal to be thankful for.'

Margot felt rather sorry for her misguided parents who flat-
tered themselves that they and the masters at Bishop's had
worked the miracle. She could have enlightened them as to the
true cause of the transformation but she held her tongue.

CHAPTER V

Lance's first appraisal of Linden's looks and manner had been
impartial. As his father might have diagnosed in a patient a
glandular disorder or a shortage of protein, he had diagnosed in
Linden a difference.

But that, the younger girls at the Elmdon High School could
have told him, was the whole point. Linden's difference fasci-
nated them. She had been instantly noticeable, appearing as she
did in the middle of the spring term and in the Upper Fifth without the bother of drably working her way up through the lower
forms.

'Distinguished-looking,' Phyllis suggested, as the newcomer
was discussed over milk and buns in the refectory during morning break.

'Not quite. You'd say that about an older person like the
Head.' Freda chewed thoughtfully. 'She's distinctive, whereas the
rest of us are ordinary. The common herd, you might say.'

'I do rather object to the word "common". But distinctive, yes,
you're right,' Phyllis conceded. 'And part of being distinctive is
that you get away with things.'

'What sort of things?' Margot asked.

'The length of her tunic, for instance. You're not going to tell
me that it's two and a half inches above her knee.'

'Shorter?'

'No, longer.'

The breach of regulations was obviously significant but the
distance between hem and knee was too prosaic to be dwelt on.
For them Linden had glamour, that subtle quality to be felt but

not described except by saying that she had grace and poise, as if accustomed to a sphere of existence unknown to the humdrum inhabitants of their own town. She had come from elsewhere, had lived in the south and even abroad. The pitch of her voice was low, its accent free of any local inflection. Not that she was talkative: if challenged no one would have been able to remember anything of significance she had ever said.

It would not have occurred to Lance when he first met her, or indeed at any other time after, that when wearing her hat with the brim turned up like a dark halo she might put one in mind of Botticelli's *St John*; that bare-headed, she would not have been out of place among the aloof and pallid women favoured by the Pre-Raphaelites. Nor did she actually resemble any of them. Regular features, eyes of a greyish blue, hair soft and dark with a deep wave – did not yet amount to actual beauty.

Her gift – a natural endowment since she was neither old enough nor clever enough to have acquired it – was to suggest qualities she did not possess, to direct the eye of the beholder to a wider vision than she herself was capable of. There was a certain magic in it and since all magic must be suspect, Lance had once again hit the nail on the head when he muttered that Alex had better watch out.

It was only gradually that Margot came to a similar conclusion. One evening in the spring term of Alex's second year as a boarder, she had stayed on at school for a lecture on 'Careers for Women' and was hurrying to catch the bus to Ashlaw. Having cut it rather fine, she felt justified in taking a short cut along the river-bank, a shaded path out of bounds according to school rules. It was still twilight but would soon be dark. At a pace between running and walking, with no other sense of danger than fear of being seen by one of the mistresses, she came suddenly on two people loitering at the foot of one of the steep tree-bordered paths leading down to the river.

At first she didn't recognize them. When she did it was with embarrassment as well as surprise.

'Alex!'

'Margot!' Linden's voice held a teasing rebuke. 'What on earth are you doing here?'

The need to explain took all her remaining breath.

'I must go.'

Triumph in having caught the bus soon gave way to the incurable habit of worrying about Alex. He hadn't said a word. Well, there hadn't been time: she had barely paused much less stopped to chat. He hadn't been wearing the regulation stiffbrimmed straw boater, had obviously sneaked out and should not have been there. If he did that sort of thing and was found out, he would be sent to the crammer. How could he be so silly? But worse than the silliness which normally she could have accused him of outright, was something new. She had felt it instantly: a complete separateness from the rest of the world, which she recognized as love. At least on Alex's part. He hadn't even seen her; he only saw Linden.

Musing on Linden's effect on him, Margot could only fall back on language so commonplace as to betray her own inferiority. Linden should be described in poetic words, such as spell binding. She herself had been spellbound and remained so, to some extent.

During the next two years she and Alex were to see less of each other than ever before even in the holidays when visits to friends kept them apart, nor did Linden come as frequently to Monk's Dene. A vacancy had occurred in the office of an Elmdon solicitor and she had slipped into it. The summer holiday before Alex went up for his second year, Margot had spent with friends in Devonshire, but she was at home on the eve of his departure and helped him to pack.

'This is a good one of you.' She found the snapshot among shirts and socks on his bed. It was Alex at his most attractive, holding a tennis racquet and smiling at the camera. The smile was quizzical, a trifle self-mocking: he had outgrown his overconfident swagger. She put it on the chest of drawers, assuming it was for the family album.

'Lance took it. He's got a really good camera. A Leicher.' Alex retrieved it and put it in his wallet. 'It's for Linden. She's always wanted one.'

Always! The word suggested an attachment long-established. And long-lasting? She had known about it of course – it had been a lovers' meeting she had blundered on that evening by the river – but except for the fleeting impression that the young man was not Alex at all but a stranger held in some sort of trance, she had not thought it important. Wasn't he always involved in some adventure? Even in nursery days he used to say, 'Let's have an adventure' and would stride to the front door, fling it open and draw splendid breaths of adventure-laden air – and then nothing happened.

All her life she had lived in his reflected light, a lesser planet in the orbit of a brighter luminary. Without consciously observing them, she had come to know his every mood, every change in his voice. Their relationship had been too deeply shared to be recognized by either as a relationship at all.

Even so there had evidently been things she hadn't known. The most important factor in this adventure had been absent from those early days which now seemed remarkably uncomplicated. As to why she should think of Linden as a complication it would have been hard to say. After all she herself was responsible for having brought her to Monk's Dene in the first place. She had pleaded with her mother to invite the Greys. Linden was her friend: she should be pleased that she had become Alex's friend too.

Silently rolling up socks and tucking them into the toes of shoes, Margot discovered that she was not pleased – nor was 'friend' the right word. She felt instinctively – and how much more keenly later on – that Linden had so taken possession of Alex that he was changing and becoming somehow diminished. Indeed, enchantment must diminish a man: in loving Linden Alex would lose more than he gained. In being loved by him, Linden would gain all she could want, more perhaps than she could value. Such thoughts were as yet beyond Margot's power to formulate, but her reaction to the remark about the photograph had been one of alarm. Did Linden always get what she wanted?

When Alex came home at Christmas her misgivings were confirmed. Far from being broken, the spell held him more firmly than ever.

'Look here, Meg.' It was his first day at home. He had arrived late the night before. Margot was on a ladder hanging paper-

chains on the dining-room picture-rail. He picked up a handful
of the red and green loops and draped them carelessly round
Dante's First Meeting With Beatrice framed in oak above the
mantelpiece.

'I'm looking.'

'You've got to co-operate. I can't hang about here for the
whole vac. On the other hand, Mother won't be too happy if I
slope off too often.'

'Where do you want to slope off to?'

'To town of course. Dash it all, I haven't seen Linden yet. It's
been three months. We've written, naturally, at least I have pretty
often.'

'She'll be coming to the party.'

'That's not till Boxing Day and the house'll be packed with
people.'

'What do you want me to do?'

'Well, to start with I want you to come down to floor level and
find an excuse for going into town. Then I can quite decently
offer to go with you. It'll look better that way than if I push off on
my own the minute I've got here. Surely there's something you
need – or want – or have forgotten to collect?' He picked up a
library book and looked at the date. 'Do you realize that this
book is practically overdue?'

'Five days to go.'

'You're running it very close. Just think, in five days you might
be struck down by a fatal disease, say cholera or bubonic plague.
Or more likely fall off that ladder and break a leg. Then where
would you be? It's always wise to return a library book at least five
days before it's due. That is my own invariable custom.'

'I like to finish a book if possible. That's what I get it out for.'

'You can finish it on the bus. A mere fifty pages according to
the bookmark.'

'There's no need to complicate things. We can just go.'

There was a coat to be collected from the cleaner's, angelica
for trifles, a present to be delivered. There would be time for
Alex to lure Linden from her desk for coffee at Pikes while
Margot did the errands. Alex's mood as they walked down Castle
Street was buoyant. Half-a-dozen people called out to him or

41

crossed the street for a chat but he swept on, Margot hurrying to keep up, to the solicitor's office where Linden worked.

Worked? Her desk was at right-angles to the window. She saw them, got up unhurriedly and presently joined them on the pavement in hat, coat and gloves. She might have been expecting them.

'Won't they mind?' Margot asked.

'I don't think so.'

Margot had forgotten how attractive she was, how well her clothes became her; in this case a grey coat with deep fur collar and cuffs and a close-fitting winter hat which concealed her hair, isolating the frail facial bones and giving her the look of a medieval page. And Alex? Margot had not so much forgotten as failed to realize how handsome he was. When she left them and hurried off in search of angelica, it was with pride in their distinction as well as a variety of other emotions.

Alex leapt on to the homeward bus just as it started and took the seat behind Margot and her parcels.

'I can't bear it.' He leaned forward, his arms on the back of her seat. 'Not seeing her for weeks on end.' His voice was low and tense, just audible above the throb and rattle of the bus.

'You're serious about her?'

'Serious? Good Lord, you don't realize. She has completely changed my life. Haven't I slaved for years to get myself into something or other – some profession worthy of her?'

'You don't know which? I thought it was definitely law.'

'I'm not sure. Law may take too long.'

'Too long for what?'

He didn't answer. They had chugged along for another mile before he said, 'She's so brave about her problems. It's really touching, the way she makes light of them.'

'What are her problems?'

'You know – being absolutely alone in the world except for that weak-kneed desiccated mother of hers. No one she can turn to for support or financial help. Imagine her – eating her heart out in that moth-eaten office for a few shillings a week.'

Margot's imagination failed her. She could only remember her impression of Linden an hour ago – her elegance, her composure, the leisurely ease with which she had abandoned whatever she was supposed to be doing at her desk. But she understood – it was as clear as daylight – that the obvious solution to Linden's problems was a husband, and if it was clear to her, how very much clearer it must be to Linden!

'Can't you get Mother to ask her to stay, Meg?'

'Why don't *you* ask Mother?'

'Linden's your friend, isn't she?'

'Yours, too.'

'Friend? That's not the word. You don't know anything about that kind of thing but believe me – my God! She's. . . .'

There were no words to describe her, or the way she had stolen into his life and changed it. Her reserve enslaved him. She was always out of reach: an ice-maiden who had never melted in his arms and so had retained the mystery that haunted his imagination. That it was the product of his imagination was nevertheless a measure of the fascination she possessed. The quest for something more than she ever gave was an act of faith, a conviction that there must be something more. How dull at close quarters the legendary sirens may have been! How wise of them to keep their distance!

'She's the sort of girl that drives men mad.'

Margot's respect for Linden revived. There was something remarkable about a girl who could drive men to madness and at the same time inspire them to work hard at their studies. Somewhat unwillingly she did drop a hint to her mother that Linden might like to stay for a few days. The answer was firm.

'No, I don't think so, Margot. She can stay the night after the party but that is all.'

Sarah had seen enough of the Greys to justify leaving them to make their own way. If any launching into local society had been required, Marian had accomplished the manoeuvre herself. There were in and around Elmdon a number of comfortably situated families similarly placed to Sarah's own before she married. Their sons would enter professions, or make the army their career, or in some few cases inherit land. The Greys' contact with such people must be marginal but somehow contact had been made. Linden was invited to hunt balls and to various charity affairs. Through a network of acquaintances her name had cropped up when Embleton and Son were looking for a young woman for their front office, to sort and post mail, receive clients, serve sherry or tea and set the correct tone for a long-established firm. It was assumed that young women who went to hunt balls would not be deterred by the slenderness of the wage: they were only in search of a little pocket money until they married, especially young women without qualifications of any kind.

Not surprisingly, the Greys were still renting rooms in Gordon Street, the rest of their silver still presumably in store. Sarah had some idea of their straitened circumstances and the endless contrivances entailed in living on an army pension, but she had little sympathy for their pretensions. If she had formerly been complacent in dismissing Alex's infatuation with Linden as a flash in the pan, she was now more wary. But she saw nothing in his behaviour that any reasonable parent could object to and tried to persuade herself that Alex was mature enough to know that he was too young to form a permanent attachment.

'And you can't be much more illogical than that.' Edward was being bothered by yet another dispute with the directors, especially with his *bête noire*, Bedlow, and was inclined to brush aside the topic of young love. 'As a matter of fact, I'm not sure why you object to the girl.' That it would be years before Alex could think of marriage seemed too obvious to be worth discussing. 'What's wrong with her?' Quiet, rather colourless, ultimately boring, he thought.

Sarah hesitated. It was the morning after the party. Linden had just left.

'There's nothing wrong with her.'

'Then that's the trouble: there ought to be. The girl can't be human.'

'She's human,' Sarah said.

Alex and Margot were relaying the drawing-room carpet which had been taken up for dancing, Alex fuming because if Linden had waited for an hour or two, he would have been free to go with her; Margot raptly happy, her grasp on her corner of the carpet erratic. She had forgotten Linden, forgotten Alex glaring at her across the room, lost as she was in memories of what had been the most wonderful of all parties.

Lance was home from Glasgow where he was studying medicine. He spent most of his time with what he ambiguously referred to as his father's skeleton and had to be dragged to the festivities. But almost at the last minute, on the morning of the very day, they had heard that Miles was home from Oxford. She and Alex had gone to Bainrigg with a belated invitation.

Miles was at the piano when a maid showed them into the drawing-room. Unprepared, he sprang up and came towards them with such genuine pleasure in his eyes and smile, and so prompt an acceptance, that the reunion after more than four years was a happy one.

Though still shy and self-doubting, he was less awkward and no longer tongue-tied: he had learnt to some extent to talk to girls. At his school, he told Margot, as he twirled her expertly in a quickstep, there had been an interchange of dances with a girls' school. He had taken a few lessons and found that dancing was one of the things (one of the few things, he said) that he could do. He played the piano for carols and for the final singsong before the guests went home. He had been the last to leave and had promised to come again on New Year's Eve, and, as he was dark-haired, he would be their first-foot.

An exasperated twist on the diagonally opposite corner of the carpet roused Margot from a rapturous daydream.

Miles kept his promise. He came on New Year's Eve and was sent out just before midnight; waited until the clock struck twelve, knocked, and was admitted – blushing and diffident – carrying a paper of salt in one hand and a gleaming lump of best Wallsend coal in the other.

Afterwards he and Margot drank their ginger wine together, braving the cold on the front doorstep and looking out into starlight unchanged through countless centuries since the custom began. With a touch of awe Miles was conscious of having taken part in an endless procession of men bringing coal out of the dark to placate the pagan gods of fire.

'It's wonderful,' Margot said, the wonder embracing bare branches interlaced with stars, the closeness of Miles as he drew the shawl around her shoulders, the new year ready to unfold a succession of days more glamorous than days had ever been before. 'Looking out into night is like looking into the year ahead and wondering what it will bring.'

'I only hope you chose the right man to start it off and bring good luck.'

There was harmony between them, an interplay of light and shade; one confident that all would be well, the other daring to hope that nothing would go wrong.

CHAPTER VI

A spell of fine weather towards the end of June had ripened an unusually fine crop of strawberries in Miss Burdon's garden, a mixed blessing as with all soft fruit. Miss Burdon was at a loss as to what to do with them until she remembered that there would almost certainly be visitors at Monk's Dene over the weekend. Alex was coming home at the end of his second year at the university.

Her friendship with the Humberts owed less to congeniality than to long association. Burdons had supplied lawn and linen for Sarah's trousseau, and Miss Burdon herself had fashioned a boudoir cap for the bride, a confection of lace and satin ribbons which Sarah had never worn: it simply didn't stand up to Edward's ridicule. Nevertheless, Miss Burdon remained a family friend and the Humberts were her most valued customers, except perhaps for Mrs Rilston who from a sense of duty occasionally sent down for tapes, elastic, sateen linings and gingham for the maids' morning dresses. But one could scarcely offer strawberries to the Rilstons. Besides, the Humberts would probably offer to pick them.

Bella, the maid, had already started on the day's baking. Toria Link was unwillingly detached from her bucket and broom and sent down the lane to Monk's Dene. When she arrived at the open back door, Katie Judd was drying dishes in the scullery.

'Missis says there are plenty of strawberries if Mrs Humbert wants them,' Toria said and vanished. She was sparing of speech, a sullen-tempered, homeless woman who did the heavy work at Burdons in exchange for her keep and a bed.

Katie carefully dried her hands and went to the morning-room. Fortunately the door there was also ajar. What to do about a closed door was still beyond Katie, much as she had improved in other ways. Three square meals a day and a tentative approach to security in being close to Miss Margot had made her less fey.

'Missis says there are plenty of strawberries. . . .' She repeated the message correctly and added of her own accord, 'Toria says.'

There was no one to hear but Margot who was altering the hem of a dress. No one else could have understood that the addition marked an advance: it could be described as an initiative on Katie's part.

'Thank you, Katie.' She looked up. 'You do look nice.'

The pink-checked aprons, each with a handkerchief pocket, had been her idea: she had made them herself. With her hair under control, in unfearful moments, Katie was almost – or at least one could see that she had been intended to be – like any other girl. She had been helping Mrs Roper in the kitchen for almost a year.

'If only you'd take her on, Mrs Humbert,' Mrs Judd had brought herself to plead. 'Nobody else will. Nobody that'd treat her right. And it's a worry not always knowing where she is or who might be after her for reasons you know as well as I do.'

Sarah knew them very well. It was more for Katie's protection than for any use she might be that she had taken her on; but in her limited way she did prove useful. Maud, the housemaid, accepted her quite graciously and Mrs Roper claimed that Katie saved her legs. She also washed the kitchen floor every blessed day and swept up every scrap and crumb the minute it landed if not before.

Margot gave her mind to the strawberries. They would have to be picked. Katie might help, but Miss Burdon did not look kindly on Katie. It would be better to send Katie to the farm for cream and she herself would do the picking. Linden would be arriving on the mid-morning bus. Would Linden enjoy strawberry-picking?

Neither Margot nor her mother knew how it had come about that Linden would be here when Alex came home. There had been time for Sarah's wariness to abate a little: it revived promptly when Linden arrived with an over-night bag.

'You shouldn't have asked her to stay.'

'I didn't. She must have thought. . . .'

The whispers in the hall ceased as Linden came downstairs, having left her things as usual in the room adjoining Margot's. It was immediately apparent that she would be of no use as a picker of strawberries: in her white blouse and skirt she must be kept well away from the merest drop of fruit juice.

'You won't mind coming to Miss Burdon's? You can be looking for something to buy while I pick.'

At that moment there occurred another of those encounters that had been from time to time rather upsetting. Katie, with a dust-pan and brush, had crept from the kitchen, bent in both senses on sweeping under the morning-room table where there were sure to be crumbs from breakfast. The unexpected sight of Linden brought her to a halt in the old state of crazy alarm. She lowered her head, shrank against the wall and sidled back to the kitchen.

'She doesn't change.' Linden's calm indifference was also unchanged. Such an exhibition of what she thought of as idiotic gibbering in no way threatened her apparently unshakeable poise. All the same, as a result of such incidents perhaps, Margot had sometimes sensed in Linden's attitude towards Katie something more than amused contempt; rather a veiled hostility. Certainly Katie's strange behaviour was unflattering and far from abating, it seemed to have increased.

It was better not to discuss Katie as they walked up Church Lane.

'Isn't it nice – Miles is at home. He took me for a spin in his car yesterday – to Langland Priory. Such an interesting place. There's an empty house, Langland Hall, close to the ruins. . . .' She said it as casually as possible, as Linden might have done, without gushing about how heavenly it had been.

To enter Burdon's shop was to exchange the quiet of the village street for a deeper silence – a solemn hush between walls stacked high with bales of casement cloth and black serge. At each of the mahogany counters a tall hardwood chair invited the customer to perch, in an atmosphere heavy with the odours of fabric and furniture polish. The whole effect was weighty. Purchases were not to be made lightly.

If made at all. In the two years since the General Strike and the twenty-six weeks when the miners had stayed out, trade had been slow. Hours might pass without a single ring of the shop bell. With Bella far away in the kitchen and Toria on her knees in distant regions at the back, there was no sign of human life. Then presently would come a faint footfall on the thick carpet and Miss Burdon would appear.

But on this particular morning she was already there, unusually active and flushed with pleasure in the new delivery, conscious too of having taken a bold step. Carvers, drapers in Elmdon, had also suffered losses and had put up most of their stock for sale, intending to restock with cheaper goods for a less discriminating clientele. Such a sign of change, together with the rapid greying of her hair, had concentrated Miss Burdon's mind and made her reckless. She had dipped into her savings and bought up more of Carvers' stock than she could afford.

Both counters were strewn with lace-trimmed underwear, night-dresses, bed-jackets. . . . She had taken them lavishly from their boxes, ignoring the probability that most of them would be left on her hands for months if not for ever, and was actually humming 'Drink to me only with thine eyes' as she checked items against the invoices.

The arrival of Margot and Linden raised her spirits still further: they were the very ones – the only ones – likely to buy and spread the word among their friends.

'Because, of course, I can offer them at a slightly lower price than Carvers were asking. What do you think of these?'

Both girls admired a georgette scarf – and a white silk blue-sprigged blouse with a deep semi-circular flounce in place of a collar. The fashion was for low necklines scooped out in an oval or cut to a V and made more practical for daytime by the insertion of a modesty vest, a rectangle of silk of crêpe-de-Chine with concealed pins. The fashion was also for long strings of beads.

'Pearls never date, do they?' Miss Burdon had taken two necklaces from their slim boxes. 'And really the imitations are quite convincing enough for most people.' The remark was addressed with a smile almost roguish to Linden, as to an acknowledged arbiter of taste. 'I shall keep them in their boxes until I have arranged the new stock and then they will look very well on the cabinet. Shall we try the effect?' She opened the glass door of the narrow cabinet standing on the counter and Linden draped the long, gleaming string of pearls on the black velvet, and it was Linden who offered to help with the checking when Margot tore herself away to the strawberry bed.

'I'm almost at the end of the list. If you would read the item and put a tick when I've found it.' Miss Burdon handed her a pencil. 'I've got as far as . . . two white lawn nightdresses with Richelieu-embroidered neck. . . .'

It was cool but stuffy between the high counters and the higher shelves. When the lists had been checked, Linden helped to fold the garments and put some of them back in their boxes. She was neat-fingered but languid, and when Miss Burdon retreated to the dining-room, murmuring something about coffee, she too abandoned the shop, leaving a froth of artificial silk and crêpe-de-Chine still on the counter, and drifted into the passage which formed the hall of the private house.

She was idly examining the rows of pictures on both walls when the shop-bell rang.

'Do you mind seeing who it is, dear? I shan't be a minute,' Miss Burdon called from a stooping position as she reached for cups from the sideboard.

For Katie, Burdons' shop was alien territory fraught with every kind of hazard. She had been inside twice before, once with her mother, once with her sister, never alone. All the way up Church Lane she had been repeating her message and had it safe inside her head. Nothing else was safe.

The loud ring of the bell above her head made her tremble. Fearfully, she closed the door. The ringing stopped. The message was still there, ready to be said aloud. 'Tell Miss Margot that Mr Miles is here. Would she like a trip to town?' She went slowly to the right-hand counter and waited, clutching the brass rim with both hands. It was smooth and cool and bright; the counter was covered with things she had never seen before, laces and ribbons and soft silk. There were shining white beads, too, like the ones in the glass case but not shut away, just lying there. Venturing the tip of one finger, she touched them, with her small cautious smile of pleasure in pretty things.

Suddenly someone else was there – in the doorway halfway down the shop and coming nearer. It wasn't Miss Margot or Miss Burdon. Katie knew who it was – all in white like the white things on the counter and with a pale unsmiling face and round it, heavy, dark hair. Cold eyes looked out at her from under thick, long-lashed eyelids.

That was what Katie saw, but she also felt in the part of her that warned her about things, a sour breath of enmity. Something came towards her that made a darkness in her, in her whole body. She drooped her head. It was safer not to look. She could not run, must not go until she had said her message.

'Yes?' the cool voice said.

'Tell Miss Margot. . . .' Katie covered her face with her hands and spoke the rest of her message into their protective shade.

'What did you say?' Linden waited, then returned to the hall and so to the back door opening on the garden. 'You're being asked for.'

Margot had filled the big bowl. She was hot, tired and sick to death of picking strawberries.

'It's Katie. She's been struck dumb as usual.'

'I'm coming. Tell her to wait while I wash my hands.'

Margot nipped into the kitchen, washed her hands, accepted from Bella a newly baked almond biscuit – and heard the shop-bell ring again. Miss Burdon heard it too. A second customer? But when she and Margot entered the shop together, except for Linden, it was empty. The second bell had signalled Katie's flight.

'When I came back, she'd gone.' Linden's tone was one of patient resignation to the longeurs of the morning.

'It isn't like her to go without saying why she came. She likes running errands.' Margot went out to the step. There was no sign of her. 'I believe I know why she was sent. That's Miles's car. Would you excuse us, Miss Burdon, if we don't stay for coffee? May we come another time? And thank you so much for the strawberries. They're magnificent. Mother will be pleased.'

Miss Burdon was a little put out. She had twice expected a

customer and it was only that tiresome Katie Judd, a half-wit who didn't know what she was doing most of the time. People like that should be put away. Miss Burdon would have enjoyed entertaining the two girls to coffee. She was fond of Margot, indeed of any young people whom it was suitable and not too exacting to be fond of. She folded three pairs of flesh-coloured cami-knickers and returned them to their boxes, feeling all at once in the need of a little fresh air.

Miles, sunburnt and smiling, had been leaning against the car at the Humberts' gate and came to meet them.

'I wondered – hoped – thought you might like me to run you into town.'

He had greeted Linden but it was Margot he addressed.

'I'd love it but I don't think I should go. These berries will have to be hulled' – she was beginning to hate them – 'and there are other things. . . . We aren't sure when Alex will turn up.'

'Unfortunately I can't wait.' His grandmother was unwell. He had been dispatched with a prescription to the chemist in Elmdon and had promised to be back by twelve. 'May I come down later? This evening?'

'Yes, do. Alex will be home by then. Or come this afternoon if you can.'

'I'd like to.' He climbed into his car.

'I wonder. . . .' Linden had not yet spoken. 'You could save me from an awkward situation. It's been worrying me. I called at the office this morning with a message for Mr Embleton – actually it's my Saturday off – and forgot to tell him that the client he was expecting at twelve-thirty had telephoned yesterday that he would be coming earlier. There'd still be time to warn him if you could. . . .'

'Certainly. Hop in.'

Miss Burdon waved from her open door as the car passed. Linden returned the wave. Such a charming girl, delightful smile, faultless teeth; and how reassuring to meet a young woman of such refinement. Margot was a dear girl but she could learn a good deal from her friend, acquire a little of the polish not to be found in Ashlaw. And young Mr Rilston. The two young people had much in common, coming from a similar background. Miss

Burdon was a believer in the importance of backgrounds. Their fathers had served in the same regiment, both, alas, killed. It was fitting that the young people should become friends – and very likely more than friends.

Their smooth passage through the village together on a summer morning suggested a romantic flight and roused in Miss Burdon memories of her own distant youth, though of course it was only dog-carts and gigs in those days. Iron railings enclosed the three feet of ground between the shop and the pavement and in that narrow confine an old rose-bush had put out new pink blooms. Miss Burdon inhaled their fragrance. Sunshine, roses, young lovers, strawberries successfully disposed of without the bother of picking them, the new consignment of delicate underwear – together restored her to good humour: until she went back into her shop and found that one string of pearl beads was missing.

CHAPTER VII

In a little more than an hour, everyone in the village knew or was about to be told that Katie Judd had pinched some beads from old Sally Burdon's shop. Ashlaw's underground channels of communication were alerted when Miss Burdon, bare-headed and wrathful, was seen striding down the lane to Monk's Dene, pausing only under the gateway arch to wrest the sleeve of her dress from a vicious briar.

'It's just as I thought, Mrs Humbert, when I refused to have her in my house. I'm bound to say that you took a risk in having her in yours. The girl is light-fingered as well as all the other things that are wrong with her. If you take my advice you'll look round to make sure that she hasn't taken anything of yours.'

The attack had been sudden. Sarah herself had gone to the door. Margot, hearing Miss Burdon's voice raised in anger, had joined her mother in the hall, her hands once more blood-red. They had difficulty in getting a word in but Miss Burdon's manner was aggressive enough to put them instantly on the defensive.

'Do come in' – Sarah indicated the dining-room – 'and sit down. Then we can talk this over.'

'Thank you but I haven't come to talk. I have come to ask Kate Judd to give me back those beads. Perhaps you would tell her that I want to see her. Considering the sort of person she is, I won't go to the police.'

'My goodness, Miss Burdon, I hope you won't.'

'Are you sure, Miss Burdon, that they aren't there?' Margot ventured. 'I mean there were so many things on the counter.

Couldn't they have got caught up in something? Please let me come and help to look. I'll just wash. . . .'

'Bella and I have looked everywhere. Every single item has been taken out of its box and shaken. I wouldn't make such an accusation unless I was quite sure that it was justified.'

'You'd better bring her, Margot.'

Katie had been helping to hull the strawberries, slowly and carefully. She and Margot had sat quietly, side by side in the old dairy, each with a big plate, a colander and a sheet of newspaper.

'Come and wash your hands, Katie.'

They held their hands under the tap, taking turns, and dried them on opposite ends of the towel. When Katie had dried each of her fingers separately, she carefully wiped a trace of moisture from the back of Margot's hand.

'You came to the shop, didn't you, to tell me. . . .'

'Tell Miss Margot that Mr Miles is here. Would she like a trip to town?' The smile of pride in remembering faded into uncertainty.

'I didn't see you. I was in the garden.' Recognizing signs of tension – a stiffening and quickened breathing, Margot added hastily, 'But it didn't matter: you did what you were told. You didn't need to wait.'

Was the anxiety a sign of guilt or no more than the worry of not having delivered her message?

'There were things on the counter, weren't there?'

Katie nodded, remembering the white things, remembering the white-clad figure coming nearer – and then the loud clang of the bell as she escaped. She began to rock backwards and forwards in growing agitation. Margot's heart sank.

'Were there some beads?'

From the hall came the sound of Miss Burdon's voice. It had grown louder. Katie heard her own name. Her eyes, pale as a startled hare's, registered terror.

'Did you pick them up? The beads?' Slowly, Katie put out her right hand, the fingers crooked as if to touch.

'Miss Burdon thinks you took the beads? Did you take the beads, Katie?'

And suddenly Margot couldn't bear it. It was as if in a flash of

understanding she saw the world as Katie saw it: a vast frightening muddle of disconnected events, incomprehensible people
and strange sensations. The moment of insight passed, leaving
her restored to a world in which Katie was a stranger. She saw
instead the shrinking figure, the anxious face, the trembling; felt
the awfulness of the situation, the awfulness of Miss Burdon and
her beads.

'Never mind.' She put her arm round Katie's thin shoulders.
'I'll look after you. I'll always look after you.' She took her hand
and led her to the hall.

Mrs Roper, putting plates to warm in the small oven, had been
drawn nearer to the kitchen door by the sound of Miss Burdon's
voice. The opening sentences were enough to convey a sense of
urgency. The word 'police' caused her to whip off her apron. It
took her little more than five minutes to reach the Judds' house
in Clint Lane and, panting, to raise the alarm.

Mrs Judd was alone and as usual at her wash tub. The small
house was full of the warm damp smell of soap suds.

'She's there, I tell you, without as much as a hat on her head
and raising Cain. But she did say she wouldn't go to the police.'

Even the reassurance was received as a threat.

'If she did it would be over my dead body.' Mrs Judd leaned for
a moment on her poss-stick for support against a tide of troubles
that never ebbed. 'Slip along to Number Seven, will you, and tell
our Emily while I get my good shoes on.'

She had barely eased her swollen feet into them when Emily
appeared with a six-month-old baby in her arms.

'If our Katie's stolen them beads, it's the first thing she's ever
stolen in her whole life.' A faint reflection of the scowl darkening her brow might even then be seen on that of the infant: he
was a Judd all over.

'She'd mean no harm, poor little soul,' Mrs Roper said, 'and
she's never taken anything from my kitchen, I can swear to that.'

'There's no knowing what she might do. She's not of this
world and never will be. I've known that since the minute I first
laid eyes on her. "What's this, Polly?" Jo says. "I think we've got
the fairies to thank for this one". "You're not accusing me of

wrong-doing, I hope", I says to him, "Nay, love", he says. "She's taken after my mother's side. They were all pale and fair. It was the Judds that were always dark and gruesome-like. This one's going to be different".'

'He never spoke a truer word,' Emily said, and seeing the rare glint of tears in her mother's eyes added, 'and he loved her best. Whatever her troubles, he loved our Katie best.'

'And that's something.' Mrs Roper propped the blazer on the ash-box and turned back the clipping mat. 'There's no taking that away from her. Say what you like, it pays to have a man behind you when there's trouble. With Rob away at sea, it's a pity your Ewan isn't here.'

Ewan had gone after a job at the rope-works in the coastal town where his father had worked as a boy. He'd got a lift there but would likely be walking back – ten miles if it was an inch.

'It's maybe a good thing he isn't here,' Emily said. 'He's got a temper, our Ewan. And little Stanley,' she referred to the baby, 'he's the image of both his uncles, isn't he, Mam?'

'I'll have to be getting back.' Mrs Roper glanced at the wall clock. 'It'll be time to put the potatoes on.'

At Monk's Dene she ushered them through the kitchen to the hall. The front door stood open. Miss Burdon's ample figure filled the space it left. Sarah had subsided on to a chair. Margot, holding Katie's hand, faced Miss Burdon and as much of the summer morning as was still visible beyond her. An impasse had been reached. The Judds to some extent constituted a relieving force but little relief was felt.

'I've heard what you're saying she did.' Mrs Judd ignored Sarah and attacked the enemy. 'You may be right and you may be wrong. If she's taken what isn't hers, I'll take the strap to her; if you're saying what isn't true, you've got your own conscience to reckon with.'

'There's no need to take that tone with me, Mrs Judd. My conscience is perfectly clear. All I want is my property back and no more need be said. Except that I never want to see your girl on my premises again. I can scarcely bolt the door of my shop, but I shall hold you responsible for keeping her away.'

'Give her the beads, Katie.'

Of all the terrors Katie had endured, none could equal this. All eyes had turned on her, singling her out. All these people expected her to do something she didn't know how to do. Her heart thumped so that her whole body felt as if it would burst open. She strained her eyes but could not see for the mist that clouded them. Something terrible would happen – was happening.

'Where have you put them, love?' It was her mother's voice.

Katie looked up at Margot who was a little taller, for help, and Margot yearned with all her heart to give it. She knew that when Katie swayed her head from side to side it was not in refusal but in distress.

'I'll take her home, Mrs Humbert, and see what's to be done.'

'I think that might be best, Mrs Judd.'

But Katie backed away from her mother, desperately needing somewhere to hide. A low dresser occupied the space under the stairs. Everywhere else there were people. Still backing, she found her way to the dining-room door. It was a few inches ajar. She slid to her knees against the jamb and turned her face from the company.

'Let her stay,' Margot pleaded, 'until she feels better. She really doesn't understand what it's all about. I'll bring her home when she's been quiet for a while.'

Alex was not surprised to find the hall full of people: the Humberts rarely had the house to themselves. But it was clearly a crisis of some sort. His mother's 'Here's Alex' was an appeal rather than the joyful welcome he had expected. He had to step on one side to see, beyond the stately figure of Miss Burdon, the Judds, the baby, and Katie crouching by the dining-room door.

'Such a worrying thing, Alex. . . .'

Never had Margot been more proud of her brother, more glad to have him home, more awed by his competence. He put down his suitcase; he listened; he understood.

'What are you charging for your pearl beads, Miss Burdon?'

Hustled by so direct a question from the loftier heights of justice and of conscience, Miss Burdon bridled.

'Four and elevenpence,' she said, with as much dignity as could be infused into words so mundane.

'Then let me reimburse you for your loss.' Alex took two half-crowns from his pocket. Perforce she proffered an unwilling palm. 'I hope by the way that your strawberries are doing well this year. I've been looking forward—'

'Well, yes, as it happens. . . .'

To be deflated and mollified in an instant proved too much for Miss Burdon who quickly saw the advantage of leaving. When she had gone, the Judds also left, pausing only for a word or two – or considerably more – with Mrs Roper in the kitchen. Sarah and Margot fussed over Alex who, having travelled overnight, went upstairs to bath and change.

No one knew at which moment in the drama Katie made her exit. She wasn't under the dining-table though the big tablecloth would have made a tempting hiding place, nor anywhere in the house or garden, though it was a garden of winding paths and grottoes of shade where one could lose oneself. Margot meant to make a thorough search after lunch. The whole morning had been of the worst kind for Katie: the visit to the shop; the mistake – that was the only way to describe it – of taking the beads; the dreadful confrontation with Miss Burdon, the extraordinary arrival of her mother, Emily and Stanley; the threat of the strap. It would be some time before she recovered. On the other hand, Katie's states of mind were so unpredictable that she herself might be exaggerating. In any case, Katie would go home at her usual time, six o'clock, even if she didn't come back to Monk's Dene. Once before she had hidden for a whole day after breaking a teapot lid.

It was more surprising and particularly disappointing for Alex that Linden was also missing. Alex had called at Embletons' in the hope of seeing her but she wasn't there.

'There was nobody there. According to the chap in the bookshop next door, the office is always closed on Saturdays.'

'How strange! Linden said. . . .' What was it Linden had said? Had she misunderstood?

But Alex, fortunately perhaps, had gone to put out deck chairs and settle down to wait for her, feeling aggrieved that she had gone off like that. It was mid-afternoon when Linden sauntered

in by the back gate and so round to the garden. Margot was lend-
ing a hand in the kitchen and didn't see the reunion. When she
did join them she was aware of having interrupted an intimate
conversation.

'I'm so sorry, Margot, not to have been back in time for lunch.
I must apologize to your mother.' Miles had been delayed at the
chemist's. She had insisted on his driving straight to Bainrigg
instead of coming round by Ashlaw. She had felt obliged to drop
in for a few minutes to ask how Mrs Rilston was and had been
persuaded to share an informal lunch and then to look round
the garden. 'It's delightful, isn't it?'

'I've only seen it in winter,' Margot said, 'when we went to
invite Miles to the Christmas party.'

'Naturally, Miles offered to run me home but I didn't feel that
Mrs Rilston should be left. Besides, it's such a lovely day and
downhill all the way. I was determined to walk home. Miles came
with me part of the way, then I sent him back.'

She had come, though not suddenly, to a halt. A few yards ahead,
iron gates in a wall marked the limit of the gardens and private
grounds surrounding Bainrigg House. Beyond lay open fields.

'You must let me go on alone,' she said, and although Miles
did not protest and merely opened the gate to let her through, it
was with a hint of persuasion, even of playful reproach that she
added, 'It wouldn't do, would it? People are so. . . . Well, you
know what they're like.' With a slight inclination of her head she
seemed to draw attention to the village in the valley below.

'Oh, yes, rather.' Miles answered vaguely. He too was looking
down over the fields. There was someone down there by the ash
tree at the end of Clint Lane, someone in pink. Margot? Come to
meet Linden? She had been wearing pink yesterday when he
drove her to Langland Priory. 'It's glorious, Miles,' she had said
with the sun on her face and the wind in her hair. Her capacity
for unreserved happiness delighted him.

Then he pictured her as she had been this morning in Church
Lane. It was easy for him: he was always doing it. Her dress had
been blue like the bowl of strawberries she held in both hands.
He remembered that she wouldn't know that Linden had come

to Bainrigg. Besides, he looked again – whoever it was had disappeared.

'One has to be a little careful,' Linden was saying.

'I suppose so.' He closed the gate, shutting her out, but she had seen his face light up in sudden eagerness, and had seen the light die. Was he disappointed that their time together had been cut short?

'Did Miles say that he would be coming?'

'Yes.' Linden smiled. 'I believe he did.'

Something in her manner was irksome to Alex, depressing to Margot who was to recall every aspect, every incident of that day and, with particular clarity, Linden's part in it, including her impression that Linden had something on her mind, some preoccupation beneath the smooth flow of unexceptionable remarks. How useful they were in concealing the speaker's thoughts; how conveniently they could be adapted to falsify the truth. She had lied about the message to Mr Embleton. Now, at ease in the shade of the apple trees, she seemed – not exactly at one with the summer day – rather a visitant sent to enhance it with a touch of elegance, but not to be trusted. The discovery was startling.

'Has Alex told you about Katie?'

He had not. He had found more important things to talk about. Certainly the unimportance of Katie was apparent in Linden's response to the news.

'I don't suppose she knew what she was doing. She was certainly there on her own. I found her crouching by the counter. And then she was alone again when I went to call you. How upsetting for you all. But really – a string of cheap beads!'

It was possible to forget Miss Burdon while eating her strawberries. Lance ate rapidly and went back to the monastic seclusion of his room at home. The skeleton had been ousted, fortunately in theory only, by what he referred to as liver and lights. In the evening, the other three set Miles on his way home. He had come on foot with just such a contingency in mind. Alex and Linden walked slowly and he and Margot went on ahead.

'How were the bluebells this year?'

'They were lovely. I never saw so many. . . .'

Her prompt reply faded into hesitation. He loved her openness and her slight embarrassment. She saw his amusement and smiled, wishing all the same that she hadn't blurted it out like that. She could have said that they were always lovely, as if she hadn't bothered to come now that she was older. He must not know how often she had come through the Bainrigg gate – they had just reached it – and had wandered casually along the edge of the field to the stone pit and on to the wood. It had become her favourite walk in all weathers and although Miles was always at school and then at Oxford, or staying with his mother's relations, it was always possible that he might for once be there.

Now, as if filling in time until the others caught up, they turned to the left along the field's edge. Trees stood motionless in the faintly golden light of evening. The stone pit – how had they come so far? – was full of flowers – mullein, blue scabious and moon daisies. High above as they looked up from its sheltering sides, swallows swooped and soared, making intricate invisible patterns on the sky.

Should he tell her how often he came there, not expecting – scarcely allowing himself to hope that he would find her, but taking pleasure in the place because she liked it; not yet daring to seek her out, knowing that some day he would find her there. Taken by surprise, she would greet him with the look of luminous delight that made her, lovely as she was, more than beautiful. She was so young and unspoiled. He must never impose himself upon her; never go about things in the wrong way. If only he knew, if only he had the faintest idea what the right way was, or when would be the right time to go about it. Even taking her hand, for instance, as he longed to do, might be the wrong thing and spoil this perfect moment.

The more nearly perfect the moment, the shorter-lived. They had startled a rabbit and saw it dart, terror-stricken to its burrow. As its white scut disappeared, Margot's mood changed. A frightened creature running for safety to its secret place. . . . She looked round.

'I wonder where Katie is?'

They had called at the farm where roses now clung to the trellised porch and five-year-old Rosie (as she inevitably had become) listened wide-eyed as her mother told them, 'No, there's not been a soul gone this way except that young lady in the afternoon all by herself' – Linden and Alex were to be seen sauntering up the cart road – 'and then Mr Miles just before tea.'

They had also called at the Judds, ducking under the lines of washing to ask if she had come home.

'She'll be back before dark for sure.' Mrs Judd was shaking out pillow-cases. 'I'll send down to let you know when she does.'

They had left her, forgotten the Judds and been happy, but now, sensitivity strung to the highest pitch by the wonder and strangeness of being in love, Margot felt in the still air a quickening as of other kinds of strangeness, as if from the heart of silence came warning whispers.

'She shouldn't be alone, not now. I should have stayed with her.' The dark, instead of driving her home might keep her away, hidden in some secret place where no one else could go.

'Did she ever come here?' Miles didn't remember ever having seen Katie but he was touched by Katie's concern.

'Oh yes, when we came for bluebells sometimes.'

Come to think of it, Katie had often been with her. There had been a closeness overlooked while it lasted; its strength, like that of elastic, only perceived when released. She turned, aware as she had so often been of Katie at her elbow, so pale and light, so easily ignored that she might have been here, unnoticed, but there was only Miles looking down at her, in his eyes a look of more than shared concern. She could tell him anything, everything, and he would understand.

'I had such a feeling in Clint Lane. . . . One of her pinafores was hanging on the line. . . .' For once there had been no wind and it had hung there, lifeless. 'And I thought, suppose. . . .' After all it was too fanciful to put into words the notion that Katie's outward self was so delicate, so tremblingly unsure of a footing on the earth that it might quite easily escape altogether, take flight, rarefy, and become thin as air where swallows flew so high as to be out of sight, then swooped to skim the green hedge. Head tilted, she stared upward, dazzled, half remembering some other time, some other upward flight when the earth fell away and there was nothing but light and air. 'She loves her pinafore. There was some material left over from my pink dress. . . .'

'I believe I saw her.'

'Here?'

'No. Down by the ash tree this afternoon. I thought at first it was you.'

'Then she wasn't far from home. Which way did she go?'

Miles could not say. The pink shape had been there one moment and gone the next. He had stood at the gate for a minute as Linden walked down the field path. Would Linden have seen Katie? Evidently not; she would have said so. All the same when they all met at the field gate, Margot naturally asked her.

'No.' The reply was instant. Then more forcibly repeated. 'No. I didn't see anyone. It was pleasant and quiet, such a change for me.' She had gone by way of the farm. 'I didn't know that I'd be taking the same walk all over again.'

She leaned wearily against the gatepost, seemed out of sorts and complained of the heat. It was clearly time to go home. Margot looked back once to wave to Miles who was watching them from his side of the gate.

Having floated cloud-like for the past hour, she was now downcast. The walk home became a silent trudge. Light was failing when they came to the ridge. The village below lay shrouded in dusk. From every chimney rose a column of smoke. The evening ritual of stoking kitchen fires had begun; the heaping of coal, source of all comfort and daily threat to the men who hewed it.

The Judds' door was open, their yard dully red from firelight within.

'No.' Mrs Judd went on ironing without looking up. 'She isn't back. She's nowhere about the farm. When Ewan came back he went straight out to look for her. He didn't get the job and hasn't had a bite to eat.' Then as they turned away she put down the iron and came to the door. 'She's never been out as late as this before. Not when it gets dark.'

Impossible to sleep. Thinking of Miles did not help. At some time after midnight Margot had reached the state, half waking, when the day's events take on the likeness of dream, feelings and images interfused. Katie was crouching in a dark burrow, or was it a counter in Burdons' shop? Phantom-like she was rising into the air, growing smaller, almost out of sight, then suddenly falling faster and faster and vanishing.

'Alex, are you awake?'

'As a matter of fact I am. What's up?'

'It may be just silly but I've had the most awful idea about where Katie might be. She was in such a state. She would want to hide in a place where she could never be found, ever.'

Alex listened, apparently sceptical. No wonder: it did seem improbable.

'You've got Katie on the brain. I never heard such rot. For heaven's sake, go back to bed. And mind you don't wake Linden. She was very tired.'

To be told it was all rot was what she had counted on. She had certainly been out of her mind and was so still to some extent. Tiptoeing to bed, she noticed that the door between her room and Linden's had swung open slightly. Linden was not asleep either. There had been just enough light from the uncurtained window to make out her white figure kneeling by the bed. The abnormality of the day had stretched into the night. She who never prayed was saying her prayers.

Why? Margot was too tired to wonder and soon fell asleep. Sounds of movement in the house an hour later did not disturb her. It was not until morning that she learned how Alex and Lance had spent the rest of the night – and what they had found.

CHAPTER VIII

The shop stood empty for a long time after Miss Burdon left. For a time she had hung on, not from stubbornness but because she could not afford to move. After Katie's death the shop bell ceased to ring; in fact, Katie herself was probably the last person to ring it. The knell it tolled was not only for her but for Miss Burdon's means of livelihood. Not another inch of ribbon crossed her counter; not another farthing fell silently into her empty till.

She may never have seen the word 'Murderer' chalked on the pavement outside her door as she remained indoors, alone and in constant dread of the Judds. Rob's ship docked in time for the funeral; Jo's two younger brothers and Ewan made up a formidable quartert. Toria Link drifted away just before a third volley of bricks shattered the big window. Bella, unwilling to sacrifice the regard of Ewan Judd by staying on, found a job at the Penny Bazaar in Elmdon. It was assumed that Miss Burdon was still at home, invisible behind shutters and drawn curtains until at last the shop was let and she moved away.

Hers was not the only life to be altered by the death of a morsel of humanity insignificant even in a community as small and unremarkable as that of Ashlaw. No one beyond the limits of the village had ever heard of Katie Judd. Many had never heard of Ashlaw, not until they read the headlines in the county press, TRAGIC DEATH OF WAR ORPHAN: GIRL'S BODY FOUND IN MINE SHAFT and more colourfully in its columns: *Accused of theft she fled. . . . Death trap. . . . Scandalous neglect. . . . Her life for a string of beads?*

Who was responsible? The weight of blame was distributed

between her accuser, the police (as a matter of course), the coal company, the landowner, and the late Bert Cosway, a former owner of the Lucknow Drift, deceased in 1902. The only people to emerge unscathed from the tragedy were the gallant young men who had found the girl and participated in the recovery of her body regardless of personal risk.

Only Margot knew how Alex felt. After she left him that night he had lain awake. Far-fetched as it seemed, it was not impossible that Katie had tried to hide in the shaft. Miles had seen her there by the ash tree; the brickwork was low enough in some places to be stepped over. To Katie's imperfect understanding, that was a place where things disappeared from sight and were never seen again.

And who had driven the message home, lording it over his humble admirers from Clint Lane, among them quite possibly Katie herself? He found it hard to believe that the ridiculous incident could have such a long-term effect and yet, improbable as it was, he couldn't rest without making sure.

There was a light in Lance's window: he was still mulling over other people's livers. The two had reached the ridge in the grey of daybreak and shone torches down into the shaft. Discarded rubbish had caught on the rough masonry of the casing and had impeded her fall. She had dropped to a point just beyond reach and lay suspended on the rail of a dismembered bed-head wedged crosswise. They had roused the constable and two of his neighbours: it seemed best to keep the Judds out of it. Alex had insisted on being the one to be lowered.

'There was absolutely no danger with a rope round the tree and four men to haul me up. It makes me sick to be praised for courage. I tell you, Meg, this thing has put years on me. The Greeks had a saying: Man know thyself. Looking back I see myself as a conceited ass.'

He looked older, and not merely because he was pale and heavy-eyed. As long as he lived he would remember the cool dawn breeze and the scent of elderflowers, the first downward look into the dark, the distorted figure strangely sprawled in the torch light. . . . Holding her in his arms, he had felt the brevity of life, the finality of death.

'Her neck was broken. But Lance thinks that in any case she could have died of shock.'

For Lance too the experience had marked a turning point. Since the cautious handling of his first cadaver, he had familiarized himself with physical death but this was the first time he had been confronted with the corpse of someone he knew; of Katie who had cleaned his shoes and from time to time had nervously removed his empty dinner plate and backed away from the table as if it might explode. Taking her from Alex – light and limp in her pink apron – he underwent a change of heart. In those solemn minutes as daylight grew, he learned more than theory could teach. It was people who mattered; people who were breathing one minute and the next minute might be gone. He had thought himself wholly committed to medical research. It was Katie, her fair hair grimed with soot, her neck lolling, who changed his mind. She rescued him, he afterwards thought, from the laboratory and nudged him into general practice.

Margot suffered the first heartache she had known.

'I said that I would look after her – always. She was so helpless. I should have stayed with her.'

It was extraordinary that Katie, timid, almost speechless, patronized, forgotten most of the time, should leave an emptiness so wide, an echo so persistently reproachful.

'You loved her because she needed to be loved,' her father told her. 'There are so many things that people like Katie can't do, but there is something important they can do: they can create love.' In loving hearts he mentally added, remembering Miss Burdon.

Margot, drying her tears and shedding more, could have added another name to the list of those who had not loved Katie. The simplicity of her grief was soon complicated by a worrying thought. From the garden gate at Bainrigg, Miles had seen Katie though without knowing who she was. Linden, walking down the field path towards the chimney, had not seen her. A curve in the path or a thickness in the hedge might for a moment or two have limited her view.

But suppose Katie had seen Linden, conspicuous in her white skirt and blouse and coming towards her. They would soon be face to face, just the two of them in empty fields under a wide sky. Margot knew as surely as if she had been there, how Katie would have felt. Could it have been the sight of Linden that drove her panic-stricken to the nearest hiding place? How strange if her unaccountable fear of Linden had been in some weird way a forewarning that Linden would be the cause of her death, indirectly of course. Margot shivered in the grip of a superstitious fear as irrational as Katie's. There were already reasons, suppressed or unacknowledged, for the gradual change in her attitude to Linden. The possibility that she might unintentionally have driven Katie to her death at the very time when Katie most needed help seemed actually to change Linden herself. For the time being she didn't want to see her.

Nor did she. Linden left immediately after breakfast on the fateful morning and judiciously stayed away. The atmosphere at Ashlaw for the next week or two would not have been to her liking. Among other things she missed Katie's funeral.

Never in living memory had there been such a funeral in Ashlaw. For Jo Judd's sake as well as for his daughter's, the Hope Brass Band turned out to a man and led the cortège. It was felt that the *Dead March from Saul*, customary for men killed in the pit, was less suitable for a young girl. *Abide With Me* fell more kindly on the summer scene she had so abruptly left. The procession included every adult capable of following the hearse. Others lined the main street and Church Lane. Boys clinging to railings or peering through bushes took off their caps as Katie passed, the flowers on her coffin lying almost as deep as the earth that would soon cover it. The publicity surrounding her death had moved sympathizers to send donations to her family. Some of the more generous remained anonymous: neither the coal company, the landowner, or the Mining Association would wish to accept responsibility, but as individuals they were not without heart.

The Judds were gratified. Their prestige had never been higher. Their resentment against the world was appeased – for the time being – by the inquest, the crowds, the wreaths, the band and not least by the service in church. It was Mrs Dobie who urged the revival of the old custom of hanging white garlands in church when a young girl died. It had not happened for over fifty years and she was the only person who remembered it. Then, afterwards, the sit-down tea in the British Legion hut was photographed and the pictures were published in the *Elmdon Gazette*. The funeral did all that funerals are supposed to do in dignifying grief and making it bearable. The folk of Ashlaw, drawn together as they had been in other disasters, knew how to look after their own.

On the second day after the funeral, Margot made a private pilgrimate to Katie's grave. The little twelfth-century church of St Michael stood isolated from the village on a rise overlooking the river. Late sunshine gilded the gentle slopes beyond the church-yard wall. A mountain ash leaned over from the neighbouring pasture to shade the spot where – unbelievably – Katie lay in quietness unbroken save by the murmur of the river below.

Margot knelt to replace a fallen spray of flowers. She smelt the dying fragrance of wreathed lilies and the sharper scent of new-turned earth, and gradually there came to her in the hush of the June evening the sense of a mysterious yet natural wholeness: the transition from life to death was perhaps no more than the gentle flow of water between green banks in the valley below. The distress of the past days yielded to blessed relief. Katie was safe: nothing would harm or frighten her again.

Inside the church it was dim and cool. Above her head as she entered by the west door hung Katie's maiden garlands looped to a rail. They were made of white linen in the shape of crowns adorned with rosettes. Later they would be hung on the north wall.

Margot's heart leapt as the awesome silence was broken by a faint beating of wings on the St Oswald window. A bird, misjudg-ing the level of its flight, had struck the stained glass. It clung for an instant, wings outspread as if balked of entry, then took to the air once more and was gone.

Behind her the door opened. The garlands swayed in a current of air.

'Miles.'

'They said you had come this way.' To conceal his delight in having found her, he looked up at the crudely made garlands.

'There haven't been garlands since 1875,' she told him, 'when

Mrs Dobie was a girl. It was her idea to bring them for Katie. You remember Mrs Dobie?'

'No one could forget Mrs Dobie. It was a good idea. So many customs have died out – and that's how places change. I'd like things to stay just as they are' – how lovely she was, her eyes pensive, her lips tremulous – 'at this very moment.' Conscious of having spoken ardently, he looked up again at the dangling shapes. 'They used to hang gloves on them in the Middle Ages as a challenge to anyone who cast doubt on the innocence and purity of the dead girl.'

'No one doubts Katie's innocence. She must have taken the beads instinctively because they were pretty. She didn't realize that it was wrong – and she has paid for them, hasn't she?' Her voice trembled; she must find something else to talk about. 'I've been looking at the memorial tablets. Thomas Rilston, Isabella, Henry . . . they're all your ancestors.'

He told her about them. All except Isabella had died in battle: Thomas at Corunna in the Peninsular War: Henry on the North-west Frontier: another Thomas in the Boer War and the latest, Miles, his father, at Ypres.

'Must all the Rilstons be soldiers?' She saw that the question troubled him.

'It's been a problem.' He opened the heavy door and motioned her to the seat in the porch. 'I know it's inconsistent after what I said about disliking change, but I don't feel that I can carry on the family tradition of soldiering.'

'I'm glad. There have been far too many deaths. Mrs Dobie was right about that too. A wicked waste of flesh and blood, she called it.'

'Actually it's unlikely that there'll be another war in our time. The world is weary of slaughter. Killing on that scale must never happen again. I'd probably be safer in the army now than any of the earlier Rilstons but I'd still be out of my depth.'

'What would you like to do?'

He looked out from the narrow porch at ancient yews and headstones so worn by time that no one could tell who lay beneath them. Long beams of late sunlight touched here and there a carved cross or the crooked lettering of 'here lies . . .' and the bolder lines of a lost name. He could have said that he would like to stay for ever in such a hallowed place beside the one person with whom he felt at ease; that in the few hours they had spent together she had taught him how lonely he had been before he knew her. It was too soon: she was too young, her future still unshaped.

'I'd like to take up flying,' he said. He had a friend, an enthusiast with his own plane. 'I've been up with him a few times and taken the controls. It's a marvellous sensation – to look down on the earth. People shrink to pin-points in the sweep of the land – and all around you there's the empty sky.'

It's people who worry him, she thought. He isn't used to them. He doesn't understand people.

He was complaining that when a Rilston died his eldest son was expected to give up his career in the army and devote himself to looking after the family property. As a rule he would by that time be middle-aged. In his own case since the inheritance would miss a generation, it would probably come to him at an earlier age.

'Shall you like living at Bainrigg?'

'More than I once thought. Yes, I could be content here. Meanwhile being at Oxford gives one time to sort things out. . . . What is it? You're looking suddenly radiant?'

'I haven't told anyone yet, not even Mother. She wasn't there when I came home from school. Miss Hepple sent for me this very afternoon. She thinks there's a possibility – I'm sure it's not at all likely – but it might be worth trying. Actually it was such a surprise that I'm almost afraid to talk about it.'

'I hope eventually you're going to put me out of my suspense and tell me what on earth it is.'

'Oh, Miles, I never thought. . . . She thinks I might take the entrance exam for one of the Oxford colleges, St Hugh's, perhaps.'

Silenced by the sheer wonder of it, she leaned back and stared unseeing at the tablet of St Michael's incumbents on the opposite wall. It is doubtful whether in its long history the porch had ever encompassed a more blissful moment.

'Well done. If you come up to Oxford I'll be able to keep an eye on you.'

'Yes! But' – her face clouded – 'it would mean another year's study – and by that time you would have left.'

'Not necessarily. I may stay on and take another degree. That's one advantage of reading history, there's so much of it. One can go on for ever.'

She would read history too, her favourite subject even before she knew that it was also his. With Miles as guide she would wander amid the historic halls and seats of learning, hear the bells chime from venerable towers, trace the haunts of the Scholar-Gipsy. Her vision of Oxford was similar to, indeed identical with, that of Matthew Arnold.

For a moment he had lost her. His pleasure in the prospect of halcyon days together was modified by this fresh reminder that she was only eighteen, too young to be told that he hoped to share with her not only Oxford for a few years but Bainrigg for all the years to come. He must wait, thankful for having found at last something to live for.

Margot sensed his mood. She understood that by temperament he was inclined to be melancholy. Unlike Alex he was patient rather than decisive. Above all she sensed his loneliness. His mother had died when he was eight. Since Major Rilston had also been an only child there were no cousins on the paternal side of his family. A sudden realization of her own good fortune in being one of a complete family prompted her to say, 'You must come and see us more often, whenever you're at home.' The words and manner were her mother's. 'You mustn't mind my saying it. You're so short of relations.'

He smiled, regretting that she had given no other reason for the invitation. 'Your long-suffering family can't be expected to fill the gap. But it's true: I've never known the kind of home life you have at Monk's Dene.'

'It's the same with Lance, you know. He was very young when his mother died.'

'Did he get over it, do you think?'

'It must have made a difference, but Lance is such a strong person, so sure of what he wants to do. He doesn't seem to think about himself, only about what he thinks important. I suppose that's rather unusual.'

Margot reached the conclusion with surprise. She had never consciously noticed Lance, never given thought to his character, but had accepted him as a familiar feature of daily life. There was no need, no occasion to worry about him as she had so often found occasion to worry about Alex. To worry about Lance would be not only unnecessary but incongruous. A person always intent on fulfilling some purpose or other had neither time nor inclination to deviate into any kind of worrying behaviour.

Miles listened with some amusement to her inexpert analysis of Lance's character, but had she known it, the topic rather depressed him. He saw in the tawny-haired habitué of the Humbert household a being possessed of all the admirable qualities he himself lacked. Miles needed no reminder of his own deficiencies: thought of himself as indecisive, unimpressive, by nature an outsider. Even the most clearly formed of his intentions so far, to marry Margot, had as yet the luminous quality of a dream, a delight devoutly to be wished for rather than a campaign of purposeful moves towards a desired end.

His happiness was modified but he was happy still. They lingered in the porch until the sun went down, then loitered homeward in the after-glow. He reluctantly declined Margot's invitation to join the evening meal: his grandmother was still unwell and he would be wanted at home. They parted with the pang of severance, the sensation of being wrenched apart that lovers feel even though their love be undeclared, unratified by touch or kiss. In regret and rapture, Margot waited under the arch, now draped with the blue flowers of clematis, until he turned into the village street. She would remember the past hour and cherish its memory as one cherishes a gift that has outlived the giver.

But now she thought of the news she was burning to tell. She would wait until the end of the meal and while they were still at table – 'What *do* you think?' she would say casually. 'Miss Hepple thinks. . . .' Or even more nonchalantly, 'By the way, I rather gather that Miss Hepple thinks I might go to the university.' But she knew that nonchalance was beyond her, she would blurt it out, still gasping with the amazement she had tried to conceal when Miss Hepple said, 'Your work throughout the year has been of a consistently high standard.'

On either side of the garden path flowers were in bloom, lupins and larkspur and tiger-lilies. The perfume of orange blossom filled the air with the promise of long summer days. Had her talk with Miles roused in her a new awareness of the familiar scene? Or was she experiencing the heightened perception that warns of coming change? She saw the house as she had never seen it before. With all its windows open, curtains unruffled by any breeze, it seemed embowered in a rare stillness. It was more than an affair of brick and stone; it had garnered all the events of family life to hold and keep for ever when all the people who had come in and out had gone.

Stillness begets expectancy, otherwise why should she be holding her breath? The tea things were still on the garden table; they had been there when she came home from school. With a pang of remorse for having forgotten her, she thought of Katie, carefully carrying out cups and saucers one at a time.

Mrs Roper had evidently gone home. It was Maud's afternoon off. Father usually came home early on the day of his quarterly board meeting. He must have gone out again. Alex could be anywhere.

'Mother!' She was not in any of the downstairs rooms. A house with doors and windows open and no one about can be a little eerie even when there is nothing to fear. A rose petal fell from the bowl on the hall table. Instinctively she removed it from the polished surface and held its velvet softness to her cheek as she went upstairs to change. The door of her room was open. With a little shock she found her mother there. She was sitting on the window-seat and looking down on the garden.

'Mother!'

Sarah turned, her face wet with tears.

'What's the matter? Is it Father – or Alex?'

'No, no, they're all right, I think.' She managed a smile, sniffed, wept again. 'I've been watching for you, longing for you to come home.'

'Something has happened.' Some awful unspeakable thing?

Sarah leaned on the window-sill, her eyes on the rising ground beyond the garden where trees heavy with foliage were dark against a sky of fading gold.

'I have loved it all so much,' she said. 'I can't bear the thought of leaving. It will break my heart.'

CHAPTER IX

From the beginning Humbert had been at odds with the board of directors. As an agent he was an asset to the company: as a man he was a thorn in the flesh. He was certainly less respectful to his employers than would have been prudent in a man dependent entirely on his salary. By temperament and education he was disposed to take a more liberal view of the country's chief industry than to see as its main purpose the creation of wealth for its owners. The source of that wealth, he had once had the audacity to remind them, was two-fold: the coal and the men who mined it, the one inaccessible without the other.

Such heresies had alarmed and irritated the owners, especially Bedlow. Humbert's background alone made him suspect to a man who had started as a trapper at the age of seven and toiled his way up as pony-driver, putter, hewer, overman; had saved and studied and through sheer ruthless determination acquired a substantial holding in the company.

Humbert would have admitted to a genuine admiration for such a man, adding the proviso that he was impossible to work with. They had been at loggerheads over Humbert's insistence on improved safety levels, often expensive, on reasonable working hours, on the closure of dangerous seams and other measures favourable to the men. He had held his position because of his competence as a consultant engineer but also because of his skill in ironing out local difficulties. Managers, viewers and overseers liked and respected him. Less appreciated was his concern for the men on whom the industry depended.

But the more fair-minded of the directors would have acknowledged in private that Humbert's outspokenness, though
resented at the time, had often been justified. He had more than
once been proved right. He had a nose for coal and knew where
it would be economic to lay out capital on boring and – more
important to the diehards – where it would not.

As far back as 1921 he had seen the danger of government de-
control of wages and had not concealed his sympathy with the
men during the ten-week lock-out. He had predicted that the
resumption of mining in the Ruhr would end the boom in
British coal. Sure enough, demand and prices fell. Men were laid
off and one sixth of all pits were closed. Coal was sold at prices
below cost. Feeling had been tense during the twenty-six agoniz-
ing weeks when the miners hung on after the General Strike
ended. Whereas Humbert blatantly declared that the men were
starved into submission, the owners, watching the source of their
wealth decline, continued to insist on longer hours and a cut in
wages.

Lord Laverborne, wealthiest of all the directors, had judiciously sold off three of his collieries. The remaining three
yielded sufficient income from royalties, way-leaves and railway
rents to maintain him in the manner to which he had been
accustomed. He rarely attended meetings and happened to be
abroad at the end of June 1928 and so missed the flare-up at the
quarterly meeting.

Quite simply – it was unique: different from any board meeting of any kind ever known. Its course and outcome were shaped,
not by Quinian, acting chairman and financial manager of
Fellside's interests in an iron company, blast furnace and shipping line, not by Bedlow, whose glowering self-interest alone
could defeat opposition, nor by his chief bugbear, Humbert, with
his fancy theories – a chap who had never got his hands dirty nor
put a penny into the company and – his unsuitability could be
put no lower – an ex-parson.

What made it different from any other meeting was the presence of Katie Judd. Uninvited, her frail spirit insinuated itself
into the boardroom. The gentlemen were no sooner seated than
the agenda fell to pieces. The last item became the first as

Bedlow, always a stranger to formality, produced a sheaf of papers and spread them on the table.

'What I want to know' – his thick fingers trembled as he arranged the newspaper cuttings on the shining surface. He was an old and angry man. His fierce eyes under thick eyebrows glared at Humbert who sat at the lower end of the table. 'What I want to know is who's going to be made responsible for this. I'll tell you who it should be. Them that didn't want Lucknow reopened even if there is coal there which those same people know there is. If my advice had been taken seven years ago, there'd have been a sinking in Larson's fields. By now we'd have had a fully operational pit there and yon old shaft would have been filled and levelled off as if it had never been there.'

The thrust went home. Humbert glanced at Quinian, received a despairing nod of permission and sprang to his own defence.

'I advised against developing Lucknow, although there certainly is coal there. The minutes of the meeting will confirm that I also said that at some future time it might be an economically sound project if sufficient capital were available. My estimate of the possible cost was rejected out of hand' – he returned Bedlow's glare – 'but was confirmed by the valuers. Penny pinching is not to be tolerated in this dangerous industry. Besides,' – as Bedlow opened his tightly compressed lips to interrupt – 'there were legal difficulties as you well know. They haven't yet been resolved.'

He reminded them that Cosway, the original owner of the Lucknow Drift had worked it on lease. Under a clause in the agreement, if a lease expired and was not renewed, the lessee was obliged to give first option in disposing of buildings and equipment to the lessor and to restore all ground to an arable state. He was also legally bound to fill up pits of no further use or so to enclose them that they presented no danger. Ventilating shafts must be enclosed within a wall six feet high.

For a moment, as Edward paused unhappily, controversy was forgotten, all minds having turned to the tragic absence of one particular six-foot wall. But only for a moment.

'If my advice had been taken, all that rubbish would have had to be cleared away seven years ago. Yon shaft would have been

filled in and the ground levelled.' It was as if Bedlow had not
been listening.

'Besides the inadequacy of the proposed investment,'
Humbert persisted, 'there were other problems. Incidentally,
there may have been a six-foot wall there. None of us was here in
1901 except perhaps Mr Bedlow.'

'Who was the lessor?' Quinian addressed the question to
Andrews, legal adviser to the board. He was a painstaking ambi-
tious man of thirty-five and had come prepared, having
immersed himself in the history of the Lucknow Drift.

'The seven-year lease had been renewed six times but wasn't
renewed in 1901. It was Cosway's responsibility to make all safe
before the site was restored to the lessor, which he may have
done, as Mr Humbert pointed out. A lot can happen to a wall in
an exposed situation in getting on for thirty years.

'Cosway died in 1902. His one daughter emigrated to New
South Wales and married there. The lessor was Thomas Burdon,
father of the present owner of Burdon's Drapery shop. In 1913
he sold the site to the owners of the Hope Carr colliery which was
taken over in 1918 by the Fellside and District Coal Company.'

Having read from his notes, Andrews looked uneasily across at
his friend Humbert.

'So' – Bedlow's face was red with triumph and resentment –
'this company has been responsible for that death-trap for ten
years. If my advice had been taken—'

'The company is also responsible for other death-traps, including those slums in Potter's Yard,' Humbert pointed out sharply,
concealing his inner concern.

'I seem to remember' – the speaker represented the bishopric
of Elmdon, also a substantial shareholder in the company – 'that
there could be no development without an agreement with the
owner of the land to the west of the Lucknow site and that he was
unwilling to give wayleaves.'

Rilston. It was a decision he may have regretted, Humbert
thought, considering Rilston's financial difficulties. He was sufficiently bothered to be grateful for the intervention. The fact
remained that he himself should have kept the local managers
on their toes though in managerial terms the Lucknow site

belonged to none of the working collieries. A rotten industrial relic mouldering for years! He had not so much laid eyes on it until the recent tragedy. If he had bestirred himself to walk that way, he'd have been on to it like a shot. All his work, skill and acumen, all the cut and thrust of his battles with Bedlow counted for nothing in view of this one piece of negligence. It was a bitter moment.

Quinian in the chair rapidly restored the agenda. There was more than a chance that Bedlow would demand a reprimand. It would not be seconded: it was too unreasonable, but it would have to be entered in the minutes and might lead to a further enquiry and a demand for compensation. Who knew what might come to light? It was to be hoped that it would all blow over.

And so it might have done. When he had submitted his quarterly report Humbert paid less attention than he ought to the progress of the meeting. He was conscious of a peculiar mood. Concern, regret, loss of confidence in his much prized efficiency should have depressed him deeply: he was depressed. Yet a curious sensation came and went as if – to use a mining image – into a deep seam there came intermittent and dangerous flashes of light and heat. It was not long before he understood what was at work within him.

He remained seated when the others rose to go, almost unaware that the meeting was over, until Bedlow, having gathered up the cutting, moved in his direction.

'And another thing.' His heavy jowl quivering, he waved the papers close to Humbert's face. One was a picture of one of the young men who had been commended for their public spirit in having recovered the body of the unfortunate girl. 'It's given you a boost, I dare say, to see your lad's picture in the papers, and him too. He's not the sort to back off from a bit of publicity, they tell me. What about the other lad? He was there as well but very likely he didn't put hisself forward to have his photo taken. I'd like to know how your lad knew where to look for the girl. How did he know, eh? I wouldn't have known. There's not many that would. But he did, your lad, didn't he?'

Who could tell what the old man had in mind beyond an impulse to stir up further trouble for his enemy? In a startled pause several heads turned. Humbert, stupefied by fury, was dumbfounded. From the top of the table Quinian intervened.

'Mr Bedlow, sir, you should withdraw those remarks. You are out of order. Completely out of order.'

'The meeting's over, isn't it? I can say what I like.'

'Yes.' Humbert drew breath and steadied his voice, 'And that's the sort of thing you like to say, you narrow-minded, blundering skinflint.' He got up. 'Get out of my way before I lose my temper.' He looked along at Quinian. 'Mr Chairman, as a favour, would you mind reconvening the meeting? It will take no more than a minute, in fact, the gentlemen don't even need to sit down. I intend to resign as agent of the Fellside and District Coal Company. My resignation will be put in writing immediately.'

His anger had gone. The visiting beams of light had widened and become constant. He felt and look revitalized. The sense of renewal was not unfamiliar: the same lightness of relief had come when he turned his back on the timber business and again when he left the ministry.

'For God's sake, man, don't put anything in writing until you've thought things over.' Quinian spoke urgently. He and Andrews had stayed when the others left. 'This isn't a resigning matter.'

'Strictly speaking we're only responsible for our own working pits,' Andrews reminded him, 'and the company never worked Lucknow. If anybody is to blame, it's Rilston. A landowner can be prosecuted for any hazard on land accessible to the public and the shaft happens to be on his land.'

'But only the shaft.' The Rilstons may have had a small royalty on that account before the lease expired but Humbert was quick to see the injustice of holding them responsible when those who had made real money out of Lucknow went scot-free. 'Even in its present state the shaft is not a hazard. No one could fall into it by accident.' In the heat of the moment the full significance of that fact escaped him.

True enough. Quinian was relieved. 'The whole thing will blow over. That is, if you don't stir things up by resigning. Your resignation will be seen as an acceptance of responsibility. The company won't like that one bit. Heaven knows what it might let them in for in the way of claims for compensation. There's been mining hereabouts since Roman times.'

'Dubious liability,' Andrews said. 'That's typical of mining. It could take years to sort out if anyone were unwise enough to try. The company will wriggle out of it, but what about you, old chap?'

Their anxiety on his behalf touched him, but he did not share it, caught up as he already was in plans for a new project. Here was a chance to put into operation a scheme he had dallied with from time to time, never expecting it to be realized, a scheme which could be advantageous to Rilston too. A quixotic impulse to give Rilston a helping hand confirmed – and excused? – his decision to resign. 'There's Langland Hall standing empty,' Rilston had said. That was years ago. The place was going to rack and ruin. It would be a public service to take it over, renovate, make the cottages habitable, find work for the unemployed. A land scheme similar to the Surrey smallholdings? Vegetables, poultry, goats, a pottery. . . . The possibilities were endless. He would take it on a ten-year lease, at a nominal rent, with a clause that if ever the land was to be sold, he would have the first option to buy.

He sat on when the others had gone, absently smoothing the pages of his report into a perfect rectangle, conscious only of having found his true vocation, forgetting that he had seemed to find it twice before. It was some time before he became aware of the surrounding silence and looked at his watch. Only then did it occur to him to wonder how Sarah would feel about leaving Monk's Dene.

CHAPTER X

The rooms at Langland Hall were long and low, the windows narrow. In winter, daylight came late. Indoors it was always twilight except for the fires that roared and blazed in the cavernous grates and were for ever in need of replenishing.

Margot emptied a scuttleful of coal on the sitting-room fire and lingered – guiltily: there was still so much to be done elsewhere. She went to the window. They had been glad that the main rooms faced this way with open views to the south and west, but throughout a particularly sunless November there had been nothing to see but low skies and bare trees. She had learned not to mind the feeling of being shut in; she would even have welcomed the grey gloom that shut out all the things she was missing – if there had been time to notice it or to feel anything beyond the backbreaking tiredness of being constantly on her feet and, occasionally, disbelief that a few months could so transform her life.

All the same it had become a habit to look down towards the road at the end of the long drive connecting the Hall with the outer world, and presently she saw the postman trudging up to the last of the three gates. There might be a letter from Alex.

As soon as the fire was red again she must bring her mother downstairs. The attack of pneumonia had been severe, and so had Dr Pelman. 'Madness' he called it, to move into this old ruin before the restoration was complete. It had barely begun. The roof was sound and the plumbing worked. Doors and windows had been made weather-proof, but after more than two decades of standing empty, the house still suffered the desolation of neglect.

The Hall had ceased to be a gentleman's residence eighty years ago and had been let to a succession of tenant farmers. Its situation at the end of the so-called drive, now degenerated into a gated cart-road, isolated it from the nearest village of Fellside. Ashlaw, five miles away by road was for all practical purposes out of reach.

Islands of comfort had been fought for and won against fearful odds, but floors were still bare in most of the rooms; cupboards were damp; snail tracks glistened on the flags of the vast kitchen. It would be months before carpenters, decorators and carpet-layers could make the place ship-shape.

Edward used the word casually. Home comforts came low on his formidable list of priorities. First viewed in summer sunshine, the house had seemed to possess the romantic charm of age. Since the removal he had rarely been at home except during the most alarming phase of Sarah's illness. The project he had undertaken involved him in problems he had not foreseen: legal, practical, technical. He had to see architects, surveyors, council officials, merchant builders. . . .

He glories in it, Sarah thought, hoping the glory would last when so many other things had come to an end. She understood his need to do everything at lightning speed in order to prove that it could be done at all, knowing that Dr Pelman was not the only one to call it madness.

'A mammoth undertaking,' Edward told her, his eyes glowing, and it was as some cumbersome elephantine creature that Sarah regarded the grey pile into which she had been summarily dumped; a building scarcely less forbidding than the ruined priory 200 yards further up the slope. Had she been as she used to be, she would have thrown herself into the battle for his sake and for Margot's. But from the moment the blow fell, the heart went out of her: she had left it at Monk's Dene. Her illness, four weeks after they moved, had been more than pneumonia: it had been a failure of spirit. She recoiled from the truth, that this time Edward had made a mistake – and took to her bed.

For Margot, discomforts and inconveniences counted for

nothing compared to the change in her mother. It struck her afresh as Sarah shuffled into the room, having succeeded in dressing herself for the first time for over a month.

'You should have waited. I was coming.' She helped her to a chair and put a rug over her knees.

'Sit down for a few minutes.'

They faced each other across the hearth. The greater change was in Sarah, but Margot too was thinner, paler, more serious. The burden had fallen most heavily on her, but the worst was over. The nurse was gone, and, as they frequently reminded each other, most of the difficulties were temporary. In six months, Alex would have taken his degree. There would be a place for him with an Elmdon firm dealing mainly with company law and he could live at home.

Mrs Roper was a sad loss. She gave them a day occasionally but could not be longer away from her husband who suffered from pneumoconiosis. Maud had left to be married. The Todds, a couple already housed in one of the cottages, were helpful and Bessie did simple cookery. The daily woman who walked or cycled from Fellside was reliable as times were hard and the work welcome. But resident help was essential. Despite their problems, Sarah persisted in waiting for a suitable person to respond to their advertisement: to be saddled with an unsuitable one would, she foresaw, be purgatory.

Meanwhile, one successful outcome of the mammoth undertaking, the only one, perhaps, was the employment of Ewan Judd as handyman. For the first time in his life he had a regular job.

'It's given him a bit of pride in himself,' his mother said. He had ceased to smoulder with resentment, was occasionally heard to whistle as he chopped wood and dug beds for vegetables and had been seen to smile.

'A transformation.' Edward was enthusiastic. 'And there's so much more we can do in saving men from the scrapheap of unemployment.' He dwelt on the theme. It replaced an earlier one that women should have careers and learn to be independent. Margot had gone back to school for the autumn term. A fortnight later came the removal. For another fortnight she had managed the hour-long journey from Langland to Elmdon, not including the walk to Fellside station, until the alarming onset of her mother's illness.

'You can take up your studies again,' her father said, 'when things are more settled. I'm not sure that your health would stand up to university life.'

In the emergency, Margot scarcely gave a thought to her studies or the university, as on a sinking ship a desperate passenger discards personal belongings and takes to the lifeboat. When the crisis was over and Sarah took a turn for the better, mother and daughter were often alone when workmen had gone home, except for the Todds and Ewan, who was proving unexpectedly reliable and inoffensive. Ferocious as the Judds could be in defence of their own, they could be equally pig-headed in loyalty to their friends. The Humberts, especially Miss Margot, had been kind to Katie and were accepted as partisans in the guerrilla war against a hostile world.

Margot was about to tear herself away from the fire when heavy footsteps in the uncarpeted hall announced the approach of Ewan with a trug of wood and three letters in unfamiliar hand-writing.

'Nothing from Alex. But these – surely one of them will be from the treasure we're looking for.' Margot skimmed them. But neither a widow used to looking after a titled lady with a completely staffed household, nor a Scottish woman aged sixty and not afraid of rough work, nor an eighteen-year-old from Cornwall would serve their purpose.

'If only we could have the titled lady's complete staff. How very satisfactory that would be.'

They amused themselves with talk of butlers and ladies' maids while Ewan stacked logs on the hearth.

'Some time when you've got your coat on' – he addressed Margot – 'you'd maybe like to come and choose a Christmas tree. There's plenty up there at the back of them ruins.'

'I hadn't thought. . . . It's still three weeks. . . . It won't be the usual kind of Christmas. Or do you think we might manage the party on Boxing Day? Just ourselves, Phyllis and Freda of course, Linden and Miles and a few others.' Her spirits rose as she remembered how wonderful last year's Christmas party had been.

'We'll have to see.' They were the words Sarah had used when they were children begging for some treat. She smiled – and as with the momentary lifting of a cloud, life became normal again.

When Alex came home all was well. Together they explored the sixteen rooms, discussed their possibilities and decided on one for Lance, who came in time to drive Mrs Roper back and forth from Ashlaw and to help with Christmas preparations. The heavy curtains were at last hung in the galleried hall; a tree was installed; decorations were unearthed from cardboard boxes. Mrs Roper made mince-pies, brought puddings and dressed the turkey. Father arrived from London laden with parcels.

On the day before Christmas, fields were white with snow. Miles telephoned in the morning to ask if he might call. Watching for him from the sitting-room window, Margot saw the desolate landscape transfigured – or rather failed to see it at all except as a backcloth for the scenario of Miles's arrival.

She was roused from the trance of expectation by a variation in the scene. It was snowing again and through the flurry of flakes she could just make out a moving shape down by the barn, a darkness in the surrounding whiteness. Not a car. A person? Then it was gone – or had never been there. There was nothing but snow: nothing to think of but Miles.

It was a quarter of an hour before he arrived. To him the house seemed warm and full of people. He had last seen it as a wreck of a place and felt some embarrassment in coming. It was an awkwardness dispelled by Alex's greeting, 'Here comes our landlord. How are you, old chap?'

He had brought flowers and grapes for Mrs Humbert who had been firmly imprisoned in the sitting-room out of harm's way.

'Everybody is being useful. Is there something I can do?'

'You can have coffee with Margot and me. She's bringing it now.'

Sarah saw the light in Margot's eyes as Miles took the tray from her, and the tenderness in his as he looked down at her, pleased that her hair was unbobbed. She wore it up with a curling fringe on her forehead. Her slimness made her seem taller. She was no longer a schoolgirl and that pleased him too.

It would be all right for her, Sarah thought, putting aside with regret a private plan of her own for Margot's future.

'Not a real party,' Margot was explaining. 'Just ourselves and a few friends. You'll come, won't you? It could be fun with everything in rather a mess and everyone will help.'

'You've brought it with you,' he said. 'All that I loved at Monk's Dene.' How could he describe the welcoming warmth and ease of friendship he had felt only with them; the closeness of sympathy he had felt for the first time in his life with Margot.

Lured by the fascination of falling snow, she had gone to the window. He put down his cup and joined her.

'Just look at Alex.' He was rushing down the drive, bareheaded in the thickening flakes and buckling his trench coat as he ran. 'He's going down to the road to wait for Linden. Lance is bringing her from town.'

'Couldn't he wait indoors like a reasonable being?' Sarah's question was acid-tinctured. Where Linden was concerned, Alex was not reasonable.

'What's he up to?'

Halfway down the slope and to the right, the old barn faced across fields with its back to the cart track. Gorse bushes growing against its blank wall were weighted with snow. Alex had come to an abrupt halt. He seemed to stoop, then crouch.

'There's something there.' They peered through dizzily falling flakes.

'I thought I saw someone there but that was quite a while ago.'

Sara was sufficiently intrigued to struggle out of her chair and join them.

'Who on earth. . . ?'

'It's a woman. She must have been sheltering by the barn. He's helping her up. He's bringing her here.'

They made slow progress. It was two or three minutes before they came near enough to give a clearer view. The woman wore a long coat and what seemed a scarf over her hat. At one point she tottered and almost fell. Alex drew her arm over his shoulder and put his arm round her. Watching their slow advance, Margot felt a touch of apprehension. It was rather weird: the coming of a stranger in the depths of winter was like an incident in one of the old northern ballads, an intrusion from ancient times.

Something was happening or was about to happen that belonged to a sphere quite alien to that of candles on the tree, mince-pies and crackers. But perhaps, in remembering it long after, knowing that foreboding would have been justified, she assumed that she had felt it.

She and Miles were at the open door when the woman sagged and fell. Alex picked her up and carried her the remaining few yards into the hall and put her on the settle. 'Brandy,' he said. Her head sank forward as if her neck had given way and her face could be seen only in gaunt outline. It was fleshless and ashen white. Her hair had come undone: long dark strands draped the shoulders of her snow-sodden coat which was thin and worn: everything about her was thin and worn.

Margot unlaced the wet boots and drew them off, exposing black stockings and gaping patches of bare flesh. Shame for the unmended holes penetrated the woman's exhaustion. She shrank back, her head against the back of the settle.

'Good heavens!' Margot said. 'It's Toria Link.'

CHAPTER XI

The brandy revived her. She became aware of the surrounding faces – interested, anxious, kind. Her eyes came to rest on Alex. In their sunken depths a light flickered. Never in all her days had she been so steadily looked at. She was not a person who had attracted interest of any kind. For years she had existed in the back regions of Burdons' shop, unpaid and largely unknown. Only Margot and Sarah could have identified her.

The arrival of a car created a diversion and presently Lance joined the bizarre group under the Christmas tree.

'Give her a hot drink and get her to bed, then feed her – but not too much at first. She's half starved.'

The two women in the kitchen stripped Toria of her wet clothes, wrapped her in a blanket and put her into a clean bed with a hot-water bottle. She was given soup and bread and butter and left to fall asleep.

Was it by coincidence that she had fallen by the wayside here at Langland Hall instead of among strangers? The topic was discussed at lunch. Nothing had been heard of Toria since volleys of bricks hurled at Miss Burdon's windows had driven her away, evidently preferring to face homelessness rather than the wrath of Ashlaw.

'Not a coincidence,' Edward said. 'She must have heard that we are here and came looking for work. I tell you, this place will be a haven for the outcast and homeless.' He said a good deal more in the same vein. Toria's unconventional arrival had put him in good humour: he was clearly doing the right thing and fulfilling a social obligation by providing work. Margot at least was infected by his enthusiasm. The meal was a cheerful one.

Except for Alex. To his disgust Linden had not come. According to Lance, who had called for her at Gordon Street, she was having lunch with a friend, would spend Christmas Day with her mother and come on Boxing Day in time for the party. There was no need to fetch her: a friend would drive her to Langland.

So unsatisfactory a report caused Alex to cut short his lunch, race to catch a train from Fellside station and be seen no more until evening when he returned home looking glum.

'The fact is,' he told Margot, 'things are pretty desperate. If they go on like this I shall lose her. I don't think she'll wait for me. Why should she?'

If she loves you, Margot thought but did not say, she won't mind waiting – for ever.

'If we were engaged I would feel safer. And so would she. An engagement would give her the feeling of security she needs. I'm going to risk it, asking her, I mean, instead of waiting until I graduate. But don't you say a word to the parents. They'd be dead against it. There'd be the usual harangue about not being able to support a wife till kingdom come. You'd think they'd realize that an engagement isn't marriage, but it is a lasting attachment. What do you think?'

'Girls like having a ring.' Margot selected the one certainty in a situation bristling with problems.

'Good Lord! Yes. Well, that will have to wait. What do rings cost roughly? Any idea?'

'They vary.' He was saving up for a car. It occurred to her that in Linden's case a car might be as strong an inducement to fidelity as a ring.

'There are bound to be others, I know. This fellow she's having lunch with. Godfrey Barford. Never heard of him, have you?'

Margot had heard of Godfrey Barford. Phyllis and Freda kept her up to date with news. He was a newcomer to Elmdon. His father owned a chain of cinemas and his only son had already become a focus of interest in the town.

'I don't think he's the kind of person Linden would be attracted to.' Her own juvenile infatuation with Linden had faded. There had been times when Linden's difference from other people, once intriguing, had shown in unappealing ways. But Linden had never lost her unique ability to seem accustomed to and only recently to have left an atmosphere in every way superior to the air she now breathed: a loftier region to which others might aspire in her company. Was it a region into which Godfrey Barford would fit? 'She probably had lunch with him because he asked her and she was too polite to refuse.' Here she was on safer ground: Linden's politeness was indisputable, but Margot knew that she would have refused just as politely if it had suited her to do so.

By the evening of Boxing Day, as a result of strenuous efforts, the Hall seemed almost homelike, had even acquired a ramshackle temporary charm. The old customs were not forgotten. Sarah stayed in her room but came out on to the landing before the guests arrived and called over the banisters, 'Do for goodness sake straighten the rugs,' as she had done scores of times at Monk's Dene. Edward responded with his customary feeble joke: 'Who else is coming besides the Campbells?'

Phyllis and Freda arrived early: Phyllis, dark-haired, in flame-coloured velvet, Freda, fair, (no, not mousy, she was constantly assured) in sea-green silk with inlets of lace. There was time for the other two to try on Phyllis's new moleskin coat and strut about like models on a catwalk.

'Not that it matters what we wear.' Freda laid it reverently on the bed. 'If *she's* going to be here we might as well be invisible.'

'Wish I was – or at least occupying a little less space.' Phyllis studied her dimensions in the mirror. 'I'm so disgustingly healthy – and obvious.'

No consolation was offered, opinion being in favour of an interesting fragility.

'And another thing: we tend to talk too much. Men like you just to stand about listening.'

'But there's always so much to say,' Margot protested, 'especially when we haven't seen each other for ages.'

An intriguing silence being beyond hope of achieving, they must rely, as Freda put it, on other forms of attraction.

'Such as?' Phyllis was frankly sceptical. In any case it was time to go downstairs.

Meanwhile, Alex remained on edge, with justification. It was Godfrey Barford who drove Linden to Langland. He was a pleasant young man, a little too smartly dressed, his dark hair a little too glossy, his wallet a little too freely exposed.

'Are you going to introduce me to your friends?' he asked, as he got out to open the first gate.

'I don't think this would be a suitable time, would it? They might think—'

'That I was trying to gate-crash?' He laughed. 'In that case I'll leave the gates open for my retreat.'

Rather to her disappointment Margot did not see him. Alex was waiting on the front steps to open the car door before his rival could get out, to say a heartily insincere 'How d'you do–' and to keep a firm hold on the door with intent to close it quickly.

'Goodbye, Godfrey,' Linden said, 'and thank you so much for bringing me.'

She had thanked him with the same sweet correctness for a number of other things. He found her sweetness and correctness irresistible. She had the social confidence he lacked and longed for, and the correctness he found so alluring did not prevent Linden from accepting gifts it was not quite suitable for him to offer, the less suitable the more sweetly. In return, as a companion she made him enviable and he was eager to show the deference she took for granted. He had learned a good deal from her and had still a good deal to learn, especially about Linden.

The Hall had a central staircase leading to a gallery on three sides, a feature which was to influence events on that evening. Margot had taken Linden to a bedroom to leave her things, though she removed her white fur wrap with obvious reluctance: beyond the range of fires the rooms were cold. She smoothed her hair and turned from the mirror and almost with a start of surprise Margot saw how lovely she was. It was months since she had seen her. In that interval Linden's cheeks had filled a little; her face, though still delicate, was more nearly a classic oval in its frame of dark hair. The somewhat heavy lids and long lashes gave mystery to her eyes, more blue than grey. The slightly fuller lower lip must have seemed – however deceptively – inviting.

It was not those details that Margot noticed just then: her impression was of grace and poise and harmony fused as in a picture or a piece of sculpture. Alex had preached to her that in a work of art there must be no false note: all should cohere to fulfil the artist's concentrated vision. In Linden's appearance there was no noticeable imperfection: she had flowered almost into beauty, a happy state. To be almost beautiful is to ensure being constantly looked at and there is always the hope that in a moment the suggestion of beauty may become beauty itself.

And yet, without reference to theory, Margot knew by this time that the graceful figure in the silver dress was no more the true Linden than the reflection in the mirror was the real girl. After the first catch of breath she was left with the sense of loss that comes when appearances are known to be misleading – as she had felt on the day of Katie's death when she had first detected a falseness in Linden.

All the same she was lost in admiration. Her own blue taffeta seemed heavy and provincial; her hair ungroomed, her manner too warm. But now Linden had arranged the floating panels of her dress and with the fur wrap over her arm was waiting politely for the signal to go down. Reluctantly Margot opened the door.

Linden's appearance may not have given unalloyed pleasure to the other girls. But to Alex? He stood at the foot of the stairs as Linden went down. Margot, following, saw his face upturned and was disturbed by its expression. It was rapt, intense and self-forgetful. It was as if nothing else existed for him, as if there were no one else there, only Linden. It wasn't like him. From the cradle, Alex had been self-possessed; now it was as if he had no self. She recognized in his attitude a quality of reverence. His very posture was that of a believer looking up to a divine presence. It was too much; it was beyond reason and, in this case, surely misplaced.

At any minute, at the first opportunity, he would ask Linden to marry him. Nothing could save him: he was going to make a mistake which could never be put right. With all the certainty of inexperience she was sure of it. Not for an instant did she think of his marriage to Linden except as a self-inflicted doom, the headlong downward plunge of a man determined to drown.

Except – common sense reminded her that it could not be headlong; it could not happen for years. On the other hand, for Alex an engagement would be as binding as marriage. There was nothing she could do to prevent the catastrophe; it wasn't her business and it would be impossible to reason with him, especially as not one sensible reason could be given to dissuade him. Wasn't Linden's behaviour, like her appearance, well nigh perfect?

It was not. For one thing Linden could lie, not from politeness or reluctance to hurt, but for her own convenience. She didn't just palter with the truth: she could actually fabricate untruths. She had lied to Miles about having to see Mr Embleton at the office, knowing that it was always closed on Saturdays. It was a manoeuvre Margot found hard to forgive. A person who could lie about one thing could never be believed about anything. What else might Linden have lied about? Even harder to forgive was her contempt for Katie. People couldn't help being insensitive if that was their nature, but she had seemed actually to dislike Katie. How strange that Katie had been so very much afraid of her as if she knew. . . . The thought, unformulated, drifted away to return later more clearly and with a greater power to disturb.

If it was impossible to prevent Alex from taking the fatal step, perhaps somehow it could be postponed. They must not be allowed to go off alone. With despair she thought of the Hall's labyrinthine passages and its sixteen rooms. Music floated up from the drawing-room where Lance was looking after the gramophone. The others were waltzing to the tune of 'Always', just the thing to encourage a proposal.

'*Not for just an hour, Not for just a day, Not for just a year but always. . . .*'

'Linden.' Alex had taken her hand and the next moment they were dancing. Margot, having traced her brother's downfall and consigned him to a lifetime of misery, had barely reached the bottom stair.

She was not the only one to witness the lovers' meeting. Toria Link had been granted the status of an invalid and urged to stay in bed, but two days and nights of rest, warmth and good food had, as she said 'put her back on her feet'. A random assortment of clothes had been found for her and these she was now wearing: one of Sarah's skirts too wide in the waist; a jumper of Margot's, too short. Without wanting to put herself forward she was sufficiently recovered as well as sufficiently stimulated by her surroundings and the festive sounds below to leave the easy chair in her bedroom and come out on to the landing. She was wearing a pair of Alex's old Scout stockings as there were no slippers to fit her and so moved quietly to the gallery where she could look down over the balustrade.

Toria was as near to being content as a woman of her temperament could be: indeed the dogged sullenness of her manner had been inevitable in her miserable circumstances. Already embers almost extinguished were stirring into warmth. She had been treated as a person who mattered and by people whom she respected, most of all by Mr Alex. He had put his arm round her – round *her*, Toria Link – had lifted her up and carried her into the house, had spoken kindly and given her brandy. Her lonely heart was softened. It was in the hope of seeing him that she had crept out of her room.

She would never forget what he had done; he was a good man. If it would be of any use to him she would willingly lie down and die for him. With an expression similar to his own as he looked up to Linden, Toria looked down at him over the balustrade. He was waiting at the bottom of the stairs for his young lady. Toria felt a glow of sympathy for his happiness that brought a smile to her lips, unused to smiling.

Then she saw who the young lady was and the smile faded.

Any plan Margot might have hatched for keeping an eye on Alex and Linden and preventing them from drifting off alone would probably have been doomed to failure. For a time she forgot it: there were other things to think of – waltzing with Miles for instance – and there were so many improvisations, such a lack of smoothness in the arrangements that she was fully occupied in dealing with these. The guests helped and enjoyed the informality.

The rigours of the Hall itself achieved what Margot had failed to do. For once Linden's social acumen failed her. Evening dresses at that time were skimpy and her concoction of lace over silvery satin was skimpier than most. When not dancing she refused to budge from the fireplace in the hall, which gradually became the focal point of the whole company. Refreshments were served there and Lance brought the gramophone from the unfurnished drawing-room. Even though a proposal of marriage needs only a whisper in a willing ear, for Alex the circumstances were not propitious.

One small incident might have marred what was proving to be as light-hearted an occasion as any in the old days at Monk's Dene. Fortunately only Margot was aware of it. Ewan, smartened up for his duties and looking handsome above his collar and tie, brought extra chairs. Head bowed, he was easing one into a space near the fire and chanced to look up directly into the face of Linden who sat nearest to the blaze. Margot, handing round mince-pies, caught his expression. His face had darkened, heavy brows drawn down, lips tightened as if he might – but surely he would not – spit. For an instant his newly acquired amiability left him. He became pure Judd. Linden, apparently unmoved, accepted a mince-pie.

Margot had caught sight of Toria and had sent up a glass of wine and a plate of food; she was evidently enjoying the party. Whenever Margot glanced up, Toria was there on the landing looking down on the firelit hall, the tree and the dancing couples and then the charades as if she could never have enough of them. When missing from the right-hand corner, she was to be seen on the opposite side of the gallery, having moved presumably to a better view-point. As the evening wore on, Margot's pleasure in Toria's enjoyment became unaccountably tinged with uneasiness. Gradually the personality of Toria herself became less distinct and she was aware only of a dark figure half seen among shadows, an emanation from the winter twilight, an uninvited visitor already established. For how long, and for what purpose other than to watch what was happening with a concentration it was difficult to account for? And suddenly she herself was so tired that she longed to drop into bed.

She was in fact the last person to go upstairs. Except for a dying glow from the fire below, it was dark on the landing. She had turned off all the lights.

'Miss Humbert.' Toria stood at the door of her room as though to waylay her. She was taller than Margot who didn't recall ever in the past having seen her standing upright, except once or twice in the distance, nor had she until three days ago ever looked into her face. She could not see it now except as a pale shape with caverns of shadow between cheeks and brows. Then she saw the whites of the eyes and the ivory of strong teeth.

'I've been waiting for you to come up.' Toria's voice was strangely impressive: she conveyed an unexpected authority. Somewhere, at some time in her history, she had known other things besides buckets and brooms.

'It's very late, Toria. Past midnight. You should be in bed. You haven't been well.'

'I couldn't rest. My mind has been in such a turmoil. He's been so good to me.'

'You mean Alex? I'm sure he was glad to help.'

'She's his young lady, isn't she? Anyone can see that.'

'Miss Grey? Well, yes, I suppose so.' Her tiredness left her. She was suddenly nervous and so, she realized, was Toria.

'She isn't worthy of him.'

'What makes you say that?'

'I've kept it to myself till now. . . .'

'Whatever can it be? I think you'd better tell me.'

Toria pushed open the door behind her and drew Margot into her room. It was not completely dark. The window was uncurtained, the sky beyond had cleared and there were stars.

'I've been asking myself why I came here. Of course, it was to find work first and foremost. Bit it's come into my mind that I was guided. It must have been Providence that sent me, for his sake. So that I could warn him.'

'Warn Alex?'

'When I saw the way he looked at her tonight, never dreaming what harm she did and what harm she might do, I thought he ought to know.'

'Harm? What harm?'

'She stole those beads. She was the one that took them, not Katie.'

CHAPTER XII

The words were simple as befitted the offence: a petty theft of
cheap jewellery. They were also potent enough to bring Katie
back from her grave, or so it seemed to Margot, so vividly did
they recall the fateful day in June and her own broken promise,
'I'll look after you. I'll always look after you'. Grief for the
betrayal of innocence and anger for the deceit and hypocrisy so
ravaged her that in later years she was to look back on Toria's
revelation as marking the end of her own girlhood. Her own
trustful ignorance and lightness of heart withered and died:
there was no place for them in life as it was turning out to be. She
was no longer the person she had been a year ago – a minute ago
– and when she spoke her voice was strange to her.

'How do you know?'

'I saw her take them.'

At Burdons' there was no partition between the shop and the
'back shop' used for storage. At the far end was a door opening
on the yard and garden. The day was hot. Toria, swilling flag-
stones at the back of the house, had been at work since seven.
The door was ajar; she stepped inside, out of the sun, and stood
with her back to the wall, motionless as the long bales of flannelette sheeting, and colourless in her sacking apron. She could
look along the whole length of the ground floor.

She heard the bell ring; saw Katie come in; saw Miss Grey
come and go (she did not then know her name); saw Katie leave
and Miss Grey come back, glance quickly behind her into the
hall, then pick up a long thin strand of something and thrust it
into her bag. When Miss Burdon and Margot appeared, Toria

slipped out quietly and started on the scullery window.

'I can hardly believe it.'

Even in the dark Toria was aware of the girl's distress: she was shivering. With a gentleness she had been incapable of for years, she felt for the chair and eased her into it.

'Why didn't you tell at the time?' There was no need to ask: the reason was obvious.

'It would have been my word against hers. Who would have believed the likes of me? Not Burdon with her snobbish notions. It would have meant the sack for me and I had nowhere to go.'

She was right: Linden would have lied – might even have turned the tables. 'The woman's lying', she would have said. 'She probably took them herself'.

It had not occurred to Toria that Katie would be suspected until Bella told her of Katie's death and added that she had taken the beads. That was just before the onslaught on the shop windows. Why had she changed her mind and left?

'It wasn't the bricks nor them that threw them; I'd have felt the same as they did if it had been my sister that got the blame for what she didn't do. There's nothing in this world worse than being blamed for what you didn't do. I've known worse things than bricks. But staying there would have done me no good: Burdons' was finished. Anyway I wanted no truck with such wickedness and I don't mean the wickedness of them that threw the bricks.'

She had left the sinking ship with no land in sight. Friendless, homeless, she had been destitute. It seemed to Margot that Toria had – apart from Katie – suffered more than anyone else from the incident of the beads.

'Yes,' – it was as if she knew what Margot was thinking – 'she put me back in the gutter where I'd sunk before. The only comfort I've had is knowing that I could ruin her if ever it suited me.'

She spoke calmly. She had never yet raised her voice from its subdued and even pitch. Somehow the absence of passion was more disturbing than if she had spoken violently. Margot could only guess at – and under-estimate – the depth of feeling such a woman as Toria might be capable of but the word 'ruin' frightened her: it was undefined but all-embracing.

'You haven't told anyone?'

'Not a living soul. Not yet. It would have done no good and would have let me in for a lot of trouble. But when I saw the way he looked at her, as if she'd put a spell on him, and his whole life was wrapped up in her, I thought he ought to know.'

'It was right to tell me. But don't tell anyone else. Promise. Just think what might happen if the Judds were to find out.' Margot's own ideas of what the Judds might do were vague, ranging from a public scandal to some terrible revenge. Any punishment that might fall – deservedly – on Linden would fall as heavily on Alex. Moreover, in her present state their mother must not be upset by another furore in Ashlaw and in the Press.

'I'm not likely to see the Judds.'

'But you don't realize – Ewan Judd is here, actually in the house. He works here.' For some reason he already hated Linden, Margot could not imagine why. He must never know that she had been the cause of Katie's death.

'God moves in a mysterious way.'

It was too dark to see Toria's expression or to be sure of her reaction to the news about Ewan. She had already claimed that Providence had brought her to Langland. It was surely a blessing that with nothing on earth to cling to she should be of a religious turn of mind. It did seem a coincidence that she should have been speaking of something that so closely concerned the Judds when unknown to her there was a Judd under the same roof, but it was going too far to suppose that God had deliberately arranged such an awkwardness. Nevertheless, Toria obviously saw herself as an instrument in the working out of God's purpose and comforting as that might be to Toria, Margot found it worrying – even alarming.

'We mustn't even mention this in case Ewan hears. I must think what to do.'

Alone at last in her own room she could think of nothing else. It was too cold to undress: her fire had long since gone out. She got into bed still fully dressed and pulled the eiderdown up to her chin. In spite of feeling years older she thought in terms of stark simplicity. If it had not happened, Katie would still be alive; there would have been no fuss about the chimney; her father would not have resigned; they would still be living at Monk's Dene; her mother would still be her old self, and she, Margot, would have completed a full term's study in preparation for Oxford. The dream of being there with Miles was unlikely ever to be fulfilled. She had realized that already but now regret for all that had been lost overwhelmed her. She wept with a child's abandonment and the hopeless acceptance of a woman, slept a little from sheer exhaustion and woke, red-eyed, to the wretchedness of her crumpled taffeta dress and the impossibility of deciding whether – when – how – to tell Alex. Was it already too late? If he and Linden were engaged, it would surely be kinder not to tell him.

The two sat side by side at the breakfast table. Stealing glances at them from behind the teapot, Margot had the impression that neither had slept well. On the other hand neither radiated the glow of successful love. Perhaps the fatal step had not been taken. Her own anger had cooled: daylight, toast and marmalade have a subduing effect on passion. Linden, languidly sipping tea, no longer impressed her as a work of art except that like a statue she was cool and remote, to be looked at rather than communicated with. Thinking of her mean little failings – lying and stealing – did not make her seem more human and approachable, more in need of sympathy, help and forgiveness: they simply disqualified her as a person to whom Alex should devote the rest of his life.

If there had previously been no sound reason for her misgivings, there was certainly a reason now. She could at any minute put a stop to the whole thing. She could say, calmly and firmly: 'The person who stole Miss Burdon's beads is seated at this table'. But it was so patently not the sort of thing one said over the teacups, if anywhere, that she felt limp with relief. The absurdity of it reduced her to an hysterical giggle which she passed off as a cough, covering her mouth with her napkin.

Had anyone noticed? Her father was trying to catch up with unread newspapers. Alex was fathoms deep in thought. Linden reached gracefully for the last piece of toast. Only Lance said, 'What's the joke, Meg?' and grinned. The wild thought came to her that she would ask Lance what to do. He would know: he was

105

the most sensible person she knew. He could be trusted – completely. She made the discovery with a sense of security as she smiled back at him. But if she told Alex and he asked her if she had told anyone else, he would resent her having told Lance first. She must talk to Alex in private at the first suitable time. At once?

But already she knew in her heart that she lacked courage to tell him, to wound him so deeply. Suppose she were to be told that Miles had done some low-down shameful thing – oh, but he couldn't – and if he did she would still love him. If he told Alex and he forgave Linden, there would be no problem. It would just be a pity.

And after all – another thought occurred to her – when Linden stole the beads she didn't know that the theft would lead to Katie's death. But how deceitfully she had spoken of Katie. 'She wouldn't know what she was doing. She was certainly there on her own. . . .' Had she the beads in her handbag as she spoke, or had she disposed of them when Miles took her to Elmdon? They had parted while Miles went to the chemist's. The office was closed but Linden might have gone home. . . . Anger seethed again. Clearly Katie had been necessary to Linden's plan. She would not have risked taking the beads if Katie had not come to serve as scapegoat.

Breakfast was nearly over. It had been rather a silent meal yet they had always been such a talkative family. Gradually there stole upon Margot a feeling of unreality. The effect of the low room with its dark panelling and small-paned windows, giving little light and limited view, was oppressive. It was as if they had all been lured into a twilit region and had been mysteriously changed. They didn't belong here any more than the familiar china from Monk's Dene belonged in its unfamiliar setting. It was all wrong for her to be presiding at the table while her mother, the heart and soul of the family, was away upstairs.

Anxious, tired, nervous, she lost touch with her surroundings as if she had drifted to some high viewpoint and, looking down, could see everything that happened. With detachment she considered Toria's faith in Providence and pictured her, motionless among the bales of flannelette at the end of the long shop, as she watched people come and go as if watching the enactment of a play. Was it Providence that sent Katie on to the stage, an innocent beginner, incapable of understanding the plot yet doomed to take a leading role? The stage was set, the bell was rung and she walked into the trap. Were they all, like her, destined to act in accordance with some terrible design?

The others were leaving the table. If only Linden would go away and never come back. If only she would marry Godfrey Barford now, at once. If only she, Margot Humbert, had not begged her mother to invite the Greys to lunch five years ago.

Linden did leave immediately after breakfast with Alex and his father who had business in Elmdon. Margot was determined not to be involved in seeing her off and contrived to be busy upstairs, but from the gallery she heard Linden's voice.

'How very kind of you to take me home, Mr Humbert – and thank you for having me. It was a delightful party. I won't disturb Mrs Humbert. I suppose Margot is with her. Alex, you must thank Margot for me. She worked so hard to make us all welcome.'

Lance had followed Margot upstairs. He, too, heard Linden's sweetly expressed leavetakings, saw too its effect on Margot.

'You're looking washed out,' he said. 'Anything wrong?'

'I don't know.' A silly answer. Seeing his expression change from friendly concern to one of sharper interest she added, 'No, of course not. Except for Mother. . . .'

'Shall I look in and see if there's anything I can do?'

'Yes, please do. Just give me a few minutes.'

She removed the breakfast tray and helped her mother into her dressing-gown: it was best for her to be up for part of the day. From the window they watched the car leave, Alex driving. A thaw had set in but he drove cautiously down the long curving way between white fields under a brightening sky, rose-tinted above bare-boughed trees silvered with melting snow.

'We seem to see so little of him these days,' Sarah said. 'It may be wrong of me when he's so very much in love with her but I do hope he won't marry her.' Perhaps even now, she thought, there might be a change of heart or something might happen. A miracle? She reproached herself. There was really nothing wrong with Linden.

For the remaining days of the Christmas holiday Sarah was sufficiently unwell to be kept in bed and Margot found neither opportunity nor inclination for the dreaded talk with Alex. On the evening after the party she had managed to murmur, 'Did you ask her?', had managed also to hide her relief when the answer was a muttered, 'She didn't give me the chance.' Even so, she could have told him: it was cowardly not to. Worse than that – she veered from one decision to its opposite – it was probably more cruel not to tell than to tell.

'You need a change,' Lance said on the last day of his holiday. He had formed his own opinion of Sarah's condition and knew that it coincided with his father's: she was going to need a good deal of nursing and there was some danger of a relapse. 'Why don't you look up those chums of yours? Phyllis and Freda.' He had never been sure which was which. 'I'm going to Elmdon. You could have lunch with them and then I'll take you to the matinée at the Court. Your father's at home, and Alex. You won't be missed and we'll be back by six at the latest. It'll take your mind off whatever it is that's bothering you.'

In the car he told her about an interesting operation he had watched for the removal of a gall-bladder. His enthusiasm gave to the ghastly affair the captivating power of an epic. Dimly she wondered if there was something special about Lance. Was he some sort of genius?

'There is something bothering me,' she said abruptly when all the instruments had been accounted for, the patient stitched up and everything sterilized. 'I wish I could tell you about it but it wouldn't be right.'

'Is it about Alex?'

'What makes you think. . . ?'

'If it's about Alex, stop worrying. He can look after himself.'

'Not always.' But Margot smiled, remembering the Tarzan incident.

'If he can't, it's time he could.'

At the riverside café Freda and Phyllis had secured their

favourite table in the window and were waiting to order. Phyllis had given up potatoes and desserts and watched the others 'wolfing' ice cream with lofty tolerance. She had also had her hair bobbed.

'It makes me feel slimmer,' she said, 'though obviously I'm not.'

Freda hesitated to take the plunge from dread of looking even more mousy. ('Your hair is *fair*, long or short', she was told yet again.) Margot had been too busy to make so important a decision.

It was interesting to hear that Angela Bavistock was known to have confided to a friend that she would rather die than marry anyone but Alex Humbert – before moving on to the fertile topic of Linden Grey. The friendship with Godfrey Barford had apparently continued.

'Otherwise she's usually on her own. That's our mistake.' Phyllis though regretful was firm. 'We're always in twos or threes. Women are more interesting on their own.'

'Is Linden, in point of fact, interesting?' Freda wondered.

'She must be or we wouldn't be talking about her. Except' – Phyllis gave Margot a piercing look – 'some of us are not talking about her at all. I wonder why?'

But Margot was engaged in working out a fair division of the bill which Phyllis's diet had made more complicated than usual.

It was to be their last meeting for some time. Phyllis would soon be leaving to be 'finished' in Switzerland. Freda was to take a housewifery course in London.

'Hard luck that Meg should be stuck at home,' Freda said, when Margot had hurried off to join Lance. 'After all she's the brainy one.'

'*C'est la vie*,' Phyllis said profoundly and with a faintly Gallic shrug.

'You could say that about anything – and in English, if you don't mind.'

Lance had been right. Lunch with the girls, the film *Under a Texas Moon* and a glimpse of Miles driving out of town as they drove in had a bracing effect, though not bracing enough to bring her to the point of telling Alex. The morning of his departure was obviously not a suitable time and they rarely wrote to each other: to compose a letter on the topic of Linden's dishonesty was beyond her. The revelation must be postponed until Easter when he would be home, though only for a few days.

She had not seen or heard from Linden since the party. The problem was not resolved but it had receded. Neither she nor Toria alluded to it again. Toria, restored to health, had been kept on. She had nowhere else to go and could not be turned adrift especially in winter. And quite soon she was found to be useful: being resident she was there to take in deliveries, to answer the door, tend fires and carry trays. She had gravitated to a low-ceilinged room above the kitchen with its own narrow winding stair and had of her own accord taken on the early morning lighting of the kitchen fire so that there was always hot water by breakfast-time.

She also did bits of shopping in Fellside. Most of the items were charged to the Humberts' monthly accounts, but it was not long before Margot came to rely on her for her own personal shopping. Toria apparently took this as a compliment. When Margot first entrusted her with a purse and list, her sallow skin reddened with pleasure.

'You can depend on me, Miss Humbert,' she said and her care of the small accounts was meticulous: the prices set down and initialled by shopkeepers – and Toria waited, head slightly bowed and hands clasped like an accused person on trial while Margot counted the change.

Gaunt and silent, stalking from kitchen to hall, from staircase to bedrooms, Toria seemed to take on – or had already possessed – something of the character of the Hall itself: large, structurally strong, of unknown age and a little frightening after dark. But Toria was by far the less demanding: food, shelter and a wage little more than nominal supplied her entire need. She was not forthcoming in manner but she was well disposed and that was fortunate for she was also a threat like an unexploded bomb. She had only to utter a few words and several lives would be altered. Margot felt a tightening of nerves when, as must happen, Toria and Ewan were seen together though the two of them did seem to hit it off; certainly there was no sign of the friction such as so secluded a life might produce between two people who were, to say the least, untypical.

Sometimes when she saw them talking together, she could have imagined that some bond united them, some topic of mutual interest. She judged this from an occasional nod of understanding on the part of one or the other and from snippets overheard. It was surely nonsense to suppose that they could be attracted to each other. Margot considered them rather an unattractive pair, though in fairness Ewan could be described as handsome in a strongly masculine way. According to his mother he could take his pick of the girls in Ashlaw, Hope Carr and Fellside. But the difference in their ages made any amorous intention on his part unlikely, though not necessarily on hers. Actually they were rather alike, both dark-browed, both probably capable of deep feelings. Particularly, if any cause for it should arise.

Langland Hall had so little to offer in the way of companionship that Margot was sometimes desperate for someone to talk to. Although Toria could not be called companionable, she was visibly there under the same roof – or roofs, the Hall being so rambling a structure. What could be more natural than that they should chat occasionally and get to know each other? Natural perhaps, but getting to know Toria was a slow business.

The few words they exchanged on household matters did develop into longer conversations though they were never long, nor could the activity be called chatting. Toria's lugubrious expression, her features apparently carved in wood, her doom-laden utterances – it was Alex who so described them – were not adapted to light conversation. But she was interesting. Margot was curious about her. There was more in her than appeared on the surface. Though she owned nothing but what she stood up in – stood tall and strangely dignified, impossible to ignore – she seemed endowed with nameless qualities beyond those required in her humble way of life.

'Now that I've got to know you' – it wasn't true but they were at least acquainted – 'I do feel that you deserve a more comfortable life than you seem to have had. I mean, you know how to do things and how they should be done. . . .' It would be too blunt to ask why she had sunk to the ceaseless scrubbing of Miss Burdon's floors. Moreover, judging by her unconventional arrival at the Hall, her prospects had not improved when she left Ashlaw.

They had met at the airing cupboard. With its doors wide open it faintly warmed the frigid back landing. One could linger there without too much discomfort. Margot had come for a nightdress for her mother. Toria was stacking bed linen: her long arms reached easily to the top shelf.

'I'm more comfortable, Miss Humbert, than I've been for many a year and I thank God for it.'

Margot murmured that she was glad. Toria's response had discouraged her from asking the direct question she had intended, which seemed on an altogether lower level. Toria's utterances made ordinary remarks seem worse than commonplace. Nevertheless she persisted.

'How long were you at Miss Burdon's?'

She had been there almost two years and would have stayed longer had it not been for you know what.

'Another year perhaps,' she added, 'would have been about enough.'

'Enough for what?' Margot could not help asking.

'For the working out of His purpose.'

Her face above the pile of white sheets she held was yellow and worn but her eyes were bright, their whites shone clear. With health – or with the fervid glitter of mania? Did she – or He – plan a similar span of years to be spent at Langland? Margot hesitated to ask, not only from inability to adopt a manner similar to Toria's own but because it might embarrass her, though she doubted whether it was in Toria's nature to be embarrassed. But at that point the postman's knock sent her scurrying downstairs.

It was a few days later that the conversation was resumed, once again at the airing cupboard which was not only warmish but free from class distinctions. Toria rarely appeared in other rooms than the kitchen and then only briefly. Consequently, most of their talk in the winter months took place on landings or in the hall.

'I wonder what made you choose Ashlaw.' Even as she spoke

Margot realised that 'choose' was the wrong word: Toria had probably been 'sent' to Ashlaw and to Miss Burdon's in accordance with some obscure divine plan. But Toria's answer was for once straightforward and free of allusions to the Old Testament.

'I was told that a cleaner was wanted at the shop there.'

A sheet had been carelessly folded; she shook it out. Margot took the other end and they refolded it together.

'I saw you once or twice from my bedroom window early in the morning. You were in the Dene beside the War Memorial.'

'Wherever there's a War Memorial I have to read the names.'

That after all was what War Memorials were for; but there it was again, the compulsion to act in an ordained way. Yet Toria did not seem to find the compulsion burdensome. Margot perceived that it would be a support. The sense of being directed gave Toria an enviable detachment from problems that would break the spirit of lesser mortals. Somehow, on her knees for one reason or another, she had kept an independence of spirit, her mind concentrated on the course mapped out for her by a divine Cosmographer.

'You feel that it's a way of paying respect to the men who died. Or perhaps' – a less public-spirited and more interesting reason occurred to her – 'you're looking for the name of someone in particular.'

'Yes.' This time it was pillow-cases. Toria inserted them narrow end first so that two piles could occupy the same shelf.

'Someone you knew and cared for.'

'Yes.'

The dead soldier must have been a relative or a sweetheart. But surely in that case she would have known which War Memorial to visit. How many were there? The search for the right one could take a lifetime. Yet if anyone could maintain so hopeless a pilgrimage, Margot felt with conviction that it would be Toria. Nothing would make her waver. She had no ties, no friends, no possessions to undermine her resolution.

'But you don't know where he lived.'

'No.'

Margot stepped back as Toria closed the doors of the cupboard. As usual, just as a little progress was being made it was time to part. But Toria did not immediately walk away as she usually did.

'He promised to come back. He said that nothing but death would make him break his word.'

'Oh how terribly sad for you!'

Their meeting, Margot thought, may have been as brief as it was poignant: there would be nothing commonplace about it. She imagined a desolate hillside mantled in low cloud and deserted save for two figures emerging from mist to meet face to face for the transfiguring moment. Toria for one would feel that it was destined. Then too soon, almost at once had come the parting: the hand clasp: the embrace? 'I'll come back,' he must have said. 'My name is. . . .' And that was all Toria knew of him?

But it was wrong to be disrespectful. It *was* terribly sad and alas, Toria had over-simplified her plight. Thousands had died un-named, their deaths unrecorded on any memorial. Perhaps, horribly maimed or blinded, he was enduring a living death in hospital or suffering loss of memory. Even if he had been only slightly wounded he would have been unable to get in touch with Toria, especially as circumstances had doomed her to a wandering life of no fixed address. Worse still, his promise might have meant less to him than to Toria. Would she be cheered by such reminders that he might still be alive?

'Have you ever thought that. . . ?'

But she was walking away. Her tall and angular form with its plaited coronet of black hair had a regal dominance, fully occupying the narrow low-ceilinged corridor. When she came to the end and disappeared down the back stairs, an emptiness could be felt.

'She's probably imagined the whole thing,' Sarah said. 'He had no intention of keeping his promise, if he ever existed. I really wonder if she's quite. . . .' Much as she enjoyed Margot's versions of her encounters with Toria, she wondered if this was a suitable or wholesome influence for her to be subjected to and how long the present unsatisfactory arrangements at the Hall could be allowed to go on. Her own physical weakness made it wearisome to think of all the problems, much less do anything about them, but she did muster strength to help Margot in framing another advertisement for a resident housekeeper to be inserted in a wider range of magazines.

'We must find someone who would be pleasant company for you, someone who won't irritate your father.'

It was clear to both of them that Toria must stay presumably – as Margot pointed out – until the allotted span of years was complete, if only because neither of them could bring herself to tell her to go. Indeed it was in their own interest to keep her. For Margot, her splendid eccentricity was a welcome diversion, and though she entertained her mother by exaggerating it, she genuinely respected a woman who might have been pitiable yet was strong, dignified and essentially free.

'The war was responsible for some very strange things,' Sarah said.

'But that was ages ago.'

'It seems so to you. You were just a little girl when it ended. But it doesn't seem so to me – or to Toria. Millions of men died. How could things ever be the same again? It was as if the whole world was rocked by an earthquake and people have never settled back in their old places. When I was your age life was so safe and manageable.'

It was as if Toria typified the folk whose lives had been disrupted in the vast upheaval, like the tramps and the down-and-out salesmen who came to the back door with shabby suit-cases of dusters and socks and scarves. Many of them were ex-servicemen who had not found jobs when they were demobilized, who had fought and suffered and gained nothing by it, not even their names carved in stone. Margot's heart sank whenever one of them came trudging up the long cart track. Unwanted goods were bought, but it was generally Toria who came to ask if they could be given bread and cheese and a mug of tea. No doubt she acted from fellow feeling – or was it from normal motherly or sisterly warmth? Did the wooden features conceal a natural kindliness? Margot could not be sure. Despite the size of the Hall its atmosphere could be claustrophobic, especially on winter days as twilight deepened and from an unlit corner or a half-open door Toria materialized with a tray or a letter come on the second post, so that in some inexplicable way she seemed to have become part of the place. And sometimes when she came upon Toria and Ewan together she felt like an intruder. They always had something to talk about though neither was by nature talkative. What could it be?

'You haven't told anyone what you told me?' she had once ventured to ask.

'Not a soul,' Toria answered gravely, and Margot believed her without ever shaking off the uneasiness she felt when she heard their murmured voices in the unused butler's pantry or in the dairy or in the woodshed.

But both were strong and capable and the help they gave left her free to look after her mother, often with an aching heart as there was no sign of her recovery. Their relationship, always close, grew closer. Its balance had altered: it was her turn to comfort and advise, to wash the feeble body and comb the hair once like her own, now dull and lank. And as the weeks passed and the days lengthened, as snowdrops pierced the greensward of the priory's roofless nave and the blackthorn came into bloom, she looked forward to Easter with both longing and dread: dread of telling Alex what Linden had done: longing to see Miles who would also be coming home.

CHAPTER XIII

In April sunshine the ruined priory lost its air of brooding melancholy, its ancient stones paling to a lighter grey. Passing under the gatehouse arch, Margot found green turf starred with daisies and beyond the northern porch where pastures sloped down to the river, there were primroses. She had already located the path she would take but she had never walked that way. Fortunately the mud that made it impassable all winter had dried. It was the first day of Miles's Easter holiday.

He had written to say that he would walk to Langland through the priory wood. She planned to meet him halfway or at the stone-pit. Overhead, larches were green. It was too soon for bluebells but sunlight through the branches fell on their fresh leaves and picked out glints of gold in her hair. Her face was serious. She was realizing that though there would be much to hear there was much that she was not free to tell. Concealment permeates the mind and puts weight on the tongue. She had unconsciously become guarded and had lost a little of her natural vivacity.

She had Miles's letter in her pocket and took it out more than once to glance at bits she already knew by heart.

'If you happened to be walking to Bainrigg,' he had written, 'and I happened to be walking to Langland. . . .' He had paused, pen in hand, to look down through budding trees at the college garden. It was time for evensong. The bell's measured strokes drifted with strains of organ music on the mild air, bringing the reassurance he constantly needed. A fellow student crossed the green – and then another – to disappear under the cloister arches: timeless figures in an unending procession ages long.

'We might just happen to meet,' he continued and smiled, picturing her as she would come from the shade of the wood into full daylight; she always walked lightly, head erect. She would call his name, and this time he would take her in his arms at once as he had so often longed to do. There was no need now to wait: she was no longer a child. He had taken the precaution of asking his grandmother how old she was when she married.

'I was twenty,' she told him. 'We had been engaged for a year.' Seeing his smile, she had asked, 'Are you thinking of someone special? It's time you did think of marrying.'

There was that charming girl, she recalled, whom he had brought to Bainrigg one day last summer, such a polite and graceful girl. She had forgotten her name but remembered having met her and her mother once at the Humberts, years ago. Her father had been in the regiment. . . .

For Miles there was a special appeal in the thought of meeting in priory wood. He was rather glad, despite her disappointment, that Margot would not be coming to Oxford: he wanted her at Bainrigg. The old place had become dear to him on her account. She had kindled his love for it at the very beginning when she had mentioned the surreptitious raids on the bluebells. He liked to think of her among flowers. His was a fleshless, visionary love. It possessed him even in his absence from her, perhaps most powerfully then when uncomplicated by the doubts and fears of actuality and obligations to other people.

He had thought continually of this most important meeting, hoping the day would be fine. Would she come if it rained? Whatever the weather, rain – mist – wind, he would find her, hold her close and pour out all that he had wanted to say and had so long suppressed.

The day was fine and Margot did walk lightly, head in air. Never slouch, Alex had said in the days when for her own good he had licked her into shape – the shape of Tom Merridew, one of the heroes in *Boys' Own Paper*, those dauntless lads unflinchingly preferring death to dishonour. ('Yielding not an inch, he smote the cobra with his machete. No second blow was needed'.) It had been an uphill task as well as a dismal failure though she could now think with amusement that in one respect she did resemble the gallant fellows. No matter how stormy the sea, how frail their boat, how fierce the mutinous natives, how deadly the snakes, they always survived – and so had she, so far.

It would amuse Miles to hear of these childish ordeals and occasional triumphs. She wondered if he too had read the *Boys' Own Paper*. With luck she would reach the rendezvous before he did. Swerving to avoid a low birch bough she came out into hazy sunshine and a flurry of birds in the hedge, and there on the left were the naked stones of the stone-pit.

She could see across the fields where lambs tottered and leapt, to the path leading down from Bainrigg House and presently a figure appeared at the double iron gates – a man's figure. Happiness warmed her whole being from head to toe. In a few minutes they would be together. But she would go no further; she would wait and let him come to her. He was coming quickly – and running.

But it wasn't Miles. The young man in shirtsleeves and waistcoat was an under-gardener. He reached her, breathless.

'There's bad news up at the house, miss. It's the master. He was taken ill in the night and' – the lad's lips trembled – 'he's gone. He passed away not above an hour ago.' He took an envelope from his pocket. 'Mr Miles sent this.'

'Mr Rilton!' It was hard to believe. He had always been there, all her life, and before him there had been other Mr Riltons, a long line of presences seldom seen, almost invisible, yet known to exercise power like the forces of nature, like the weather.

'Nothing's going to be the same, miss, now that he's gone. There's rare comings and goings up there at the house. I'll need to get back as quick as I can.'

'Of course. Tell Mr Miles how sorry I am and if there's anything we can do for Mrs Rilton. . . .'

Dear Margot, Miles had written in haste, *I tried to telephone you at the Hall but you had already left. Grandfather has died suddenly. It has been a fearful shock. I shall be kept here, there is so much to do. I'm deeply disappointed not to see you, more than I can say, much much more. But it must be soon, please. . . .*

Brightness had gone from the morning. She read the letter again and again, then turned to walk slowly homeward. By the low birch bough she paused, reluctant to go beyond the radius of Miles's influence. Since she had passed this spot only a few minutes ago everything had changed. The news saddened but could not grieve her, as she had barely known the old gentleman. The families were not on visiting terms, with the exception of that one momentous visit – as she had come to think of it – when the dedication of the memorial had brought them all together. He had called at the Hall when the tenancy was discussed. She remembered his voice and his courteous goodbye.

But to have missed seeing Miles did grieve her. It was more than disappointment, rather a sense of his having been abruptly withdrawn, leaving her forlorn and anxious. In the dreary days of winter she had looked forward eagerly to their reunion. It had not happened. She would always think of it, the lost hour, as more sadly beautiful than any actual meeting could be.

With each step that carried her away from him, that mediocre portion of her existence in which he had no part reasserted itself. The mild air, the sky of tender blue between branches and the elasticity of youth caused her to loiter, reluctant to creep home tamely, having left it with wings outspread. She was still much nearer to Bainrigg House than to the Hall. Though it would not be a pleasant thing to do, here was an opportunity to carry out an experiment she had long had in mind. She turned back.

From the stone-pit she saw that the double gates of Bainrigg House were closed. There was no one about: they would all be occupied with the emergency. She had the whole landscape of fields, hedges and trees to herself. In a few minutes she had reached the iron gates, turned her back on them and looked down the field path leading to the chimney two fields away. It was slightly to the right of the ash tree. She could see it clearly though not its base. It seemed in some way changed. For the whole length of the first field the path ran parallel with the hedgerow unimpeded by any outgrowth. Walking steadily, she could see the chimney all the way to the first five-barred gate. In the next field the hedge curved here and there, bulging over the ditch, but the path also curved at those points so that the chimney and ash tree remained clearly visible to anyone walking from

Bainrigg to the beginning of Clint Lane – though, she reminded herself, last June the trees would be in full leaf.

How long had Miles remained at his garden gate that day after Linden left him? From it he had seen Katie near the chimney. Linden had not seen her – or so she said. She might not have been looking. But it is hard not to see another person moving in an otherwise deserted countryside. Margot had already unhappily considered the possibility that Katie had seen Linden and had been in such dread of meeting her that she had clambered into the nearest hiding-place. Supposing at this moment someone in pink were to appear by the chimney – she could now see it from top to base – would it be possible to avoid seeing her?

The effect of such thoughts was to raise once again the frightened ghost of Katie, her eyes panic-stricken, her fair hair rising from her head as if electrified; to revive the sadness; to wonder why, if Linden had seen Katie, she should deny having seen her, and to remind herself that a person who lies can never be believed.

How strange – it really was a coincidence – that the thief should come unexpectedly upon the scapegoat in this lonely place, that Linden should come within hailing distance of the one person who might be the means of her undoing. If ever Katie should be sufficiently clear in her wits to declare her innocence, she might not be believed, but suspicion could fall on the only other person who had been in the shop alone. Linden had taken the risk, confident that Katie's guilt would be taken for granted. But if she saw Katie run in panic to the chimney would she try to stop her? She knew that the chimney was dangerous; Margot herself had told her and had blushed for her own officiousness. Linden had certainly not stopped Katie, might indeed not have seen her, but Margot remembered the first time the two had met under the pear tree on the garden path at Monk's Dene, and her own dismayed impression that for Linden Katie simply didn't exist. She was not merely to be overlooked but to be seen and dismissed as less than human. Would Linden, cool and composed as ever, watch Katie go to her death?

Margot faced the horror in which she was involving herself and recognized it as sheer supposition of the most shameful kind

– to suppose that Linden could have walked sedately back to Monk's Dene that day, relaxed in the garden (how elegantly even in a deck-chair!), eaten strawberries, knowing all the time where Katie was and *never mentioning it.* Impossible, even though to a person willing to let Katie take the blame for what she herself had done, Katie's permanent disappearance must have been a relief, though not an unqualified relief. Later in the evening as anxiety for Katie intensified, Linden had seemed out-of-sorts and pleaded fatigue, realizing perhaps how her behaviour would be seen if it were ever found out. Had she gone down on her knees and prayed that it never would be?

There was another possibility even worse, and not to be thought of. It was bleak comfort to feel that sheer indifference would prevent Linden from deliberately contriving Katie's death; to know and not care what happened at the chimney was bad enough. Was not indifference in itself a source of evil?

With a sense of increasing darkness, Margot groped her way to an imperfect understanding of what it was that from the beginning had made Linden seem different. The difference lay, not in anything she did – what did she ever do? – but in the nature of her being. She had only to be there to cause harm. At closer quarters the glamour faded as tinsel fades, leaving unadorned a heartless disregard of others.

The most maddening thing about Linden, she felt with a rush of resentment, was that one could never stop thinking about her. She herself was as much her prey as Alex was. One way and another she had been thinking about her for years, passing from admiration to doubt, mistrust and condemnation. She was never free of her. It was as if she cast a spell inducing love or fear or hatred (why did Ewan hate her?) – a contamination she was able to spread without having suffered the disease. Was that the secret of all witchcraft – the ability to change others while remaining unchanged?

Margot had come to the chimney and saw why it had seemed different. Disputes over its future were still unresolved and it had been encased in heavy barbed-wire. Visually it was not a change for the better. The dignified if melancholy relic had become a fabulous monster pointing a multitude of wicked darts: a thing to be fled from. She turned and saw Mrs Dobie coming from the direction of Larsons' farm. Sombrely dressed in her long black coat and deep-crowned black hat, she might have been sent to restore order in a situation of moral confusion. More simply, here was a person who knew right from wrong.

She may have been surprised at Margot's readiness in coming to meet her and by the warmth of her greeting. Her black-laced boots came to a halt.

'You're a stranger here these days.' She was a little out of breath. Exercise had deepened the petunia shades of her complexion. Otherwise she was little changed from the day when she had poured scorn on the memorial service, a solidly real human being mercifully free of so much as a nodding acquaintance with Linden Grey. To see her was like being rescued from a stormy emotional sea.

'It's a lovely day for a walk, Mrs Dobie.'

'Aye, but you'll have heard the news. It's a sad loss for them up at the House.' Mr Rilston had been less than two hours dead but Margot knew that by this time the news would have spread throughout Ashlaw. 'The world's forever changing. Mr Miles is young to be taking over. The lad could do with a bit of hardening for the toil and worry ahead of him. If you ask me he's too gentle and dreamy for this world. And how's your mother going on, love? Mrs Roper tells me she's been real poorly. She's been sadly missed in Ashlaw, has Mrs Humbert. We don't see much of the new agent's wife. They say Mrs Ainsley doesn't like the house being right in the village. Ashlaw isn't smart enough for her. It seems she's from Australia and never wanted to come here in the first place. It wouldn't surprise me if they upped and left all of a sudden. There'd be no tears shed if she went back to where she belongs. Only it would be a sad sight to see the blinds drawn again at the agent's house and your old garden getting out of hand – and then strangers coming.'

Margot walked back with her towards Clint Lane, stifling the homesickness for Monk's Dene she had unintentionally revived. They exchanged other news of births and deaths in the village, of the laying out of smallholdings at Langland, where two cottages were now occupied. Margot asked after the Larsons.

'Well enough, but too much out of the way of other folks. Little Rosie would be better for other bairns to play with. She's getting airy-fairy with being so much on her own. Talking to herself and dressing up in her mother's clothes, with flowers in her hair. There'll be no brothers or sisters for her either, from what Nancy tells me.'

By the chimney they parted.

'Mrs Dobie,' she said, as the old woman turned to go, 'may I ask you something?'

'There's no harm in asking.' She had seen that the girl was troubled: knew that she had been overworked. She was a sweet-looking girl, a regular ray of sunshine when she was little, now quiet and large-eyed.

'It's nothing personal, just a thing I sometimes think about. If you knew that something was wrong, you'd speak up about it, wouldn't you? You wouldn't let it be covered up?'

Mrs Dobie looked her up and down, then with a gesture indicated the village below, its roofs sheltered by the ridge.

'There's hardly a house down there where there isn't something wrong, nor a human being that hasn't some weight of trouble to bear. There's as many wrongs covered up and never spoken of as there are grains of sand on the shores of all the oceans in the world.' She was not, as Alex used to say, breathing fire: she spoke quietly, an old woman whom life has saddened.

'Do you mean that it's better to leave things covered up?'

'There's no knowing which is better. Sometimes you have to speak out. When? When your own conscience tells you to. But if covering it up makes you unhappy, let it out. You'll get no thanks for it but you might feel better.'

She must make up her own mind. It was comforting to know that even so wise a woman as Mrs Dobie was sometimes doubtful as to what was the right thing to do. She was looking at the chimney, now cruelly encaged and when she spoke again her words touched so nearly her own thoughts that Margot felt a superstitious chill.

'And there's been wrong done here at this very place where we're standing. What'll come of it no one knows. Things sometimes come out of their own accord without anyone telling – and one wrong leads to another as sure as I'm standing here.'

She was standing there no longer – was already moving away.

'Goodbye, Mrs Dobie. I'm so glad we met.'

'And so am I, if it was just to see that you haven't lost that friendly smile. You'll tell your mother I was asking after her?'

Alex came home two days later. Margot met him at Fellside station. They walked home, leaving his luggage to be delivered.

'You're very quiet.' Alex broke off an entertaining account of a battle of wits with his tutor. 'Something up?'

'Well, yes. I'll tell you later. This evening perhaps. You'll want to talk to Mother first.'

'The suspense will kill me,' he said cheerfully.

And when in his room that evening she told him, Margot had some idea of how it might feel to commit murder. It was a kind of death that she inflicted, though not on him: it was Linden as she had seemed to be who abruptly ceased to exist. Half-a-dozen words were enough to shatter her image beyond hope of repair.

For once he had nothing to say. They sat in painful silence. She was alarmed at the damage she had done and waited anxiously until he spoke. The walls were thick but they kept their voices low like conspirators discussing the disastrous failure of a secret enterprise.

'You've known this since Christmas? Why, for heaven's sake, have you kept it to yourself? Are you sure you haven't imagined the whole thing?'

'How could I imagine such a thing when I thought her so wonderful?' At first, she mentally added. It seemed a long time ago. In her distress she found it hard to remember the circumstances that one by one had shaken her faith. 'I'm simply telling you what Toria said she saw.'

'Do we have to believe that ghoul of a woman?'

'She was there when it happened. Why should she say it if it isn't true?'

'She could say anything. Nobody can contradict her.'

'Except. . . .' She could not bring herself to name the one person who could – and certainly would – deny Toria's story.

'You don't imagine I can confront Linden with a thing like this? What am I supposed to say? "I understand it was you who stole those damned four-and-elevenpenny beads"? I'd rather cut my throat.'

She understood – and had not foreseen – that it didn't matter now whether the story was true or false, he would never be at ease with Linden again, if he ever had been: an idol may not be the easiest of companions.

'You always said one should never tell on another person. You were forever telling me things I should or should not do. I knew this would upset you, but as you may be going to marry her. . . .' She was skirting round the truth as Linden might do. It had been her deliberate intention to stop him from marrying, to save him.

'Thank you very much. A nice little prig you've turned into.'

'If I'm a prig, you helped to make me one with all your dos and dont's. You tried to make me strong and silent like a hero in one of those stories.' Actually, she thought, Tom Merridew couldn't have made a better job of it: she had struck a fatal blow and no second blow was needed. 'You certainly tried.'

'I certainly failed.'

'You wouldn't even let me cry in peace.'

'Don't be such a chump.' He was in no mood to tell her, was barely aware of it himself, that seeing her cry had always gone to his heart and undermined his magnificent confidence.

'If you really love her, you can forgive her.'

'Of course I really love her.' Was it true? He had seemed to fall in love as he did everything, with gusto. His devotion had been whole-hearted. 'If it had just been taking the beads, wouldn't that have been forgivable? That futile business of keeping up appearances without two pennies to rub together. . . .'

Both knew the remark to be ridiculous; and he had seen at once, more keenly than Margot had done, how much was involved. The shabbiness of the affair disgusted him, the meanness of sheltering behind a person as helpless as Katie. He saw the irony of it – that an act of shallow vanity could result in an innocent creature's death. He remembered the scent of elderflowers in the cool dawn, his first glance into the dark shaft, the limp body he had held; its pathetic frailty. Seeing his misery,

Margot spared him the rest: there was no need to voice her suspicion that Linden might have seen Katie go to her death.

'I'm going to bed.' She was weary of it all. For the first time they had almost quarrelled. 'I suppose it was wrong of me to tell you. I couldn't make up my mind. I'm sorry.'

He had not been listening.

'I really thought I loved her.' It was as if he needed to remind himself. 'You don't understand what it's like to feel that way.'

'I do understand.'

'But I can't face her. I can't even ask her to deny such a rotten thing. But if it's true, I can't forgive her. I wouldn't ever be able to forget it.'

He scarcely noticed that she was leaving. From the door she looked back. His face had gone sharper, the healthy colour faded. It would haunt her, she thought, and wished she hadn't told him: it was wrong to interfere in another person's life.

'I'll have to go away. In any case I'll be glad to get away from this place. It's like a morgue, especially with that woman prowling round like a death's head.'

'She thinks you're wonderful. It was for your sake that she decided to tell.'

'There's no such thing as a wonderful person.'

He remained as she had left him, rigid in his chair. For the first time in his ardent life there was nothing in the world he wanted to do. It was dark outside and the room was poorly lit, but he saw his situation as clearly as if the cold light of a winter day had laid it bare – his own crazy wrong-headedness and her vanity, lying and deceit. Linden herself he could no longer visualize. For years she had been his first and last thought every day. He dreamed of her, longed for her. When he was with her he had been oblivious to everything but her eyes, her grace, her smile. Now it was as if he had never seen her. It horrified him. She seemed lifeless like one of the cardboard figures Margot had played with in the nursery, clipping to the shoulders a party dress, a warm coat, a summer frock. She had faded from his vision leaving only a hand reaching for a string of cheap beads.

The disquiet he felt was not even a decent regret that it was over: it was dismay for what he was not feeling. He should have been prey to the memories that haunt unhappy lovers; he should have been able to hear her voice, its tender softness, a foolish endearment. He should have felt a hand stealing into his to lie there, intimately warm, a caress. That was how it should have been. Such things had never happened. She had given nothing. He had never known her thoughts. She had not even tried to attract him. The awful truth was that he had not only deceived himself as to her nature, he had wrongly identified his feeling for her as love.

He knew at last what Margot had known all along: that if it had been love he would have found it in his heart to forgive her. Her behaviour would have angered and disgusted him, but he would not have seen it as he saw it now in all its paltry meanness. If it had been a criminal offence, even murder, might it not have called forth some grand gesture on his part? He saw himself posing as Sir Galahad for a change, offering help and support. But Linden would never do anything so positive, not that compassion would stay her hand; she wouldn't mind watching some other wretch doing it, he thought bitterly, and wouldn't turn a hair at a public hanging.

He never wanted to see her again: he couldn't bear to witness her moral squirming or to hear her lie. It was bad enough to face his own superficiality. A new longing seized him – to be single-minded and self-forgetting like Lance. He could do with one of Lance's withering doses of advice. As he foundered under wave after wave of disenchantment, it would be like Lance to throw a life-belt.

As the grey of morning stole into the room, his feelings changed. Linden had passed from his mind: there was nothing about her that he wanted to remember. Neither did he think of Lance, nor of himself, nor did it occur to him that there was any need to think of Margot. As if she had stolen into his room with the first faint light, it was Katie who came into his mind. She made no reproach or appeal. He was too tired even to think, 'What a shame'. It was just that somehow because of all she lacked, she was also without fault, the only person he had ever known who was entirely blameless. There was a kind of peace to be found in the thought that someone could live and die without

128

hurting or harming or cheating or exploiting another human being. It was of Katie that he was thinking as he fell asleep.

The few days of his visit dragged painfully. Alex was uncharacteristically dull and silent; Margot worried and remorseful. As always she was affected by his mood: the cloud darkening his horizon darkened hers too, and inevitably not only hers.

'There's something wrong with Alex. Isn't he feeling well? If only I could be downstairs.' Months of illness had made Sarah fretful.

Margot, who spent much of the day in her mother's room, was anxiously aware of the need to shield her from stress. Dr Pelman had warned of a weakness of the heart and insisted on rest and quiet for his patient. Alex's enforced cheerfulness during his visits to the sick-room was so patently bogus that they left his mother restless and upset.

'I believe it is something to do with Linden,' Margot said.

'Can they have quarrelled?' Sarah brightened, then hastened to add, 'Poor Alex. But it may be all for the best.'

The phrase was comforting but only briefly. On the eve of his departure, brother and sister held another of the low-toned urgent conversations that seemed a feature at the Hall.

'I've been thinking things over. My life here is finished. I'll never settle in Elmdon.' It had been intended that in joining a firm specializing in company law, he would be able to handle his father's problems at Langland. 'I'm going to apply to the Colonial Office.' He had heard from a friend whose father had influence, that there were vacancies in administrative posts in East Africa. It would mean beginning as an assistant district officer but if his application was accepted, he would leave in June immediately after his finals and be away for two and a half years.

'Don't say anything just yet. There's no need to upset Mother until she's stronger.'

When at the beginning of June he heard that his application had been accepted, he wrote first to Margot.

'Try to break the news gently to them both. Just give a hint or two. I'll write to them after finals when I know the details.'

Margot did her best. Her father was at home at the time. On

such occasions they had breakfast together and both enjoyed it with a slight feeling of being on holiday. It seemed a shame to spoil so harmless a pleasure but it had to be done.

'Has Alex ever mentioned that he would like to go abroad?' she asked casually.

'For a holiday?' her father asked from behind his newspaper. 'Where?'

'No. To work.'

'Work!' The newspaper was lowered. 'He's going to work at Bavistocks'.' The perusal of the editorial column was resumed but not for long. 'Do you mean to tell me that he's trying to back out when they've been keeping a place for him for almost a year?'

'He just happened to say that he had heard of vacancies for district officers in Kenya.'

'And I suppose that was enough to blow him off course again. We might have known he wouldn't stick to anything for long. This constant chopping and changing will be the ruin of him. He lacks stability. That's always been his trouble.' The newspaper was abandoned, a cup of tea left to get cold. 'Your mother won't be happy about this. Better not say anything to her. It's probably a flash in the pan.'

Which would be worse: to submit her mother to two or three weeks of worry and sleepless nights, or to a sudden shock when the news came? It seemed best to take her father's advice. When the letter came, Edward read it without a word and left the room. She waited in suspense while he made a long telephone call to Alex, then took the letter upstairs, came down and shut himself in his study. Alex had written to her too. 'Perhaps it will soften their hearts to know that I've got a first.' Yes, that was the thing to concentrate on.

'I can't quite take this in.' Sarah handed her the letter and lay back on her pillows as if the remaining strength had gone out of her. 'He has done splendidly, but your poor father is bitterly disappointed about this change of plan. He shouldn't be. It is just the sort of thing he would do himself. But he was relying on Alex's help and looking forward to having him at home. And so was I. So very much. It doesn't feel like home when he's away.'

She closed her eyes and rested for a minute. 'It's because of Linden, isn't it? Has she refused him?'

'I gather that he feels she has let him down.' The careful answer had cost Margot some thought.

'Two years, he says. Time for him to get over it and find someone else. Someone with more warmth and openness and not quite so polite.' She smiled. 'He's done so well but oh, how we shall miss him. Thank God I still have you. Without you I don't think I could go on, or want to. What kind of life will it be out there, I wonder? I do hope it won't change him too much.'

'It will be an adventure. You know he was always talking about adventures.'

There was little outward fuss: as a family they were not given to making scenes. When Alex came home to say goodbye and collect some of his belongings, there were no recriminations. They all had tea in Sarah's room on each of the three days and talked of other things besides the parting. Alex would need a few days of strenuous shopping at the Army and Navy Stores for suitable clothes, tin-lined trunks to keep out white ants – apparently they ate everything – and as there would be field trips through wild bush country, he would need boots, guns, a pith helmet. . . . Edward advanced a generous sum without complaint although he was beginning to feel the pinch after almost a year of continuous spending.

But there were intervals when Kenya was forgotten and they talked about Langland and Monk's Dene and family friends. Edward failed to notice that Linden was never mentioned; Sarah and Margot did notice and were glad. The connection could be dropped without regret.

For Margot, to have done with Linden once and for all meant liberation from the compulsion to think about her. The harm she had done could never be rectified. Katie was dead. . . . Margot turned her mind resolutely from all the other changes for the worse. The list was complete. Linden had passed out of her life and could never hurt her again.

On the last morning, Sarah insisted on going downstairs fully dressed.

'I don't want him to remember me as an invalid,' she said and somehow managed to delude both Alex and his father into believing that she was on the road to recovery.

Edward would see him off when he sailed, but Margot went with him to Elmdon station. Alex looked down from his carriage window at the young woman in straw hat and summer dress on the platform and recognized her as the little sister he had patronized and preached to and made use of – and needed. She stood erect, grave and rather gallant. It occurred to him now that it was too late that he was deserting her. He had often enough been away but never out of reach. If she should need him, he would not be there.

'Meg.' She took his outstretched hand. He saw her swallow hard and blink back tears, shedding none. 'What will you do?'

Without him? She felt the void. It yawned at her feet, unimaginably wide and damp and cold.

'I'll be all right.'

'Don't do anything silly – like getting married – or anything.'

'I'll try not to.'

The guard blew his whistle. Their hands parted. For some bonds the word love is not enough. Such bonds are unchosen, unacknowledged like air and water, and unbreakable.

'Be there when I come back.'

She walked a few steps with him as the train moved. He watched her until it reached the end of the platform, forgetful of the life ahead, thinking with unexpected pain of the life he was leaving.

As Margot left the platform, the sparse gathering of people on the concourse parted to make way for a man rushing at furious speed towards the barrier.

'Lance!'

'Damn. I've missed him. Just didn't make it.'

'You came all this way. . . .'

They stood for a moment in gloomy silence. He had travelled overnight from Glasgow; he was red-eyed, unshaven, dishevelled, hungry. She saw that he was also terribly disappointed.

'Come on. I'll take you home.' They both said it almost in a breath and laughed. He took her arm.

'When blokes go to Africa, it takes hold of them. They never settle anywhere else.'

'Perhaps Alex won't settle even in Africa.'

'That's a thought.' He fell asleep in the taxi and had to be roused when it stopped at the front door.

Sarah was lying on her bed, still dressed, her face puffed from weeping, her hair loose. Margot brought a bowl of water, a towel, comb and mirror.

'It doesn't matter about my hair.' Sarah closed her eyes and continued to pray without hope that she would live to see her son again.

CHAPTER XIV

Marian Grey enjoyed her visits to Bainrigg House. Her social life was limited. She could not go on accepting invitations from the few old friends in Elmdon who had kept in touch without returning their hospitality. To invite them to no 5 Gordon Street was simply impossible.

The seven years she had spent in those dreary rented rooms had been a test of endurance: a period of exile from the world she had once, too briefly, known. It was unreasonable perhaps (she was not a reasonable woman) to feel that Justin had let her down: not by being killed in battle, that was an eventuality he could not avoid and as an officer could be said to have sought, but in not having left her well provided for. The discomforts and limitations of Gordon Street were such as one never got used to: the musty furnishings, the smoking fires, the flaked enamel of the bath, the chipped handbasin, the view of a narrow street and the constant racket of carts and cars. In Gordon Street she was not herself.

The Marian Grey she felt herself to be emerged like Athene fully armed from the brow of Zeus when she stepped out of the Rilstons' car at Bainrigg, Chapman holding open the door – and remained as actively alive as she was capable of being until he helped her out again on the return to no 5 – to the red and blue glass fanlight and the bird-cage in the window.

In the sitting-room at Bainrigg, long windows opened on smooth lawns. Beyond a cedar's trailing boughs there were no more than glimpses of commonplace fields and mercifully distant wild country. When, as occasionally happened, conversation lapsed, one rediscovered the silence of the room, of the house, of the whole domain; a well-bred expensive silence scarcely broken by a soft-footed maid bringing coffee – or tea – or a glass of wine, until the two low-pitched voices resumed their unforceful and purposeless interchanges; purposeless, that is, on the part of Mrs Rilston.

The friendship, recently begun, had grown rapidly, encouraged by a number of ill-assorted circumstances. The most pressing included the alarming accumulation at no 5 of unpaid bills and the refusal of Wares, the principal store in Elmdon, to give further credit, and the death of a capricious relative who had been generous in passing on expensive clothes but had left everything to a nephew in Tasmania.

One morning in the week before Easter, gloom at the breakfast table was alleviated by the arrival of the weekly *Elmdon Gazette.* They had given up the luxury of a daily paper but it was necessary to keep abreast of local functions.

'Mr Rilston has died.' Two whole columns were devoted to the passing of one of the county's most distinguished gentlemen. 'How sad! We met him and Mrs Rilston, you remember, at the Humberts. Did you see him that time you called at Bainrigg with Miles?'

'No. Only Mrs Rilston.'

'Speaking of the Humberts, I suppose Alex will be home at Easter.'

'Yes. Tomorrow or the next day.'

'He'll be sure to call. Do try to meet him somewhere else.' Marian's glance expressed dissatisfaction with the room.

'He doesn't notice.'

'No, of course not. He is so devoted. I wonder . . . .'

Her wonder took a different direction as days passed without a sign or word from Alex. She had never been sure of Linden's feelings for him, or of Linden's feelings about anything. Close though they were, Linden had never been confidential. Naturally she understood the absolute necessity of making a good marriage for both her own sake and her mother's. Marian's experience had made her anxious that Linden should be spared the deprivations life had thrust upon her mother. But with the passage of time, hope of a good marriage might degenerate into a clutch at any marriage at all. Alex Humbert's father was a man of means; Alex himself had prospects – long-term prospects. The rather dreadful Godfrey Barford could, as a husband, keep both Linden and her mother in comfort, at least his father could. In spite of herself Marian could not repress a shudder.

But Miles Rilston, heir to the entire Rilston estate, would have much to offer and – her eyes turned to the morning paper – had it now. Linden knew him, had actually visited at Bainrigg. Would it be suitable to write a letter of condolence to Mrs Rilston on the sad loss of her husband?

'I don't think so,' Linden said. 'We aren't on such close terms.'

'But we have met. If I could happen to meet her again – by chance . . . .'

'She goes out very little, and especially now, I suppose.'

Nevertheless Linden's concentration on whatever it was that occupied her at her desk in the window at Embletons' was not so profound as to prevent her from noticing passers-by. There was no mistaking the Rilstons' Daimler with Chapman at the wheel. A fortnight passed.

'It's usually a Wednesday,' she told her mother. 'Miss Leonard at the office knows the chauffeur. Mrs Rilston comes to the hair-dresser and the bank and to visit an old servant in hospital. She has coffee at Pikes.'

The following Wednesday morning, Mrs Rilston was at her usual table when a newcomer approaching the one next to it appeared to hesitate. She was a thin woman in her forties, wear-ing a well-cut and well-worn grey costume, a plain felt hat and amber beads.

'Good morning. Mrs Rilston, I believe. You won't remember me. I'm Marian Grey. We met at the Humberts years ago.'

'I do remember. Won't you join me?'

To the accompaniment of a piano, violin and viola, they became acquainted. The two had much in common: an igno-rance of everyday working life, a dependence on men, a limited range of ideas. Both were widows, both lonely.

'I'm sorry that I can't invite you to our rooms,' Marian said. 'We do no entertaining.'

'I do understand,' said Mrs Rilston who would not have gone however warmly urged. 'You must come to Bainrigg.'

The visits, at first occasional, became frequent. On Wednesdays when she had finished all that she had to do in town, Mrs Rilston would bring her home to lunch. While she rested, Marian dozed over *The Lady* or *The Tatler* – or strolled in the garden until it was time for afternoon tea. In the well-padded armchair which became hers, she lost the fretfulness that sometimes marred her not unpleasing features. Being the younger of the two she unconsciously assumed the vivacity of a younger sister and sometimes gave the conversation a lighter turn. But her prowess as a listener was unsurpassed. Mrs Rilston often spoke of being hard-up, of the need to economize and to cut down on servants, of the drop in railway shares. But the richness of the furnishings, the gleam of mahogany and walnut, the thick pile of the carpets, the solidly built house and its surrounding acres made talk of poverty merely theoretical. She also spoke a good deal about Miles. It was some time before Marian identified him as the elder Miles, her son. Of the younger, less was said. Sometimes it was difficult to disentangle the two.

'And your daughter?' Mrs Rilston said. 'Tell me about her.'

'Well . . . .' To her surprise Marian could find nothing to say. Linden, the central interest in her life, was difficult if not impossible to talk about. What could one say? 'She has a little job at Embletons', the solicitors . . . She has friends . . .' Actually Linden had no girlfriends unless one counted Margot Humbert.

The two ladies liked to talk about the Humberts and their extraordinary decision to rent Langland Hall. Mrs Rilston had not mastered particulars of the agreement between landlord and tenant but she knew that it was unusual. She did not know that Edward's friends, Quinian and Andrews, had described it as an invitation to disaster, nor did Edward, but Marian had heard enough to justify her remark that there was something a little – well – unreliable about the Humberts.

'Not Sarah. We knew each other as girls. But her husband seems to change course rather frequently and Alex may take after him.'

Alex's silence had persisted. It was now June. He had not

written, and if he had been at home, he had made no attempt to see Linden.

'He has behaved oddly.' Marian did not mind writing off Alex as unreliable (one did rather wonder about his politics) and discourteous. If his father took risks, Linden had perhaps escaped the fate of marrying into a financially embarrassed family. 'But Linden is too level-headed to have become seriously involved with him. It was no more than a youthful flirtation.'

'A charming girl, I remember. She must come to tea one day.'

By the time the ladies met again Mrs Rilston had heard from her housekeeper that Mr Alex had gone all of a sudden to Kenya. His mother was terribly upset and her health had taken a turn for the worse. Everyone had thought he would settle down in Elmdon where a position was being held for him.

Marian breathed a sigh of relief. So far as she knew there was no money to be made in Africa unless it was in South Africa. Moreover, Kenya was known to be the region to which ne'er-do-well young men were sent and not heard of for years. Linden, so level-headed in not having become seriously involved, was surely too level-headed to grieve the loss of so imprudent a young man. His absence simplified things. Certainly Linden showed none of the symptoms of a broken heart. With a tiny inward shrinking, Marian admitted to herself that Linden had shown little sign of having a heart in the metaphorical sense.

Such feeling as Linden experienced in this situation could be described as resentment. Her confidence was a trifle shaken by Alex's desertion. It could scarcely be due to jealousy of Godfrey. With Alex, jealousy would have worked the other way: he would have stayed to fight, not run away. What had happened to change him so unaccountably? Meanwhile she watched her mother's successful infiltration into Bainrigg House with approval.

Miles also approved. A congenial woman friend was good for his grandmother. So far as he knew she had no other and even now she was too much alone. He had not gone back to Oxford for the summer term: there were too many things to see to at Bainrigg and also at the Rilston properties in Lancashire. It would have been possible to fulfil the minimum number of weeks to permit him to take finals but not to reach a standard that would satisfy him. There was no hurry. If he felt inclined he could return next year with a freer mind – but that would depend on Margot.

He felt his grandfather's death keenly: he had loved and relied on the old man and was not ready to take his place. For the past two or three years he had been happy in the knowledge that still greater happiness might be in store for him and not too far ahead. That he had not told Margot that he loved her had been a bitter disappointment. An aura of perfection clung to that lost meeting and no similar opportunity had arisen nor had he had the confidence to make one. He had seen Margot three or four times but never alone. Her father and brother had both come with offers of help and sympathy in April. He was astonished by the news that Alex had since gone abroad. The friendship with the Humberts and the hope that Margot returned his love had sustained him in the harassing weeks between Easter and midsummer. By the beginning of July the more pressing problems had been dealt with. One more trip to Lancashire would be his last for some time. He planned to spend the rest of the summer at home and to take the first opportunity of seeking out Margot.

Having made the trip, he came home earlier than expected. Things had gone well. He felt more cheerful and at ease than he had done since his grandfather's death. The day had been warm and he had enjoyed the drive with the hood of his car down. Coming back to Bainrigg had sometimes been an ordeal when he was a schoolboy, but now it was a genuine homecoming. Everything he loved was here in this quiet place where his forefathers had lived and died, where he would spend the rest of his life.

It was early evening when he turned into the by-road leading to Bainrigg – and cool under the wayside trees. From time to time he caught sight of the house: a window glittered in low sunlight; smoke rose from the kitchen chimney. Half an hour to the usual time for dining. Time to bath and change. He was hungry. Tomorrow . . . .

Mrs Beale, the housekeeper, had heard the car and was in the hall to greet him.

'It's good to see you, sir. We weren't expecting you until tomorrow.'

He heard voices in the sitting-room.

'Visitors?'

'Only Mrs Grey – and Miss Grey.' They had come to tea and been persuaded to stay to dinner. 'I dare say madam would have let them go if she had known you were coming.'

He didn't mind. Company would ease the monotony, not to say the slightly depressing business of sharing the long table with his grandmother. He must rearrange things now that he was to be more at home. The small sitting-room could be converted for use as a dining-room when there were just the two of them. And later, when Margot joined them . . . .

It was of Margot that he was thinking as he went downstairs – when was he not thinking of her? – and it was as friends of Margot that he thought of the Greys. He had barely remembered Mrs Grey. He had met Linden at the Humberts several times: had danced with her two or three times and had found himself entertaining her to lunch here one day last summer. He knew that Alex was in love with her. Odd that he should have gone off to Africa.

The ladies were speaking of the Humberts as he went into the room. He heard the name – was aware that the voices were subdued – sensed bad news even before his grandmother spoke.

'There you are, dear. We have just heard such very sad news from Langland Hall. Sit down, dear. I know it will upset you. Mrs Humbert has died. Late last night.'

'A very dear friend. We were at school together. However will he manage without her?'

'The removal must have been too much for her. I understand she had been ill ever since they left Monk's Dene.'

He heard the voices, reverent, concerned, vibrant with interest, with only one thought in mind: he must go to Margot at once – as soon as he could get away, but he was drawn in the wake of the ladies to the dining-room. He had already kept them waiting. He was genuinely shaken by the news. Mrs Humbert, still youthful, had seemed to him all that a mother should be: kind, loving with a quiet humour – all qualities she had passed on to Margot. Would her mother's death delay his plan to propose, marry her if she would have him and bring her as soon as possible to

Bainrigg, or – anxiety gave way to a thrill of excitement – would the prospect of an early marriage be all the more acceptable? Not immediate, naturally, but in a few months. She could not be left on her own at the Hall, some arrangement would have to be made. How soon would it be decent to speak to her father?

At dinner nothing else was talked of. Absently he was aware of their voices – sympathetic, speculative, mournfully absorbed and passionless. Two voices. Linden, never talkative, dined like him in silence. He had never heard her say anything of interest. He knew the sound of her voice but could attach to it no memory of anything she had ever said.

But when Linden did choose to speak, she did so effectively.

'A very sweet-natured girl, I remember.' Mrs Rilston was speaking of Margot whom she had seen once, years ago.

'Margot is sweet to everyone,' Linden said. 'She will make a wonderful doctor's wife. Lance Pelman is a very lucky man.'

She smiled, a charming smile suitably modified in the circumstances by sadness.

For a few minutes he must actually have lost consciousness and revived to find the scene unchanged: china, fruit, flowers were as they had been before the anguish seized him. He was troubled by a loss of direction: an explosion had shattered his entire being and yet he was still aware that in the distance people were talking about the disaster with quiet interest, with kindness, as if the subject were a pleasant one.

'Is it an engagement?'

'I don't think so. Not yet. He's not in a position . . . . An attachment. They have always been close from childhood ... so much at ease together . . . . I felt it from the first.'

'... a comfort to her now that her dear mother is gone.'

'... a dreadful loss. She will be heart-broken.'

'But in other respects she is so fortunate. I have envied her a little. What must it be like to have father, brother and sweetheart all doting on one and giving the security every woman needs?'

'They may marry soon. It won't be suitable now for him to be at the Hall as if it were his home.'

At first it was not the full realization of his loss that overpowered him, that would soon come and would never leave him, it was shame for his own dense stupidity that he found almost unbearable. To have blundered into a situation with such insensitivity was like staking a claim on territory in total ignorance of the landmarks, not knowing the language and incapable of reading the signposts. What had he been thinking of – a man who knew nothing whatever about women, who barely remembered his own mother, a man without friends, a clodhopper in human relationships? He had actually believed . . . . 'She is sweet to everyone.' He had had the presumption to imagine that the sweetness was for him alone.

Whereas from the beginning it had been little more than the kindness she felt due to a lonely stranger, a guest. She had found him stranded in the hall and had rescued him, talked about wireless sets and music – and years later had persuaded him to act as first-foot, still wanting to encourage him and draw him, an outsider, into the hospitable warmth offered to every visitor. He had seen it as a special quality in their relationship because it was the only one he had known. It was over. There would never be another. Loneliness was his lot. He saw himself deluded by hope: a traveller lured by a glimpse of *ignis fatuus*, then left to stumble on in the dark.

Thank God he had been saved from embarrassing her. In a frenzied moment he could almost have been grateful for his grandfather's death: it had prevented him from rushing to take her in his arms as if confident that his embrace would be welcome, when all the time she belonged to someone else. He felt physically ill, robbed of all comfort. He could bear neither to remember the times they had spent together nor to face a future without hope. As for the present . . . .

'Will you excuse me...?' Pride came to his rescue. With an effort he got to his feet, murmuring something about having business to attend to.

'He looks tired,' Marian said with concern.

'A long journey ... tiresome business. He is so careful of every detail. Punctilious like his father.'

He caught the word as he closed the door. It was true that he had been punctilious in not making love to Margot. That was the one unregrettable thing. What could have induced him to think that she cared for him? How presumptuous, arrogant, inept was it possible for a man to be? All the old diffidence she had helped him to overcome, all the old sense of being an outsider, revived with such force that he would gladly have died. Racked as he was by every disquieting thought a fertile mind could conceive, one thought escaped him: not for an instant did it occur to him that it might not be true.

The house was unbearable. He must have rushed out in desperation and found himself on Beggars Way without knowing how he had got there. As he passed the stone-pit he was for a moment soothed by the memory of Margot's presence there, only to suffer the realization that they had lingered there for the last time. But he went on walking in the direction of Langland, instinct drawing him there because every other place now seemed to exclude him.

For once the quiet of the wood, the subtle changes of light and the cool fragrance of the air meant nothing to him. Instead he remembered their conversation about Lance. 'I suppose that's rather wonderful,' she had said, speaking of his sense of purpose. Even then he had been blind to the implications. He remembered, too, that he had seen her in Lance's car – and a particularly malicious quirk of memory brought back an incident when he had first seen them at the War Memorial. For some reason Margot was crying and Lance handed her a handkerchief. Neither had spoken, there was no need; they were so close.

Torn between the need to cut himself off from her forever and the longing to see her again, he walked with such speed that he was soon within sight of the priory. The rapid movement had had a stimulating effect. Was there any harm in telling her, now that it was too late, that he had loved her and had not known that it was Lance she loved? A faint hope stirred. Perhaps after all she would tell him that he had not been mistaken . . . .

From the gatehouse he looked down on the Hall. There were several cars. Distress had dulled his perceptions: he should have foreseen that there would be visitors. Alex and his father had been quick to come to him when his grandfather died. Ought he to pay his respects as friend and landlord and offer help?

As he hesitated, a taxi wound its way up the long drive. Margot had seen it, had perhaps been watching out for it, and went quickly down the steps to meet the visitor. It was Lance, obviously come hotfoot from Glasgow after receiving a telegram. They stood close. He put his arm round her and they went indoors.

Miles turned and walked slowly back, through the ruined priory and into the green solitude of the wood.

CHAPTER XV

Margot came out of her mother's room and closed the door. She did it noiselessly and crept across the landing without a sound. The habit had grown on her in response to the overwhelming silence now that her mother had gone; to the emptiness of her room: the emptiness of all the rooms. The merest tap of a heel on the polished floorboards might raise an echo. Even a whisper would disturb the stillness that occupied the house from roof to cellars.

At the top of the stairs she paused, as if to go down would be too significant an act to be taken without thought. It was mid-morning. The task she had set herself – except that it had come upon her without her conscious intent like everything else in this time of passive waiting – was completed. All her mother's things had been taken care of: sorted, washed, ironed, brushed, labelled and put safely away according to the need of each precious object. In time, the clothes would go where they could give comfort to the needy, but the rings, watch, necklaces, locket, work-basket, letter-case, pen and all the trivial things a woman feels unable to throw away, together formed a legacy of memories to be cherished for a lifetime. She had found letters from Alex, only two of them from Africa. He had presided over a native dispute involving a cow: he had shot a wildebeeste and wished that he hadn't.

She went slowly and quietly down and stood with her back to the newel post, inactive, not even wondering what to do next. Presently she would be mechanically impelled to do something and must wait until the impulse came. She heard the distant metallic ring of a saucepan lid, the eerie crowing of a cock. Someone had opened the windows. It was July, the weather perfect. Faint recollections of how one behaved and what one did on perfect summer days came and went. What did one wear? Without looking down to see, she didn't know what she had on. Not black. Her mother had said more than once, 'If anything happens to me, for goodness sake don't wear black.' As a girl she had spent years in black for dead relatives, one after another.

The dining-room door was open. Margot could see straight through the room and beyond the window to the flagged terrace where two people were standing in conversation, their backs to the house. Ewan Judd and Toria Link. For some reason it had been necessary to worry when those two were together. Was it still necessary now that her mother was dead? It was also, confusingly, supposed to be a good thing that those two got on well together. Conscious of a lack of sequence in her thoughts about Ewan and Toria, Margot looked to her right. The study door was also open. Her father would be at his desk. He was always there.

The desk, placed cornerwise with the window to the left, was covered with a disorderly mass of papers. He sat, head bowed, unmoving.

'Margot.'

She went and put her arm round him. He laid his head on her shoulder.

'You're my one comfort now,' he told her. 'What would I do without you? I've made such a mess of things. What can we do? You can't be expected to live like this.'

They had talked everything over, several times. It was worse for him, she thought, he blamed it all on himself: her mother's illness, Alex's absence from home. ('He didn't take to this place,' Edward said, unaware of Alex's reason for leaving.) She grieved for him with the bewildered feeling that their family, compact, strong and secure had fallen apart. He didn't know that it was not his fault. Her conviction that it was Linden who had set in motion the whole sad train of events had sunk too deeply into her mind to be easily uprooted.

It's worse for her, he thought. Without Sarah, without Alex, no neighbours apart from the two families in the cottages, Lance banished except for daytime visits and at present taking a midwifery course in Glasgow. He was missing Lance.

'We must pull ourselves together,' Margot said. It had become a weary joke; they had made it their slogan. 'Let me help you with all this stuff.'

They made a little progress. She was too apathetic to do more than make lists and put papers into separate piles. She had already gathered that there was need for economy and was aware that amid the welter of papers there were more bills than receipts.

Even before Sarah's death, Edward had realized that his plans for Langland must be curtailed. To do him justice, he could not have foreseen the collapse on Wall Street in three months' time and the subsequent Depression. As a result mines would be closed and the shipping company on which his personal income depended would come near to collapse owing to the reduced demand for pit-props.

He was not without capital but it must remain safely invested. Fortunately he would be able to extend his work as a consultant: closures raised almost as many problems as working pits. He had the advantage of experience at a time when fewer young men were training as mining engineers and he would never be short of work, but it was work that would necessitate his being a good deal away from home. They must remain at the Hall until the lease expired. He was already doubtful as to whether he would renew it.

In future he would be dealing with young Rilston. It was too soon to discuss future plans with him. It occurred to him that they didn't see much of Miles these days. Well, naturally, they couldn't have young men calling at will now that Margot was alone. Something must be arranged. A housekeeper-companion? Did such a creature exist, a sort of hybrid like a mermaid?

They were interrupted by the arrival of Dr Pelman who called to chat and stayed to lunch.

'I'm not happy about her,' he said when the meal was over and Margot had left them. 'If she goes the way she's heading it'll be a breakdown or a decline.'

'She's missing her mother.' Edward had brightened a little and was instantly wretched again.

'Of course she's missing her mother – and she's worn out with nursing and seeing to one thing and another. But it isn't her nature to droop as she is doing. She scarcely spoke a word at lunch. Is there anything else bothering her that I don't know about?'

'Good Lord, not as far as I know. It's dull for her here, I admit. She must see more of her friends when this tiredness wears off.'

'I don't know if it would interest you but I could make a suggestion.'

They put their heads together.

Margot went out of the cool house into the warm afternoon and presently found herself by the roofless gatehouse. It was this way that Miles might come if he ever came again. She often stood there or wandered to where the trees thinned to look along the woodland path. Sometimes she stood at the sitting-room window or on the front steps in a kind of limbo between the hope of seeing his car and the certainty that he would not come. And if he did come, he would be unlike the Miles she had known: a different person, as he had seemed when he came to offer his condolences like someone on an official visit. They didn't even sit down and she had actually wished that her father would join them so that she could excuse herself.

'And you,' she had ventured when he had told her how sorry he was about her mother, 'what have you been doing? You seem . . . .'

It was not coldness that cut her off from him, he could never be cold, it was distance, as if the few words they exchanged should have been shouted across a chasm: murmured, they drifted away and became meaningless. His face had lost its gentleness and was unsmiling. His eyes? She could not see into them. He never really looked at her until he said, 'Goodbye, Margot,' and after hesitating, 'I hope all will go well with you,' as if he were going away like Alex and Lance – but permanently. It was then that she saw the bleakness in his eyes, their blue faded.

'You're not well,' she said. 'What's wrong?'

Again he hesitated, then with a deprecatory smile and a movement of his head, he was gone – to walk home, had she known it, wishing he had the courage to put an end to himself. It would be a fit climax to all his other shortcomings. The past ten minutes had been an ordeal, but if for one moment he had shown how he actually felt, she would have had to draw away, embarrassed, thinking of Lance, as he had done the whole time they were together.

Margot had rushed to her room and lain face down on her bed in the depths of disappointment and shame. She had been so sure, so childishly mistaken about his feelings for her, so naively over-confident. How could she have been so wrong? No one must know, no one must *ever* know that she had thought – that she had actually expected . . . .

She heard Dr Pelman drive away and at last went downstairs. The visit had done her father good: he looked more alert.

'Pelman has made a suggestion. How would you like to have Jane Bondless here for a time? As it happens, she may soon be free.' And as Margot was slow to answer, 'You like Miss Bondless, don't you?'

'Very much.'

'The arrangement wouldn't be permanent. She and her sister Constance have scraped up a little money, enough to set up house together. If she were to come here for six months or so, her salary would help to pay for altering and furnishing the house.'

It would undoubtedly be a stroke of luck if she agreed. He had dreaded engaging a stranger who might be officious or ceaselessly talkative or annihilatingly dull. He was disappointed by Margot's lack of enthusiasm.

'It would be an immense relief to me, darling. I can't leave you alone here, but I can't afford to turn down consultation fees either. If we can get through the winter, things should be in better shape next year. Miss Bondless is rather a special sort of person. You've always enjoyed her company, haven't you?'

'Oh yes.'

'Then shall we risk it?'

'Yes, if you think so.' She was looking past him at the angle of the gatehouse visible from the study window. What did it matter who came if Miles did not?

Phyllis and Freda had written sympathetic letters full of gratitude to her mother who had made Monk's Dene such a wonderful place to visit. Each urged her to come – Switzerland was so beautiful, London so stimulating. At the end of the month came a third invitation from Jane Bondless in a letter to Edward. Nothing would have suited her better than to come to Langland and lend a helping hand for a while. Unfortunately, Miss Crane was unwell and could not be left just now. She enclosed the address of an agency which might have a suitable person on its list. In the meantime why not let Margot come to Cannes on a visit?

She had also written to Margot.

It would not be like coming to strangers. I knew your mother so well. It would make me very happy to be reminded of my visits to Ashlaw. Miss Crane often regrets that her spare room is never used. She is more or less confined to the apartment at present and would enjoy the company of a younger person – as you would enjoy sunshine, sea and glimpses of the leisurely lives of the well-to-do. Actually I sometimes feel the urge to give them a good talking to and I do have spells of longing for home. Do come and soothe me . . . .

Edward smiled when Margot showed him the letter.

'Just like Jane.' She had known how to make the invitation difficult to refuse. 'A splendid idea. It's extraordinarily kind of her – and Miss Crane. You'll write – at once?'

Margot did so, with many thanks for the kind invitation which she would have been happy to accept if it had not meant leaving her father alone. He was often away on business trips and must not come back each time to an empty house. She looked forward to seeing Miss Bondless on her return to England and hoped that Miss Crane would soon be well again.

It was all perfectly sincere but not absolutely straightforward. It was hard to admit even to herself that she could not bear to move so far away from Bainrigg House. To salve her conscience she tried to give her mind to the decorating and furnishing of a room for Miss Bondless. In the absence of other company the emptiness of the house was gradually occupied by the two who were there: not merely occupied but filled. For Margot in her downcast state they became larger than life. She was always conscious of them, expecting them to appear before they actually did, Ewan with step-ladder or tool-box; Toria with a string-bag of items to be checked and change to be counted; the two of them at the end of a passage or in the kitchen when Bessie Todd had gone home. Talking or silent, they did no harm, were known to be reliable, yet they seemed significant like messengers from a painful past or a worrying future.

It was impossible to think of them without thinking of Katie, of her pitiful end, the cruelty with which she was sacrificed and its consequences. The old days at Monk's Dene seemed a lifetime away, the family no longer a living organism, friends out of reach or estranged. Instead there was Ewan, self-contained, bitter, liable at any minute to erupt into reckless anger, and there was Toria forever responding to some weird dictate of Providence. A spark from one could set the other alight.

Foxgloves grew tall, pink and purple in the shelter of the priory walls. The birds were silent, it was high summer. Next there would be harebells to warn of its approaching end. Weeks passed and Miles did not come.

CHAPTER XVI

Margot's instinct had not misled her. From the beginning, Toria and Ewan were allies, drawn together by a common interest. On one subject at least they were in complete accord and since the subject was one of many facets – more than either of them knew – as a topic of conversation it never grew stale.

On the morning after Boxing Day, having watched the departure of Mr Humbert, Alex and Linden, Toria had gone downstairs. In the hall she met Ewan who had just closed the front door after them.

'Good riddance,' he said.

'Who do you mean?'

'Her. Swanking about in her silver dress and white fur.'

'Miss Grey?'

Toria was not surprised. From the gallery on the previous evening she had seen a good deal, including Ewan's ferocious snarl in Miss Grey's direction. She had not known then that he was a Judd. Heedful of Margot's warning, she did not pursue the subject, which cropped up again a week later when Alex went back to the university.

'He'll be safer in London,' Ewan remarked grimly. 'Out of her way. I had her summed up from the minute I first laid eyes on her.' Under their scowling brows the eyes were now baleful. 'That was before I ever came here and when she turned up last week I thought trust her to be in with the bosses and driving about in motor cars.'

They moved to the kitchen. Having by this time begun to make herself useful, Toria started on the washing-up. Ewan riddled the fire in the huge grate and banked it up with coal.

'When did you first lay eyes on her?'

'Well, I can tell you exactly. It was the day they had prayers and that at the War Memorial. I was coming back from Elmdon where I'd been to sign on and there were these two women waiting at the bus stop. It's against the animal-feed warehouse. The bus came all of a sudden. There was a bit of a splash and her high and mighty ladyship stepped back, never looking behind her. And there was this woman like a pedlar, standing up against the wall with tapes and stuff like that on a tray hung round her neck. Hair-pins and bootlaces. Her ladyship barged into her and knocked the woman off balance. The tray tipped up and all the things were scattered on the ground in the mud and muck.

'Did yon stuck-up bitch apologize? Did she not know the woman was just trying to make a living? Had *she* ever had to wonder where her next dinner was coming from? You'd have thought she might have slipped the woman a bob or two – or a tanner – or a threepenny bit. Not likely.'

'It was a shame.' Toria had listened with deep attention as if the story confirmed what she already knew of Miss Grey. 'A wicked shame.'

'The woman had to get down on her knees and pick up a few of the things. I tell you it sticks in my gizzard, a thing like that. That's life, I says to myself, some down in the gutter and some riding their high horse. And the woman felt the same. "You may be down in the muck yourself some day", she says to her, "and that's where you ought to be".'

'She was right. "He hath put down the mighty from their seats and hath exalted the humble".'

'And so he should,' Ewan said, guessing from her tone that *He* was someone in the Bible. 'Take the French Revolution.' He had not made the most of his years at the village school but he had been interested in *A Tale of Two Cities*. 'Can you blame them for cutting the heads off them aristocrats? I'm not saying it was right: all I'm saying is that it was understandable.'

At an early age Ewan had made the discovery that the bosses existed in order to grind the workers into the dust. In the hope of unseating them he had joined the Labour Party. He found the meetings tame, but they had enlarged his vocabulary.

'I saw her at that party,' Toria said, 'and the way she treated Mr Alex.'

'You haven't heard the rest of it. A constable came up, a chap I know. He used to play quoits with our Bob. "This gypsy is annoying me", she says. "Leave it to me, miss", Charlie Sparr says and gives me a wink.'

'She was a gypsy?'

'God knows. I never had a good look at her. She had a shawl over her head.' There had been only a minute before the bus left and he, too, had been stooping to pick up some of her wares. 'She could have been. There's a few of them about. You can take it from me – yon upstart very likely put that woman in the workhouse. And that wasn't all. I saw her again at Ashlaw that same day.'

Ewan's voice had changed. He could not speak of Katie. Linden's high-handed treatment of the pedlar stuck in his gizzard, but that she had somehow contrived to frighten his sister stirred him to the depths of feeling. He could not forget that she had followed close behind when Katie rushed out from the Humberts' gate, speechless and trembling, nor his resentment at the contrast between the two: one shrinking, defenceless, never telling her fears: the other confidently at ease as if the world belonged to her.

On the morning in June when Alex left for Kenya, Toria and Ewan were again on the front steps to watch for the taxi and help with the luggage.

'He's doing hisself a good turn,' Ewan said. 'Getting away from her.'

'It's a long way to Africa. He could have got away from her without going so far.'

'He's maybe found out what she's like.'

During the summer months Linden did not appear at Langland and for a time she was not discussed. Neither Ewan nor Toria was given to talking for talking's sake.

A year had passed since Katie's death. To the Judd family it had brought more than one change of mood. Shame and grief had found vent in fury against Miss Burdon: pride in the funeral had tempered the shame. As public interest faded, the tragedy became an intimate family affair with Katie herself as its centre, to be mourned and missed and inevitably transformed. She took on a rare unearthly quality and was becoming sanctified. As the sharpness of grief subsided, memory was to undergo other shifts and variations.

It was some time before interest reverted to the actual circumstances of the theft. It had been taken for granted that Katie, being as she was, strange and unpredictable, had been prey to some abnormal influence.

'What made her do it?' 'She'd never taken so much as a pin that wasn't hers.' 'Something must have got into her.'

Such speculations, endlessly repeated, were comforting and might have proved so for years to come. It was Lily Hart who cast a new light on the matter and raised questions of a different kind.

Lily was the daughter of the landlord of the Halfway House Inn on the Elmdon road, a pretty, pleasant, idle, slovenly girl whom Mrs Judd was always warning Ewan against on the grounds that she had never done a day's work in her life and was no better than she should be. These demerits were counter-balanced to some extent by Lily's claim to have second sight. Nobody believed her but she was sure of an audience when she read the teacups or the cards.

At the end of June, on the anniversary of Katie's death, a few friends dropped in at Clint Lane, including Mrs Roper who lived next door, and Lily. When tea was over she reached for Mrs Judd's cup, inverted it in the saucer, turned it three times and held it in long, grimy, beringed fingers.

'Well, I don't know I'm sure . . . .'

But Lily disregarded Mrs Judd's protest and bent her unkempt mop of dark curls over the upturned cup.

'There's something missing. There's cause for searching here.' She paused, looked raptly up at the ceiling and down again into the cup. 'There's looking for something – or someone. No, it isn't Katie, bless her, she's dead and gone. Not someone. It's a thing. Something lost.'

'Nothing that I know of.' Mrs Judd was firm, and when Lily had gone and the undoubted thrill diminished, 'If there's any searching to be done, it's her that should be finding something useful to do. A bit of soap wouldn't come amiss either.'

'I'll tell you one thing though.' Emily spoke slowly as if newly awakened. 'There is something missing. Them beads. Nobody knows what happened to them. What did she do with them?'

It was a new line of thought demanding a more careful reconstruction of Katie's last day.

'She didn't have them on her when we went to Humberts' to fetch her home, I'll swear to that,' Mrs Judd said. 'And I wish to God I'd brought her away instead of leaving her there. The only pocket she had was in her apron and I'd have seen them. Anyway if she'd had them she would have given them to me when I told her to. Didn't she always do as she was told?'

There would have been time for her to hide the beads after she left the shop and before she joined Mrs Roper in the kitchen. But where? At Monk's Dene? Mrs Roper didn't think so: every cupboard, nook and cranny had been emptied and scrubbed clean when the Humberts left. In any case there had been other people about. Katie, last seen crouching by the dining-room door, could not have gone anywhere else. There was no knowing when she had left or where she had gone or when she had reached the chimney.

'She should have been better looked after, my own poor bairn. I'll never forgive myself for leaving her.'

Someone tactfully changed the subject by remembering that Mrs Robson had felt the same when she had forgotten to put up the fireguard and her six-year-old Georgie had fallen into the fire. The comparison was comfortless but it diverted attention from Katie.

Interest in the missing beads, however, once roused, spread to every household in Ashlaw. Were they still under a hedge, or in a hollow tree, or hidden in the clutter of any one of a dozen backyards? For a while, looking for Katie's beads became a game for a few of the more imaginative children. The notion that they might be in the chimney, now unapproachable in its barbed-wire cage, gave to the chimney itself a different character – mysterious and gruesomely romantic, fit scene for the birth of a local legend. Alex's prediction that a forbidden place might over the years become sacred was on the way to being fulfilled.

But for the Judds and their neighbours the questions, 'What did she do with the beads? What *would* she do with them?' suddenly became obsolete: an entirely different question took their place.

On an evening in October, Mrs Judd sat in the rocking-chair with her feet on the fender. Firelight filled the room. The tea was already laid, a special tea with pineapple chunks and evaporated milk. Rob, on arriving home the night before, had produced a whole ham from his kit-bag, the first ever to grace the family table. For herself Mrs Judd asked no more than the simple luxury of half an hour with nothing to do.

'Draw the curtains, Emily, and let's have a bit of peace before they come.'

Emily paused to glance out at the twilit landscape. The flush of sunset had faded. Nothing could be seen of the village below but a few yellow gas lamps at the far end of the main street. At such times Clint Lane seemed to breast the darkening world as if sailing in air towards the western fells.

'The nights are putting in.' She twitched the brown casement-cloth curtains together.

'It's always about now when it's getting dark that I think of her. It's as if I'm still looking for her to come home.'

'It's been over a year.' Emily sat down on the other end of the wide fender. 'And it could have been yesterday.'

She too was free for a while though not for the best of reasons. The caller had been round with his crake the night before, intoning the bad news: 'Hope Carr pit idle the morn.' She'd had Sam under her feet all day, but she had at least been spared one night's battle with the pit clothes and the filling and emptying of the bath. They were saying that there'd be baths at the pit-head some day – not a day too soon, although some of the men, Sam for one, reckoned they'd stick to their own bath-tub in front of their own fire. Having him at home for the day meant a drop in the weekly pay packet. On the other hand she had been able to slip out, leaving him to keep an eye on Stanley. A brief escape from the male members of the family, one of them half a Judd, was not to be despised.

It was at such quiet times in the blessed warmth, the shabby room enriched by the crimson and gold of leaping flames, that they talked about Jo, the father whom Emily had almost forgotten; about Katie who was his favourite because she most needed to be favoured; about Rob who was too lavish with his money, especially now when trade was slack and he might not always be sure of a berth; about Ewan and whether he was going steady with Bella Capfield.

Bella, formerly Miss Burdon's maid, had soon had enough of the Penny Bazaar in Elmdon, of draughts from the ever open doors, chilly waiting for buses, the day-long absence from Ashlaw, the late return home.

'He could do worse than settle down with Bella,' his mother said. 'She's somebody we know.'

It would have been difficult not to know Bella and all her family who lived four doors further along Clint Lane.

'She's fallen on her feet getting that place at Bainrigg House. They've both gone up in the world, her and our Ewan.' They heard the sputter of a motor cycle as it slowed down at the back gate. 'That'll be him now.'

She moved the kettle from the hob to the cross-bar. By the time it boiled Rob had arrived and – breathlessly – Bella, who had to be back at the House in just over an hour. In the comfortable aftermath of a satisfying meal, Mrs Judd returned to the rocking chair, Emily to the fender with a final cup of tea; the others remained at the table. Ewan lit a Woodbine, Rob a pipe. Bella turned the pages of the late Mrs Judd's photograph album. She enjoyed looking at the Victorian forbears of the Judds more immediately at hand and saw the album as a sign of respectability – and she was right. The gold watch-chains, feather boas and wide-brimmed hats, the mittened hands and bearded chins evoked more prosperous days when mining boomed. Jo had been less fortunate than his father and grandfather and since his death the family had gone further downhill.

There was only one photograph of the present generation, taken when Jo joined up fourteen years ago. Father standing, mother seated, Emily with twin plaits, Rob and Ewan in sailor suits, all unsmiling and strongly united – and in her mother's lap . . . .

'Here's Katie.'

She had moved and spoiled the picture. Her features were blurred. Consequently it was to Katie that the eye was immediately drawn. The uneasy tilt of the head seen as though through a mist and the light hair more than ever like gossamer, intensified the impression she had given in life, one of strangeness, of not belonging.

'Let me see.'

Bella leaned towards Mrs Judd, holding out the album.

'I wish there's been a proper photo of her.' Mrs Judd outlined the group with her finger. 'When we're all gone there'll be no one to remember what she was like and nothing left to show that she was ever here.'

In the silence they all remembered her or tried to.

'You're wrong there, Mother.' Since he had taken to a pipe Rob felt entitled to be – and was – respected as head of the family. 'There's a good chance that Katie'll be the one to be remembered when all the rest of us are forgotten.'

'Folk'll remember the funeral,' Emily said.

'And those white things hanging in the church,' Bella added. They had made her rather nervous.

'They likely will,' Mrs Judd said bitterly. 'And if anybody asks who they were for, they'll say, "Katie Judd, the girl that stole the beads". And why she did it and what she did with them I'll never know.' She set the chair rocking and stared unhappily into the fire.

'You're sure,' Emily appealed to Bella, 'they couldn't still be somewhere in the shop, ravelled up in any of the things?'

Bella assured her for the twentieth time that she and Miss Burdon had shaken every bit of underwear and crawled about on the floor without finding anything but a farthing and a fair amount of dust.

'Not a sign of them. They must be somewhere else. It's like

159

one of those mysteries you read about,' she concluded. 'What the poor little soul did with them will never be known.'

It sounded final, the way she put it. There seemed nothing more to be said until Ewan spoke the words that changed everything. After the pause his voice was sudden and loud.

'If she ever took them,' he said.

It was a thunderbolt. The small room vibrated.

'Well, I'm damned.' Rob solemnly laid down his pipe. 'How do we know she ever took them at all?'

'Because old Sally Burdon said she did.' Ewan was as shaken by his own perception as by its implications. Their anger against Miss Burdon had been for her heartless treatment of Katie, leading to her death; the accusation she made had not been questioned.

'Somebody must have took them,' Emily said.

'If Katie didn't take them, who did?' Rob demanded.

The temperature of the room, already high, rose higher but the general mood became less sombre. A thief, still unknown, could be hunted down and dealt with; Katie's name could be cleared.

'Well, I hope none of you think it was me.' The threat of united action was so strongly to be felt that Bella was alarmed.

'What a thing to say,' Mrs Judd was reassuring.

'I was in the kitchen the whole morning baking until she called me to come into the shop to help to look for them.'

'Somebody could have come in and nicked them when the shop was empty,' Rob pointed out.

'We'd have heard the bell.'

'So there was nobody there but you and Sally Burdon and Katie.'

'And Miss Margot. But she was picking strawberries all the time. She came into the kitchen to wash her hands – and she took one of my almond biscuits. I mean' – Bella looked round, unnerved by the battery of four pairs of dark attentive eyes – 'nobody could think Miss Margot . . . .'

'What do you take us for, Bella Capfield?' Mrs Judd was stern. 'Nobody in the world was kinder to our Katie than Miss Margot.

160

Katie thought the world of her. If somebody took those beads and let Katie take the blame and go to her death, it was somebody as different from Miss Margot as two humans can be. Somebody that would let Katie suffer and not care . . . . Mind what you're doing' – the reproof was automatic as Ewan stubbed out his cigarette on his saucer – 'that's my best tea-set as well you know.'

'I wish I had my hands on whoever it was.' A phrase his mother had used stirred a memory as if the guilty stranger, undreamt of a minute ago, already existed in flesh and blood and hovered, waiting to be identified.

'What about Toria Link?' Mrs Judd ventured.

Rob had never heard of her and Emily couldn't remember ever having seen her. Mrs Judd had seen her only once when she went to Miss Burdon's back door to collect a quilt for washing. It was Bella who came to the door, but she had caught sight of Toria Link going into the wash-house with a bucket. Why Miss Burdon had wanted her to wash the quilt when her other washing was done at home, she couldn't say, except that there was nowhere like Clint Lane for drying. As a matter of fact the quilt had dried in two days on her line: there happened to be a good strong wind. In the village as a whole, Toria Link was known but no one knew her personally. What would she want with pearl beads?

'She could sell them,' Rob said.

'And lose her job and the only home she had if she was found out?' Bella alone knew one or two things about Toria. 'Anyway she was never allowed in the shop. Miss Burdon made that clear when she first came. There was a notice in the window for rough cleaning – and she turned up. It looked as if she had walked from Elmdon but she started on the scullery straight away.' Bella had been sorry for her and had slipped her a cup of tea and a slice of fruit cake when Miss Burdon was upstairs playing the piano. 'But she was always at the back. With it being carpets in the shop there was no scrubbing there and you know as well as I do that Luke Farshaw had the cleaning of the shop windows for years and his father before him.'

'Ewan knows Toria Link. He's at the Hall now.'

'You can count her out.' They saw that he was serious. His face had flushed. 'She wouldn't do it. She's religious for one thing.'

'She went neither to church nor chapel,' his mother reminded him.

'Likely she hadn't decent clothes to go in. You can be religious without going to church or chapel. She's read the Bible. She talks like the Bible, about sins and that. Anyway, what about them that do go? Sally Burdon went to church regular, didn't she?'

His heavy sarcasm was impressive.

'If there was nobody there but Katie, Miss Margot, Bella and Toria Link and no other customer came in—' Rob was interrupted.

'Wait a minute.' Bella had clapped her hand to her mouth in self-rebuke. 'There was somebody else: Miss Margot's friend.'

The pause was pregnant with surprise, hope, dismay and conjecture.

'I never saw her but she might have been in the shop while Miss Margot was in the garden. When I went into the dining-room to set the lunch, there were three cups on the sideboard. Missis had been meaning to give them coffee.'

Which friend? There had always been young people at Monk's Dene. Several girls of Miss Margot's age came often enough to be recognized. On this particular morning Bella had not seen the girl in question. When she was helping to look for the beads, Miss Burdon had mentioned that Miss Margot's friend had helped to check the invoices – and what a delightful girl she was. Then had come the fuss and bother when they failed to find the beads and the worry because Miss Burdon was so sure that Katie had taken them. Bella had 'lived-in' at Burdons' and didn't even know that Katie was missing until the next morning when she heard that the poor little thing was dead. What with one thing and another she'd never given a thought to who else might have been in the shop until they had started talking about it just now.

'There was no friend at Humberts' when we went there. Not that we saw anyway,' Emily recalled. 'I wonder where she'd gone, whoever she was.'

'Gone off to hide the beads.' Rob's suggestion was intended to lighten the atmosphere. It was not taken seriously. Not yet.

'Let me think.' Mrs Judd thought back to the two terrible days she had tried to forget. In the evening, while Katie was missing, Miss Margot had come twice to the door to ask for news. 'I was unpegging the line, I remember. The first time, Mr Miles was with her. They were going Bainrigg way.' The second time, she was ironing. It was getting dark. She had gone to the door to speak to Miss Margot and beyond, in the lane, saw Mr Alex and a young lady in white.

Ewan looked up sharply. For a while he had not spoken, apparently lost in thought. If his mother had been paying attention she would have recognized his expression and known what it portended: an inward simmering liable at any minute to boil over. He had, in fact, been struck by her earlier remark, that if somebody else had taken the beads it would be somebody who would let Katie suffer and not care. He knew of one such person – the only one – who could behave as if other people didn't matter, as if they had no feelings. And now – Mr Alex and a young lady in white. Who else could be with Mr Alex?

'That's her,' he said. 'That Miss Grey. If she was at Ashlaw the day Katie was missing, she must have been the one in the shop.'

'It makes you think,' Rob began, when they had all shared similar thoughts in a brief silence.

'It sounds as if she's the only one that could've . . . . I mean if Katie didn't.'

'Now don't say anything you'll be sorry for, our Emily.'

'He's right though, Mother. I'm not saying she did take them but she's the sort that would take anything she wanted, choose what. I know a bit about her and one thing I know is that Katie was frightened of her. It's a long time ago now . . . .' He told them how Katie had rushed into his arms as if running away as Miss Grey followed her out of the Humberts' gate. 'I'd seen her in Elmdon that very same day.' They listened with indignation to his account of the pedlar's scattered goods – the mud – the total loss – Miss Grey's complaint to the policeman.

'But would anyone as posh as that pinch beads?' Rob asked.

'The posh ones are the worst.' Ewan was sure of it. From the start he had identified Miss Grey as one of the upper class who should be done away with – all of them. 'They're nothing but a sink of corruption.'

163

It was felt to be strong language. It was also felt instinctively that caution was needed before conclusions were jumped to when the upper classes were involved.

'Mrs Roper would know if she was the friend that was at Monk's Dene that day. Shall I . . ?' Emily reached for the poker, intending to knock on the fire-back.

'No, don't knock. She might be busy with Ben. He's been real poorly this week.'

Bella offered to slip round and ask her and in a few minutes returned with Mrs Roper, Ben having found relief in sleep after a spell of battling for breath. A chair was squeezed into the space between the fender and the treadle machine. The situation was explained.

'Well, what a going-on! Do you mean to tell me we've been blaming that poor dead girl for what she didn't do?'

'We don't know,' Rob said, 'but we damned well want to find out.'

Casting her mind back and remembering that she had run up to Clint Lane to give warning that Miss Burdon was on the war path, Mrs Roper arrived circuitously at an answer to the question 'Was Miss Grey there that day?'

'She wasn't in the house when Katie came back from the shop, I'm nearly sure.' Katie had crept into the kitchen. She had been running; even with the table between them she had felt the girl's heart beating. Katie hadn't said a word but then she hardly ever did. Maud was upstairs making up a bed for Miss Grey although they hadn't been sure if she would come. Downstairs, she thought, there was only Mrs Humbert.

'Isn't it sad, her gone – and at her age? What would she be? Still in her forties?'

'And Miss Margot?' Rob headed her off from a line of thought liable to stretch indefinitely.

'She came back with strawberries. She and Katie went into the dairy. Just the two of them, quiet and peaceful, pulling the stalks off. Very likely that was the last bit of happiness Katie ever knew.'

'It seems funny,' Emily said, 'that Miss Grey wasn't there. Where was she?'

A picture gradually took shape – its colours murky – of Miss

Grey at large. Doing what? And where? There was no background to the picture.

'We'll never know.' Mrs Judd leaned back in her chair,
resigned. 'It would take a miracle to clear it up.'

'There's somebody at the back door.'

It was Emily who spoke but they were all in a mood to be startled by the knock. The handle turned.

'Don't say a word,' Mrs Judd warned, 'whoever it is.'

'Can I come in?' It was Mrs Larson, her cheeks fresh and glowing from the cool night air.

'You've never been turned from my door yet, Nancy Larson,
and I've known you all your life.' A general moving up and
adjustment of persons to available space left room for her at the
table. 'I'd forgotten it was Thursday. You could have come for
your tea.'

Nancy had been at the Chapel Guild. It was the highlight of
her week.

'I thought I'd pop in for a minute, but you've no need of
company when you've got your family round you. All but one and
she's with us in memory.' The guileless remark played havoc with
Mrs Judd's warning. As she hesitated, Rob took charge.

'We were talking about Katie. I didn't get home until two days
after it happened . . . .'

'And we were telling him about the day when' – Emily was
reluctant to mention the theft – 'when we saw her for the last
time.'

'Except that no one seems to know much about it, such as
when she went to the chimney.'

'If she came our way, no one saw her. Mind you, there's plenty
of ways she could have got to the chimney over the fields. But not
a man, woman or child passed the farm all day except the ones I
told the police about at the time. The young folks from Monk's
Dene and Mr Miles.'

The day had been more interesting than most. She had stood
at the window two or three times to watch them go past: Mr Miles
going to the village in the afternoon; then the four of them walking to Bainrigg at about milking time.

'The four of them?'

165

'Miss Margot and Mr Miles. They called to ask if we'd seen Katie. The other two went by just after. Mr Alex and the other young lady.' And oh yes, she had passed the farm earlier in the afternoon on her way to the village. All by herself. Dressed all in white.

The phrase was becoming significant: it had a falling cadence: it was memorable: it isolated the wearer from other folk. In the listeners – and they were a tough lot – it produced a superstitious tremor.

'Oh, her!' Bella's tone was more eloquent than words.

'So that's where she was,' Ewan burst out when the door had closed behind Mrs Larson. 'What was she doing up there all by herself? When she went past the farm, that was the time when Katie went missing, wasn't it?'

'It's a funny thing she wasn't seen coming up from the village, only going back. She can't have come up along the Lane or somebody would have seen her.'

The subject was inexhaustible. Amid the vagueness, the endless wondering, the hopeless attempt to drop it and talk of something else, one image persisted – of a young lady dressed in white who had walked alone, who must have passed the chimney where Katie's body was found. The only person known to have been in the vicinity at the time; the only other person to have been in the shop when the beads disappeared; the only person to supply an answer to the question, 'If Katie didn't take the beads, who did?'

Bella's hour was up. She closed the album, squeezed her way round the table, went into the scullery for her coat and came back to put it on.

'You'll have to come with me, Ewan. I dursn't go past that chimney by myself in the dark.'

'Whatever she did or didn't do' – Mrs Judd's mind was still on the young lady in white – 'I don't like the sound of her.'

Her summing up left Miss Grey at a distance like a dubious historical figure whose suspected misdeeds could never be confirmed – until Bella brought her abruptly nearer.

'Whether you like her or not, you'll likely be seeing a lot more of her. As sure as I'm standing here she's setting her cap at Mr

Miles. She'll be mistress of Bainrigg House one of these days. Just you wait.'

CHAPTER XVII

Rumours spread quickly in Ashlaw. Suspicions once breathed in the privacy of the Judds' cramped living-room crept into the outer air. Borne on the famous breezes of Clint Lane, they found their way to other firesides, to be whispered and adapted to taste. But a central theme persisted: it had been found out that Katie Judd did not steal those beads. (It transpired that no one had ever believed that she did.) Who had stolen them? The young woman now a frequent visitor at Bainrigg House had something to do with it. She had even – at this point voices were so low as to be barely audible – had something to do with Katie's death.

Apart from the compulsion to pass the word on, there was nothing to be done. The sinister relish of the tales provoked no action, except on one occasion when the young woman in question appeared in the main street on her way to the post office. Children playing on the pavement were called or dragged indoors, the doors firmly closed. It was said that she was only sending a telegram on behalf of Mrs Rilston. Could you believe it when there were three maids and an under-gardener to run messages?

Strange things had happened. Nell Bowes who used to live in the end house in Clint Lane swore that she had gone into her backyard early one morning and seen Katie running across the field *after she was dead*. In pink, and fair-haired. It was enough to make your blood run cold. The Bowes had since moved to Fellside where Harry worked. It was now obvious that they had gone because Nell had been frightened nearly to death by seeing the ghost. Her mother had died of heart failure.

It was on the very day after the Judds' family gathering that a more reliable version of their suspicions reached Langland Hall, to raise ripples of unrest in that quiet backwater.

Langland was at its most colourful in autumn. Throughout the centuries of its ruin by Picts and Scots and Danes, by dissolution and desecration, it had undergone a gentler intrusion. Rowan and birch, sycamore and thorn had quietly occupied the remains of frater and chapel; bramble and elder now softened the tumbled stones marking the outline of nave and refectory. Robbed of its earlier riches, the priory had never known a richer display of crimson, copper and gold than on a still day in October.

The stillness of stones and trees was matched by the stillness of the woman who sat in a sheltered embrasure facing south. She felt the faint warmth of the sun on her face and hands. Her inner response to the beauty of her surroundings had in it a touch of reverence: for her the scene was hallowed. But she also felt its sadness. Every leaf, having reached a glorious end, must fall. The blaze of colour was that of a funeral pyre.

The touch of melancholy was characteristic, but Toria was herself far from sad. The peace which had fallen on the priory and on its surrounding fields and woods had fallen on her too. She too had mellowed and was aware of the merciful change. From this sunlit niche she could review not only the Hall and the cottages below but the whole course of her life before she came there: its early quietude and promise of continuing simple comfort, the disaster that had uprooted and almost destroyed her and the years of penance, the miraculous transition to a way of life that answered all her needs.

With the mellowing had come the slow revival of a lost faculty: the power of loving. It had withered and died in the frost of betrayal, leaving a bitterness she had never hoped – or wanted – to overcome. But gradually in the past months it had passed from her, not forgotten but outgrown. Edward Humbert's enterprise had not been, as he now feared, entirely ill-starred: it had given new hope to the one unfortunate woman who most needed it.

Her thoughts moved to someone else who needed it as, through the gatehouse arch, she saw Margot walking up the slope, at her heels the cat that followed her everywhere. Toria gave no sign, but she was disappointed when Margot stopped, then turned to wander aimlessly back to the house. They might have talked; the girl needed help. If Toria had one wish left unfulfilled it was to be of help to Margot, to support and comfort her as she would a daughter of her own.

With the perception of a caring observer she was aware of the girl's loneliness, separated from her friends, from her brother, bereft of her mother and, for some reason hard to understand, from young Mr Rilston. The idea that Toria Link could be a source of comfort to her employer's daughter might be dismissed as presumptuous. Toria would have understood such an attitude and would have remained indifferent to it. Solitude and suffering had not exhausted but rather intensified an inward energy that wrongly directed could be harmful. But to love and protect the loved one? What harm could there be in that? It was a question she had asked herself before, long ago, but then the answer had been forced upon her: now she could act as she chose.

Margot had paused on the step of the back door as if unwilling to go in. The dull thud of the heavy door as she closed it behind her roused Toria from her meditations. It was past midday and her resting place was now in the shade. She and Bessie Todd were going to put up curtains in the room being prepared for Miss Bondless. She went back to the house, pausing to snap off dead flowerheads in the back garden – they looked untidy. Her concern for the Hall and its well-being had grown with her concern for its inhabitants.

As she swept the path clear of dead leaves, Ewan came round from the front with a barrowload of clippings and soon had a bonfire going. Toria added her sweepings. As the smoke rose blue against the green slope beyond, Ewan said abruptly: 'I went home last night. Our Rob's home. We got talking . . . .'

Toria listened while the blue smoke turned grey in air still golden but cooler than it had been an hour ago. Jackdaws gathered on the gatehouse and after a medley of raucous calls flew off again.

'... and we think now it wasn't Katie.' Garden fork in hand, Ewan stared into the fire, unconscious of the peculiar intensity of

170

interest he had roused. 'There was someone else that could have taken them.' He hurled another forkful of dead leaves on to the heap, deadening the blaze. 'How do we know that it wasn't her that took them? The only one in the shop ... the only one up there by the chimney . . . .' That was a thought to brood on and be sickened by. 'She needn't think she can get away with it.'

'You'll never be able to prove it.' Toria had been slow to respond. 'Unless somebody saw her.'

'Nobody could prove it was Katie unless somebody saw her. Never mind about proving: she's going to suffer for it, I can tell you that. You know what I told you about that pedlar woman. She said, "Maybe you'll be down in the muck yourself some day". What if she was right, eh?'

'It's what she deserves, the one you're talking about, but remember, she's not worth you or your Rob going to prison for or losing your job here for. Give a thought to that before you do anything you'll regret.'

'Don't you worry. There's all sorts of ways, but it needs to be done soon before she gets herself set up in Bainrigg House and being lady of the manor and living on rents from the likes of the boss here and owning all this land we're standing on.'

'What do you mean?'

'She's set on marrying Mr Miles, that's what I mean.'

He stepped back as a tongue of flame leapt from the bonfire – and turning, he was struck by a change in Toria. It was for a moment as if the fierce heat came from her too; as if, revelling in the blaze, she too was alight.

But he was disappointed in her reaction to his news. He had expected her to share his renewed sense of the injustice of life, or at least to say a few harsh things about the abominable Miss Grey. Instead, she had looked ... cheerful was hardly the word, but he couldn't find another for the absence of a glumness he had grown used to. It hadn't lasted (he glanced at her again) and she no longer looked as if she had been lit up inside, but she hadn't said a word, not a word. He wished he hadn't told her. Well, you never could tell with Toria. If she was absolutely sane, pigs might fly. He spat on his palms, seized the handles of the wheelbarrow and trundled off, his mood morose.

Toria stood gazing at the bonfire until the flame narrowed and became a sword. Was it a sign? Was it an answer to her prayer that she might be of help: a confirmation of her belief that she had been sent to Langland to be of service to those who needed her? Not just to serve with hands and on willing feet, but to act as an intermediary in bringing low the evil-doer, the woman who, for over a year, she had held it in her power to shame, whose good name she could in a breath destroy?

But she had grown cautious. While struggling to survive, she had seemed to hear the voice of Jehovah telling her what to do. His commands had been clear and simple to match her needs, as a person on the point of death sees life shorn of its distracting trivialities. But in returning to a more normal existence, albeit only to its fringe, she was aware of complexities which had not concerned her as an outcast.

She had learned that help, however well meant, could be two-edged. She had helped to rescue Mr Alex from his entanglement with the same cold-hearted woman, but in setting him free she had also left Miss Grey free, to worm her way into Bainrigg House and perhaps to break Miss Margot's heart, to queen it, as Ewan had said, over the very earth on which she herself now stood. It was wrong. It should be stopped. But how? Surely not by some clumsy interference by the Judd brothers who would very likely come off worst in any attack on Miss Grey.

Whatever they did, they would be meddling in matters she had taken upon herself. The secret had been hers. She had promised to keep it, but they had found it out and had stolen from her the right to use it in her own way and at the right time.

The crimson flame died down, leaving no more than a glow in the heart of the smouldering heap. The colour was gone but the heat remained. She turned away, uncertain, her hard-won peace of mind disturbed. How would young Mr Rilston feel if she told him who had been responsible for Katie Judd's death? Would it matter to him? She didn't know what sort of man he was. What sort of man would prefer Miss Grey to Miss Margot?

She had thought of him as one of the honourable sort, a perfect gentleman but rather shy. It was possible he didn't even know (though it was plain enough to Toria) that he was all the world to Miss Margot. A friendly hint might be enough to make him realize the mistake he was making. She yearned to be of help to those who had befriended her. Was it not for that very purpose that she had been sent here? Her coming had surely been ordained.

Toria's upbringing had been godly: she had never played a game of cards or dominoes, but she knew what happened when the pieces were stood on end and one of them fell. It might be safer not to interfere again – not yet. She would know when the time came.

CHAPTER XVIII

'Beg pardon, ma'am.' It was Bella nervously acting as parlour-maid while Jenny was at the dentist's. 'It's Henderson. He's asking for the master.'

'Mr Rilston won't want to be disturbed. What does Henderson want?'

'It's about a drainpipe, ma'am.'

'Then Mr Rilston will be either in his study or in the summer-house.'

Mrs Rilston went to the window. From her sitting-room the summer-house was out of sight, screened from the north by trees. It was a timber building and stout enough to be wind-proof though hardly suitable for use at this time of the year even with the paraffin heater she had insisted on. But presently she saw Henderson limping across the garden in its direction. If not in his study Miles must be there.

She was worried about him. For the past three months he had been withdrawn, altogether uncompanionable. Meal-times had become constrained and awkward. If only Frederick were here! She wept a little. At the back of her mind was the thought that Miles's mother had been subject to what was tactfully called depression: in fact, there had been times . . . . It had not been an inconsolable sorrow, though dreadfully sad of course, when typhoid fever carried her off. They had hoped that their son would marry again but it was not to be.

So far there had been nothing actually strange in Miles's behaviour apart from his being so remote and unhappy. She had confided her anxiety to Mrs Grey who had agreed that he needed the company of younger people; it had also been agreed that if Linden could spare the time from her many engagements, she should come more often to Bainrigg.

'It would be very good of her. I know she is popular and has many friends.' She was indeed the very girl, one of their own sort, to take Miles out of himself.

Consequently, rarely a week passed without a visit from the Greys. Sometimes Linden came alone; a friend would drop her off for an hour or two and pick her up again. She would bring Mrs Rilston something from town – an altered dress, matching embroidery silks, a library book. Mrs Rilston grew accustomed to having her there and so presumably did Miles though he never sat with them, was certainly never alone with Linden, greeted her pleasantly on his way upstairs to his study or out into the grounds but never stopped to talk. It was understood that he was collecting material for an article or possibly a book, on ecclesiastic life in northern England in the Middle Ages.

'So much work entailed,' Mrs Rilston would explain helplessly, 'but it gives him something to do and he is so very clever. Scholarly, you know.' If only he would hunt or shoot! There had never been a Rilston who didn't hunt or shoot.

At his table in the summer-house, Miles commanded a view of his own fields but more often his eyes rested on luminous clouds above distant hills, on the blaze of sunset, on a crescent moon. Before him a pile of unread books and a too-slim sheaf of notes served to remind him that in this sphere as in every other he was a failure: the article would never be finished, the book never written. There were days when he merely reread a few paragraphs written weeks ago without adding another word.

'It's about the main drainpipe, sir,' Henderson explained. 'It must have been fractured for quite a while. The damage first caught my eye when I came up from Ashlaw yesterday by the field path. I generally come in from the upper road, as you well know. I wondered why that ditch just outside the gate on the right-hand side was so wet, fairly brimming with water when there hasn't been that much rain. And coming through the gate into the garden, that bit of ground by the shrubbery is all soft and squelchy, and it doesn't smell too good.'

'How does the pipe lie?'

'So as to drain off at right-angles to that ditch and across Pennybit field to the main road.'

'I'll come and look. We'd better get the council people.' It was an excuse to leave the causes of dispute between monks and lay brothers and to seem to be in charge of the estate.

Sure enough the ditch alongside the field nearest to the garden was water-logged and would probably remain so all winter. When Bella went home for her hour off that afternoon she found to her disgust that the path was ankle-deep in mud. Nobody had warned her. A good pair of shoes ruined!

'I'm not going back that way.' She had popped into the Judds', hoping that Ewan would be there, but there was only Rob who would be joining his ship next day. 'I'll have to go along nearly to the farm and then up the far side of the field.' She had to be back at four and spent most of her precious hour cleaning and polishing her shoes. 'They say mud sticks and there was never a truer word.'

Visitors were coming to dinner: friends of Mr and Mrs Rilston who were staying in Elmdon on their way to Scotland and several other people, including Mrs and Miss Grey. 'Needless to say.'

The dinner party passed off pleasantly. Mrs Rilston had been apprehensive: she had done so little entertaining since her husband's death but the Fenwicks were old friends, the Gillings and Roberts were local people and the Greys could always be relied on, Mrs Grey a sympathetic listener and Linden quietly voicing unremarkable remarks, so that there was no disharmony. Gavin Roberts, a few years older than Miles, entertained them with tales of his adventures at the newly formed flying club at Howlyn.

'Why don't you join, Rilston? You've been up?'

'Yes, two or three times.'

'Flying's definitely the thing from now on, especially with the new de Havilland DH60. It's their latest, just out last year, with a welded steel fuselage. Come and have lessons. You'd get the hang of it in no time.'

'So dangerous,' Mrs Rilston protested.

'Not at all. It's almost monotonously safe, a jolly sight safer than going down a coal mine. You're in a world of your own up there in the clouds. Seeing the earth beneath you, you get things into proportion. Problems seem less important. You wonder what you've been worrying about.'

'Gavin has no problems,' his wife said, 'and very little to worry about.'

'Not when I'm flying, dear.'

'If ever there's another war, which God forbid, aircraft are bound to play a bigger part,' Mr Fenwick said. 'There's something to be said for building up a strong air force, just in case.'

'Don't even think of it on such a pleasant evening.' Mrs Fenwick preferred to talk to Miles about Oxford where her grandson was an undergraduate. Had there been any lull in the conversation there would have remained the pleasure of looking at Linden in her autumn dinner gown of parchment velvet with gold lamé at the neck and wrists.

'Are she and Miles . . ?' Mrs Fenwick whispered as the ladies went to the drawing-room.

'I don't really know. Perhaps not yet but I do hope . . . . It would be very suitable.'

Marriage would be his salvation. It would give him an aim in life. Drifting from day to day was the very worst thing for a young man of his temperament. She had thought at one time that Miles himself was disposed to marry. Only a few months ago he had been so much more cheerful and active than he had ever been before. Of course, Frederick's death had been a great shock to him.

As for Miles, the duty to exert himself as host had at first been stimulating but as the evening wore on he relapsed into the dreamlike state that had become habitual. It was as if he moved alone against a background peopled by others with whom he felt no affinity: they were there, as the Greys often were, slightly more animated than the pictures on the wall but beyond his reach. Between himself and them no messages were interchanged from heart or mind. Half-a-dozen people substituted for those in the room would effect no change: he would barely notice the difference.

At ten o'clock the guests began to take leave. There was a

general movement into the hall. They had their own cars. As a rule Chapman drove the Greys home though sometimes Miles took them in his own car so that Chapman need not leave his fireside again: he was getting on in years. On this occasion the Fenwicks naturally offered to take them.

'How very kind!' Marian Grey looked round. Miles and Mr Fenwick had already gone out; of Linden there was no sign: she had gone upstairs for her wrap and had not yet come down. 'I should be delighted.'

'Miles will drive Linden home.' Mrs Rilston and Mrs Fenwick exchanged meaningful looks which Marian was careful not to notice.

Miles had gone out to see the guests off. His goodbyes were interrupted by a summons to the telephone to speak to his agent in Lancashire, who apologized for the lateness of his call and explained that he had that evening been in the company of a gentleman who had shown interest in Fothering Farm which was up for sale. Were there any special instructions if he should make an offer? It was good news . . . .

Miles was still at the telephone when Linden came slowly downstairs, wearing the white fur stole she had worn at Christmas. She smiled, with a little wave of her hand which he interpreted as a farewell. He nodded and gave his mind to the possible sale of Fothering Farm while Linden joined the Roberts and Gillings on the gravel sweep in front of the house.

'Can we take you somewhere?' The offer was polite but unenthusiastic. Both couples lived a few miles away in the opposite direction from Elmdon.

'Thank you. I mustn't trouble you. Miles will take me.'

She didn't mind waiting on the drive. The night was cool, but after an evening indoors she found its freshness pleasant and walked up and down, admiring her kid evening shoes and occasionally looking in at the windows. Minutes passed. Her loitering took her further from the front drive, beyond the light from the hall, along the unlit eastern side of the long façade. At the corner she turned to look back. The sound of the cars was now distant. Moments later, Bainrigg was lapped in the deep silence of a country house at night. Beyond this point lay the gardens and beyond them empty fields shrouded in darkness. In her light dress and white fur she was the only creature visible, mothlike against the dense background of the shrubbery.

Miles hung up the receiver as his grandmother passed on her way upstairs.

'You are taking Linden, aren't you?'

'Good Lord! Is she waiting?'

In the drawing-room, coffee cups and glasses had been removed and all the lamps but one switched off. He glanced into the other downstairs rooms and ran down the steps. The drive was empty of guests and cars. He went indoors.

'She must have gone with the Fenwicks.'

'Then I'll say goodnight, dear. Don't stay up too late.'

Miles went back to the drawing-room. He put logs on the fire, a record on the gramophone and lay back to listen. It was one of Chopin's nocturnes, No 8 in D flat major, his favourite. The limpid notes seemed to convey both the memory of lost happiness and yearning for its return. His mood was passive. Fate was unalterable: there was nothing he could do but bow to its implacable and arbitrary decrees. He entertained such thoughts but knew them to be self-indulgent and unsound. He genuinely suffered, but perhaps in the very depths of his being he felt, slight and ineffectual as a candle in a vault, a melancholy pride in his graceful acceptance of rejection, forgetting that what is never offered cannot be rejected.

He moved only to lift the needle when the gentle sounds ceased and to switch off the lamp, then lay back again, thinking of Margot. She had gone from him, become a half-forgotten dream, a beloved memory . . . . An hour passed and another. The silver chime of the French clock on the mantelpiece roused him. He must have slept. It was past midnight; the logs had burnt to white ash and the room was almost dark. Between sleep and waking he was vaguely troubled. Having thought of Margot, he had dreamed of her and in trying to recall the dream he was aware that it was not only the chiming clock that had roused him. Turning sharply, he saw a movement at one of the long windows.

There was someone outside, a pale figure against the outer dark, a wraith pleading to come in.

His head cleared. It was no phantom but a woman leaning against the window. She raised her arm and tapped on the pane. He sprang to his feet.

'Linden!' He pushed open the window, put his arm round her, lifted her over the low sill, switched on a light – and was flabbergasted.

'Oh Miles. Thank God you're here.' She cringed, barely recognizable, shivering, dishevelled, cheeks streaked with mud and tears, one shoe gone, the velvet dress spattered and evil-smelling. In one limp hand she held the white fur stole, now wet with slime and earth-grey like the pelt of an animal drowned in mud. 'I would have died if anyone else had seen me. You'll help me.' She burst into tears.

'Come to the fire. Tell me – how has this happened? Where have you been all this time?'

Immaculate, elegant, poised, self-contained, she had made no impression on him at all. But now he was genuinely distressed for her. His heart warmed to her as it would to a stray kitten or a lost lamb.

'I had to wait. I waited in the summer-house until all the lights were out. Until they'd all gone to bed. I didn't know what to do. I couldn't bear to let anyone see me like this and I would have stayed there all night, but it was so cold – and what would I have done in the morning?'

She had ventured out of the summer-house and had seen the faint light of the dying fire in the drawing-room, she told him, sobs shaking her slim body.

Disregarding the state of her clothes, he put his arm round her and stroked her wildly ruffled wet hair, his hands tender and comforting. She clung to him, ruining the corded silk lapels of his dinner jacket with her tears and muddied sleeves. He put her in a low-chair, replenished the fire, rubbed her numb fingers.

There were two men, she told him. They had come out of the shrubbery. No, she hadn't seen their faces: they had something on their heads so she hadn't really seen them at all. She thought they meant to kill her but no, they had not hurt her. They had hustled her through the gate into the field. One of them had pulled off her fur and thrown it into the ditch, a sort of pool of muddy water. She couldn't see it – it was too dark – but she could feel the mud under her feet and there was a horrid smell. Then suddenly, still without speaking a word, they had gone. She heard them running down the path, towards the bottom of the field.

She slid from the chair and crouched nearer to the fire, shuddering. It was an outrage – and on his own land. He had never been so angry or so deeply stirred to pity. Such compassion as he would naturally have felt for any creature ill-treated had never yet been roused by human need. To see the victim actually here at his feet, a girl entitled to his protection, a guest in his own house reduced to such a state; to see her tears and feel the softness of her cold hands; to be near enough to take her in his arms and stroke her hair; to burn with anger and the compulsion to help and comfort her – together roused in him a spirit altogether unfamiliar. Her very nearness was a revelation. The mud and tears and the pathetic small foot without a shoe moved him as no glamour could have done, and because he felt her weakness and dependence on him, he felt too his own contrasting strength. This was a situation he must – and could – handle.

'You must have something hot.' He went swiftly to the kitchen. The fire there was never out; a kettle was still warm. He brewed a stiff rum toddy. Her hand shook so violently that he had to hold her and guide the mug to her lips.

'They were not Ashlaw men,' he assured her. 'None of the local men would dare do such a thing – or want to. They may have come from Fellside. I believe they have a rough lot there. It's probably too late to catch them but I'm going to ring the police.'

'But they didn't take anything.' She indicated the gold chain at her neck, the gold bracelet on her wrist. 'And they could have done. Please, you mustn't ring the police. I can't bear to have it known. I feel so humiliated. If I thought people knew about it I could never come here again.' Tears hung on her long lashes; her look of defeat was touching. His anger revived, but he understood that it would be folly to risk waking the servants, or worse still, his grandmother.

Linden drank the rum but went on shuddering as if she would never be warm again.

'You'll have to get out of those clothes. I'll find something warm for you to put on and then I'll take you home.'

'You're wonderful,' she said. 'I'm so relieved and grateful that I could come to you for help. Just to have you here . . . .' The tears spilled.

If she had stayed out there much longer she might have died of cold. Even now she might go down with pneumonia not to mention the shock to the poor girl's nerves. He brought the copper hot-water jug from his room, a sponge and towel, and gently washed her face.

'There, that's better.' The words and manner came instinctively from the forgotten world of childhood.

Back in his room he found sweaters, a warm singlet, the long socks he wore with plus-fours, a dressing gown and travelling rug. When he went down she had struggled out of her dress and was taking off her stockings. 'Look. They're ruined.' She pushed away the unsightly pile of garments and once again dissolved into tears.

'They can be replaced. I'll see to that – and your fur.' No one had ever called him wonderful before. 'What happened to your shoe?'

'It must still be there in the ditch. When they'd gone I tried to reach my fur and I fell . . . .'

'Here, put these on. I'll help you.'

She stretched out a slim white leg. He knelt to ease the coarse sock on to her small foot, looked up, smiling at the incongruity and saw that she was beautiful, her eyes pleading and unhappy. Lovely and lost. The phrase pleased him. Lovely and lost and needing him. He drew her to her feet to pull the warm garments over her head, covering her bare flesh. It seemed quite natural to take her in his arms to kiss and console her. It was hard to let her go when she drew away.

'We mustn't. I'm not . . . .' She drew his attention to her half-dressed state though there was no need. Unwillingly he helped her into the thick dressing gown and went to bring out the car.

She made no protest when, having wrapped her in the rug, he

picked her up and carried her out. If she had, he would have ignored the protest, buoyed up as he was by a confidence he had never felt before. Never had he felt so completely master of his own house; never had he acted with such efficiency on someone else's behalf; never had he thrilled to the sight and feel of a woman's body close to his own, his lips on hers. At the wheel he drove with a dash and speed to match his mastery of the entire situation.

'You've managed it so well,' she breathed, as they drew up in Gordon Street. 'Oh Miles.' She lingered over his name. 'I don't know why you have been so kind to me.' She raised her face to his again, her lips soft and tremulous. 'So very sweet and kind. And I know I can trust you to keep our secret. No one else need know. Only you and I, dear Miles.'

The intimacy and secrecy intrigued him. To be drawn into closeness and relied on because of his strength seemed infinitely precious to one who had always been an outsider, incapable of measuring up to other people's demands as he imagined them to be. For once, thought was abandoned; he could only feel, the feeling as much for his own newly discovered self as for her.

'You have a key?'

She had rescued her little silver mesh evening purse from the mud.

'It was so pretty.' Her mouth drooped.

'Don't think of it. Leave all that to me.'

He carried her to the door, held her while she reached to unlock it and set her down on the carpet at the foot of the stairs, smiling down at her – she was so frail and slight – when she turned to thank him again.

He had crossed the river on the outskirts of town when he remembered the bundle of sodden clothes on the back seat. He reversed, drove back to the bridge and dropped them one by one over the parapet; the ruined dress, the foul-smelling fur – the one small kid shoe.

At Bainrigg House, the maids shared the big attic. Its window was on the front of the house. The sound of a car engine long after the other three cars had gone woke Bella. Who could it be? She couldn't see the fingers of the alarm clock but it must be late.

'What are you doing?'

She had roused Jenny by pushing open the casement to lean out and look down. The headlights were on and the engine was running.

'Here. Just you come and look. It's them.'

Elsie also woke. The three crowded into the window, but as Bella said afterwards it was all done so quickly that the others were too late. She was the only one that saw Mr Miles carrying *her* to the car.

'And she wasn't wearing what she was wearing at dinner, that's for sure.'

'I didn't think he was that sort of a man.' Jenny got back into bed.

'It only takes that sort of a woman,' Elsie struck a match and looked at the clock. It was twenty-five past one.

'And she's one of that sort, you can mark my words.' Bella already knew plenty about Miss Grey and the temptation to pass it on was irresistible.

The two men running across the lower end of Pennybit field arrived neck-and-neck at the main road. Only when sheltered by the hedge did they pull off the balaclavas that had masked their faces. But they didn't look at each other nor had they spoken a word since they left Bainrigg. Darkness was no problem: they knew their terrain too well. In fact, the rapid retreat had been the best part of the whole rotten business: it had restored their badly shaken self-esteem.

'If you ever breathe a word of this to anybody else, I'll break every bone in your body,' Rob said when he had got his own breath back.

Ewan swore. He was too disgusted with himself to speak otherwise. They'd made a right mess of it. For one thing they hadn't been ready. All they had intended was to spy out the land and see if they could get into the gardens at Bainrigg House without being seen. It had been a bit of a lark like when they were lads sneaking off with their balaclavas on to do a bit of poaching. They had a plan all right, to shove her into the ditch and give her a fright. It was nothing but fair, the least they could do for Katie's sake: the sort of thing the woman concerned wouldn't mind seeing done to others. But it was all in the air, for some time in the future. To start with it meant getting her on her own and there wasn't much chance of that. They'd have to work something out the next time Rob came home.

From the shrubbery they had watched the nobs leaving. So far as could be seen from the headlights and the light from the house there was a Bentley, an Armstrong-Siddely and what looked like an American car. Some folks had money to burn and there were bairns in Potters Yard without boots to their feet. Then, just as they were themselves leaving, *she* was there, all by herself and coming towards them. It was a shock. They might have gone there night after night for years and never seen her alone and it had to be this one night when they weren't ready.

He hadn't expected it to be like that. Smashing windows with bricks was one thing, but laying hands on a woman with intent to punish her was another thing altogether. Especially a woman like that. The plan had been simple, but their sudden actual contact with her made it unworkable. Her perfume, her delicacy, the feel of her clothes, the indications even in the dark that she was a creature used to protection and therefore helpless – made it distasteful even to touch her. To hustle her through the gate and into the field was as much as he could bring himself to do. It was Rob who had pulled off that bit of white fur and chucked it in the ditch. He himself had done nothing; had stood like a stook. There had been a terrible moment when, nonplussed, they hadn't known what to do next until by mutual consent they had taken themselves off at full speed, saved by their own decency.

He was ashamed of it. He had gone soft. He hated her, more than ever, but for the life of him he could not have harmed her. The likes of her were untouchable by the likes of him. It was not a compliment. The girls he was familiar with would never have got him into a mess like this. For that matter they would never do anything as shabby as what she had done and deserved to be punished for.

And there was something else, harder to explain. At close quarters faintly visible in the surrounding darkness, she hadn't seemed real. It was uncanny, the feeling that if he had brought himself to touch her, there would have been nothing to hold. Inside the soft outer covering there was nothing: not merely no warmth, no angry protest, no response, but an absence of life as he knew it. On her feet and breathing, she was less alive than Katie in her grave.

'I'll tell you what' – Rob was deeply in earnest – 'I'll be glad to get back to sea.'

Neither felt like going home.

'What about seeing if Lily'll let us have a pint?'

'At this time of night?'

'She won't mind. She sleeps downstairs. The old man won't know.'

Both thought of Lily with something like affection. She was the kind of girl they knew, a better class of girl altogether.

Feet firm on the road, they stepped out briskly, the only moving objects in a silent world, and gradually they became less conscious of the fields on their left, dark and disaster-ridden, of the big house shrouded in trees and of their foiled escapade (whose further outcome was certainly not of their choosing). The air was fresh on their faces. Above them stretched the vast canopy of the sky, the wheeling constellations and myriads of stars.

'What good would it have done Katie anyway?' Rob demanded. 'Humbling her, I mean. It couldn't make any difference to Katie.'

Katie had escaped to another region somewhere between the earth and the distant stars – and yet – it was a queer feeling, Ewan thought, and would take a bit of understanding – but in a way she was here, as close as the bramble stems in the hedge where she had picked blackberries and the milestones where as a little girl she had liked to sit.

Ahead on the right, darkness thickened in the shape of a building. It was the Halfway House Inn. He saw it through tears.

186

CHAPTER XIX

Miles's new-found firmness of purpose lasted. How long? Certainly while Linden was recovering from a feverish chill, the result of shock and exposure. He went to Gordon Street every day with flowers, fruit and wine. She was charmingly grateful, her eyes on his face, her smile winsome. The bedroom door was left ajar while he was with her. Occasionally Mrs Grey came to arrange pillows or to bring a cooling drink.

'Linden has never been troubled with colds. It's going to take time.'

Languid against her pillow in a mist of artificial silk and lace, her face wan in its frame of dark hair, Linden was fortunate in having been spared the less attractive aspects of a chill: reddened nose, puffy eyes, thickened speech. He felt heavy-footed, too tall for the flimsy bedroom chair, but he continued also to feel strong and firm in his intention to see her safely through her illness and to make amends for the outrage she had suffered. He saw no reason to tell her that he had alerted the local police, nor for that matter, had PC Pratt seen any reason to tell him that there was talk about Miss Grey in the village.

Miles felt no urgent longing, no physical compulsion to take her in his arms: she did not stir his flesh. The embrace in the drawing-room had been pleasant but involuntary. He saw her as a precious external object, a prize dropped in his way by the whirligig of time, a safeguard against unbearable loneliness.

As long as she remained an invalid needing rest and restoratives, he was happy, in the gentleness of his nature, to look after her. He could overlook her failure to read any of the books she

187

so politely thanked him for, and later her indifference as to where they went when he took her for a drive, her ignorance of the countryside and her inability to distinguish one historic ruin from another. Absorption in his new role kept him cheerful and attentive.

'It's taking a long time,' Mrs Grey murmured. 'But we mustn't take any risks, must we?'

It took a surprisingly long time, almost a month, before Linden was well again – well enough, presumably, to go back to work. Unfortunately, her absence was found to have made so little difference that the Empsons, father and son, now felt able to dispense with her services altogether.

'I don't know what we shall do, I'm sure.' Mrs Grey accepted a glass of wine and sighed.

It was one of the frequent occasions when Miles brought the Greys out to Bainrigg and left Mrs Grey with his grandmother while he took Linden for a drive, returning for afternoon tea. By this time the Greys were sufficiently at home to stay almost until dinner-time.

'I shall have to find something else,' Linden said bravely, stifling the worrying trace of a lingering cough behind a lace-edged handkerchief.

Miles instantly felt responsible. Her dismissal was the direct result of the wretched affair that had also caused her illness. Some delicacy had been needed in persuading Linden to let him provide the means of replacing her damaged clothes. As it happened the dress was from Liberty's and was not yet paid for: it was a simple matter to send a cheque. The value of the fur wrap (a gift from Godfrey Barford) was more difficult to assess until Linden found a similar one in a furrier's catalogue. The slippers had come from Wares before their refusal to give further credit. Miles was also determined to pay the doctor's bills.

As the attack on Linden was a secret between the two of them, Mrs Grey must not know of these transactions. In addition, Miles felt the awkwardness of paying bills from local firms with cheques bearing his signature. It seemed best to give the money in notes directly to Linden and leave her to settle. Altogether the sums involved a bigger withdrawal from his personal account than he had made for years.

But the secrecy strengthened their intimacy. His thoughts, his attention were fixed on Linden. Day after day there was something to be done for her and information to share. And now . . . .

'I don't know, I'm sure,' Mrs Grey said again.

Ought he to take on the responsibility of finding Linden something else to do, as she so pluckily put it?

'We must try to think of something.' Mrs Rilston's vague contribution reflected her ignorance not only of the present peculiar situation but of the entire labour market.

'At least she's looking more like herself,' Mrs Grey said.

They all looked at Linden, now fully restored to health. Indeed it was hard to believe that she had ever been ill, and on Great-grandmother Rilston's velvet-cushioned chair she seemed, in her simple and expensive-looking dress of cornflower blue, as fitting a feature of the room as one of the porcelain figures on the mantelpiece. As familiar – as permanent?

Perhaps even then, trapped as he was by conscience and the need to make amends, Miles's confidence wavered. She was beautiful, composed and at ease, an ornament to the room, but despite her unemployed state she was no longer pitiable, no longer a lost lamb to be shepherded softly into the fold. The enfolding had already to some extent been accomplished. The role of the shepherd was less clear. The thought 'What's to be done with her now?' without actually taking shape threatened a faint disquiet.

As the bond that united them – her need, his pity – stretched thinner, other bonds were strengthened. In the eyes of their small world they had become a pair. 'The young people'. 'You two . . . .' Linden's sparse remarks were sprinkled with 'Miles and I', and there were stronger hints from Mrs Grey who had drawn her own conclusions from the late return on the night of the dinner-party and Miles's sudden attentiveness.

'You must not keep Linden out late, Miles. There must be no more – talk.'

Miles was unaware that there had been any talk, as for a while was Mrs Rilston, until she was waylaid one morning by her housekeeper.

'I think it right to tell you, ma'am' – Mrs Beale's manner was distant – 'that there's talk among the maids.'

The talk, Mrs Rilston was astonished to hear, was about Miss Grey. It also involved Mr Miles, but the unpleasantness derived from Miss Grey. Things were being said in the village which it was not Mrs Beale's business or intention to repeat. At first she had listened to the tittle-tattle, but when it came to such nonsense as a ghost in Lucknow meadow, the ghost of a girl in pink seen early in the morning and once just as it was getting dark, she had put a stop to it at once. But when gossip centred on the House she felt it her duty to report it. She would do her best but she could not guarantee that Miss Grey would be shown the respect that guests at Bainrigg House had always in her time received.

'But why ever not?' Mrs Rilston demanded, already confused.

When the drawing-room had been 'done' on the morning after the dinner-party, there had been signs – Mrs Beale hesitated – of irregularity. An intimate item of underwear had been found, the furniture had been disarranged and Mr Rilston had been seen to carry Miss Grey to his car in the early hours of the morning. Informally dressed.

'Thank you, Mrs Beale. You were right to tell me. And I must tell you that any servant in my house who fails to show proper respect to any of my guests will be dismissed instantly.'

Since the war there had been a laxity unknown in her young days though she had no personal experience of it. She felt the news too unpleasant to be passed on to Mrs Grey, but after some thought she did pass on an edited version to Miles. Linden Grey was evidently not the girl she had taken her for but she was the only girl available whom Miles might be induced to marry – and marry he must for a number of reasons including his own mental health, not to mention her own. She could not be solely responsible for his variations of mood and lack of direction: she was too old and too tired to be worried any more.

'I'm surprised that you allowed yourself to be drawn into a situation which would cause talk among the maids – and even more surprised that Linden should behave in such a way. But it can be remedied and I for one shall be happy to forget it when you confirm the attachment in the proper way' – and almost immediately, it seemed to Miles, she produced the emerald ring which had been her own mother's.

Even so he made no decision, and indecision throughout the winter months proved fertile ground for the growth of an 'understanding'. It was not until April that, desiring nothing else, he accepted the inevitable: and Linden accepted the emerald with modest acquiescence and the words: 'Oh, Miles, it really is beautiful.' Nothing was said about love and briefly he felt at ease. For once he was behaving like everyone else.

His satisfaction would need to be very great indeed to equal that of Mrs Grey and presumably that of Linden though it is likely that her accustomed reticence concealed some misgivings. She was not long in discovering that Mrs Rilston's references to being hard up had some basis in fact. Miles, whom experience had already made wary, made it clear that the wedding must be quiet: there could be no lavish expenditure. It was unnecessary to point out that the bride's contribution would consist entirely of debts and the Rilston wealth was chiefly in land.

And of what use was land? It could provide her with none of the luxury she pined for and felt entitled to. When Mrs Rilston mentioned that the coal company had made an offer for the Langland estate, it seemed obvious to her that it should be accepted.

'You will feel much better off with money in the bank,' she told Miles.

'There's no question of selling Langland.' Miles spoke quite sharply.

'Of course not.' Linden never argued, never chattered about her likes and dislikes, never gossiped or laughed very much. On the other hand, she was never rude, never sulked, never behaved incorrectly (except through no fault of her own on the evening of the dinner-party). When at last the emerald, expensively reset, appeared on her finger and the news flashed through the village ('What did I tell you?' Bella said), Miles was not happy in his engagement but he was less unhappy than he had sometimes been. It would be a suitable marriage. The need to be convinced of its suitability had nevertheless given him sleepless nights. Was there not ample proof in historical records that even arranged marriages designed to protect property and lineage and to maintain the social structure were as often as not successful? Man and wife knew their separate roles and fulfilled them.

Suitable? In the small hours he came to hate the voice of reason that lectured him from within his own skull. Historical records had nothing to do with the quandary he had got himself into. All the same, he was calm and resolute and convinced that on a humdrum level of reality he was doing a sensible thing.

Then came the morning when with time on his hands he strolled down through the fields to take a few photographs before fitting a new roll of film.

CHAPTER XX

'Try to relax,' Lance said. 'You're doing very well. You haven't stalled once so far.'

'But we're coming to a hill.' Grim-faced, bolt upright at the wheel, Margot spoke through her teeth. 'I'll have to . . . .'

'You know what to do. I'll tell you when. Now. Foot down, gear to neutral, foot up, rev, foot down, gear to second, foot up.'

'I did it.' She turned her head, radiant. 'I double-declutched.'

'Watch where you're going. Stop when we get to that gate and I'll drive. I need to get on faster.'

He was always short of time but it had been his idea that she should learn to drive. She could come with him on some of his calls and practise for ten or fifteen minutes now and again. There had been some surprise when Lance, a gold medallist, his results brilliant, had turned down the offer of a promising opening in Glasgow and had come home to join his father's practice. No doubt he had his own reasons besides the obvious one that Dr Pelman, after years of working single-handed in harsh winters with crowded surgeries and always available for emergencies at three pits, was now suffering from arthritis and was very much in need of a partner.

Margot had set herself the goal of being able to drive by the time Miss Bondless came, Miss Bondless herself being so competent in so many spheres. Had she not once driven an ambulance under shell fire? Margot's bright look of triumph in having made the gear change raised Lance's spirits too. He saw it as a revival of the vitality she had seemed to lose. She was not changed, only subdued and would come to life again. But there were problems ahead. He was pretty sure that the news from Bainrigg House had not yet reached her. He had heard it from Mrs Roper when he visited her husband, a sufferer from pneumoconiosis. Margot would hear it soon enough. He had no intention of telling her.

'I read of a very interesting case the other day.'

Margot moved over with alacrity: she was more interested in the human condition than in the internal combustion engine.

'This story has a gloomy beginning.'

A doctor had been called in to certify a man as insane. Two medical signatures were needed. The patient, a quiet, self-effacing man, had completely changed and become violent, even dangerous. His distressed family had agreed that he must be put under restraint. But this second doctor had noticed certain physical symptoms – a swelling in the man's face, a curious condition of the skin, slurred speech, a thickening of the fingertips. 'In short,' Lance warmed to the tale, 'he was convinced that the man was suffering from thyroid deficiency and not insane at all. After a course of treatment he was completely cured.'

'How amazing! I hadn't realized that a person's mental state could be affected like that – by some physical condition.'

'Indeed it can. That was an extreme case – and the opposite is also true: emotional states can effect the physical condition – pulse, digestion, breathing – can cause pain and insomnia . . . .' He ransacked with enthusiasm the catalogue of human ills.

His attempt to divert the direction of Margot's thoughts was not entirely successful: she thought immediately of Miles, of the change in his manner at their last meeting. Since there was no other explanation, he must have been unwell. Illness had sometimes made her mother peevish and unlike herself. How childishly she had reacted! She had behaved like a medieval maiden waiting to be wooed. As a friend she should have insisted on finding out what was wrong. It was obvious now: he had been ill, had hoped that she would be concerned but would never inflict his trouble on her unasked.

Lance called on two patients in Fellside before driving her home and found her silent and preoccupied but not noticeably depressed. Margot was in fact regaining much of what he would have called her 'tone'. She had enjoyed preparing a room for

Miss Bondless and a trip to London with her father to buy clothes, go to theatres and hobnob with Freda, She had also had her hair cut. She had escaped the bob and shingle epidemic: longer styles were coming in and the light brown waves falling to the nape of her neck were very becoming. The wound of Miles's apparent change of heart was not healed, but gradually her natural optimism had allowed her to dream of a reconciliation. There had been no reason, she repeatedly told herself, no quarrel – that was unthinkable. He had been worried by his new responsibilities, saddened by Mr Rilston's death. It must have grieved him to miss another year at Oxford. When they last met, her own behaviour must have seemed more unaccountably cool and unsympathetic than she had realized.

Between the Hall and Bainrigg House, separated by no more than a walk through the wood or a short drive by road, there was now no contact. It was Alex who reported from Kenya that Miles had joined the flying club at Howlyn. 'Lucky devil!' He had heard it from Angela Bavistock who wrote to him regularly. She had heard it from Gavin Roberts's younger brother who had been in Alex's year at Bishop's. Alan Cobham, on a visit to the club, had singled out Rilston as promising to be a first-class aviator and was keeping him in mind for one of his field displays. And when a DH60 Moth flew low over the priory and Ewan Judd said, 'I bet that's Mr Rilston', Margot had stared up into the sky, dazzled, as when a child she had followed the flight of a bird. Miles would find it exhilarating to soar above the earth where, she realized with concern, he had never yet been really happy.

There had been one other point of contact with Bainrigg. She was arranging daffodils in a vase for the hall table when her father came out of his study with a letter in his hand.

'I don't know what to make of this.' It was from his solicitor who had heard from the Rilstons' legal adviser that the Fellside and District Coal Company had made an offer for the demesne of 120 acres comprising the Langland Hall and priory estate.

'Don't worry.' He smiled at Margot's alarm. 'Our lease has eight more years to run. Besides the Rilstons won't sell. The old man was dead against parting with land. In any case it's one of the terms of the agreement that in the event of a sale I should have the first option to buy.'

He was less confident than he seemed. He had put too much capital into restoring the Hall and cottages, as well as buying equipment and levelling land for the smallholdings to be able to make an offer for some time to come.

'Why should they want to buy? Is there coal here?'

'Undoubtedly. They wouldn't want land for any other reason. It's unlikely that they would develop it in the short term but it would be worth their while to own it.'

He would have been easier in his mind if Frederick Rilston had still been alive: the old gentleman had appreciated his gesture in resigning over the chimney incident, so saving him from a possibly costly law suit. There had been a friendly understanding between them.

'It wouldn't surprise me if that old blackguard Bedlow was behind this. He'd dig up the Garden of Eden if there was coal to be got out of it. If only we could get the Ministry of Works to take over the priory!' He must see Quinian, find out how the land lay and pull a few strings in Westminster and Whitehall. Nostrils dilated as by the scent of battle, he vanished into the study.

The matter remained in abeyance. Whether from inertia, reluctance to part with land or shrewdness in delaying the sale in the hope that its value would appreciate, the Rilstons appeared in no hurry to sell.

On the very day following Margot's decision to seek out Miles, an opportunity arose which made it possible to call at Bainrigg House, a perfectly natural straightforward reason for calling as a friend and neighbour. Her father's dream of establishing the Hall as a cultural centre in a district much in need of one was to be realized at last. With the co-operation of the Elmdon Music and Arts Society a musical evening with the Phoebus string quartet was to be held at the Hall.

As a friend then, Margot walked to Bainrigg by way of the priory wood; as an old friend and nothing more. It was unfortunate that every step revived memories of the last time she had walked that way almost exactly a year ago. Then as now there had been sunlight between branches, the fresh green of cuckoo-pint and hyacinth leaves, the pairing birds. She had shared with them the mysterious thrill of awakening life as she had walked on air towards the long-awaited meeting. Here was the drooping birch bough; the wicket gate into the field where once again lambs skipped and ewes stolidly munched; the first glimpse of yellow gorse above the stone-pit and – amazingly – she could scarcely believe it – he was there, in the place where they had sat together on a smooth shelf of stone in the sheltered hollow. He was holding a camera.

'Margot!' He leapt up to level ground and came towards her. 'Stand still.' A click and he had caught her, standing erect, smiling, forgetting why she had come, overjoyed that they had met at last as they had planned, only a year too late. What was a year but a gap in time leaving nothing changed? He was looking at her with the old tenderness. For her the moment was supreme.

For him? The first visionary moment passed, having done its terrible work in shattering the fragile peace he had seemed to find. It had made a mockery of any hope that he could live without her. Already, even before she came quickly across the grass to stand obediently still, her feet among the daisies – already his self-confidence was being threatened by the paralysis of doubt, and with good reason. Impetuosity had led him into a relationship he had never envisaged and could not have imagined, but he had accepted it as a release from the deepest loneliness he had known in all his lonely life.

Imperceptibly release had become constraint. He had recognized his dilemma even as he spoke the words that made it permanent. And now he would have to tell Margot, explain what could never be justified, though of course it could not directly concern her, not emotionally. He could not even assume that she cared what he did. He must not make the same mistake again.

'How strangely things happen,' she was saying. 'I never told you but I used to come here often – when I was younger, you know – hoping you'd be here, and now when I least expected it, here you are. Actually' – she remembered her role as friend, neighbour, promoter of the arts – 'I was going to call at the house to leave you one of these leaflets.' She produced one from her bag. 'An evening of music. I hope you'll come, for Father's sake as well as your own. I remember something you once said, ages ago. "Sometimes there's music". It was a lovely thing to say, like a promise that music might come out of the air . . . if one waited . . . .'

Had he changed a little? He looked older. She saw the beginning of an anxious frown between his brows. He had certainly been glad to see her but he was now serious, desperately serious, without the grace of manner which had been so endearing.

'When we last met' – she took courage – 'I felt that you were changed and I wondered if you were unwell. You haven't been ill, have you? We've seen so little of you since Mother died.'

He must speak. A premonition of disaster put weights on his tongue. No words could lessen the enormity, as he now saw it, of his conduct. To speak of it could only make more inescapable a situation which had sometimes seemed unreal. He must remember that Margot was not involved. What seemed a catastrophe to him affected her only distantly if at all. Her concern was that of a caring friend. It had always been so from the beginning. The warmth and vitality he had loved had from the start misled him.

'I should have known that even if you belonged to someone else I would have gone on loving you.' He spoke – now that it was too late – with a passion he had never known before. 'I could have lived alone, hurting no one . . . .'

'You never told me' – she trembled with the thrill of it, disregarding the odd way he had put it – 'that you loved me.' Oh, she had been right to come. Why had she waited so long?

'I was going to, longing to, waiting until it would have been the right time to tell you, hoping you might feel the same for me. I thought of nothing else. I had no idea then that I would have been too late.'

'Too late?'

'It simply hadn't dawned on me that there was an understanding between you and Lance, not until Linden told me that you'd always . . . .'

'Linden told you that Lance and I. . . ?'

'He's a fine fellow. But I couldn't face being with you, knowing there was no hope for me. And then . . . . There's Linden. I felt sorry for her and I thought since there was no one else for either of us, we might . . . . Linden and I are engaged.'

Happiness drained from her so suddenly that it seared her from head to foot. Daylight seemed to have dimmed. She looked round in disbelief at sheep still browsing as if in mist on grass from which the green had faded. She understood it all: the cool lie, the successful ruse, his ignorance of women like Linden. But there were no women like Linden. Wherever she went someone must suffer. It was as if she darkened the air and filled the surrounding space. Nothing was safe from her as Katie in her simplicity had known from the beginning.

She shivered, her eyes dull with misery. She and Miles should never have met. Their ways had crossed, that was all. She would say nothing: there was nothing to be said. He need not know how she suffered. An unfamiliar pride held her rigid.

'Margot.'

The stupor left her. She turned and walked away. The walk became a frantic run.

'Margot. Please . . . .'

She fumbled with the wicket gate and was gathered into the merciful shade of the trees. For the rest of her life she would remember his voice calling her name: remember that she had not looked back or spoken a word of comfort or reproach. Still running, she stumbled over a tree root and into the arms of Lance. In her distress there was no room for surprise that he was there. He set her on her feet. She shook herself free and they walked homeward.

'He told you?'

'You knew?'

'Yes.'

'He thought you and I were in love, or engaged or something.'

'Did you tell him that it wasn't true?'

'No, I didn't tell him. He should have known that it isn't true.'

Presently as the ice that gripped her melted, she began to cry. Silently Lance handed her a handkerchief. She took it without a word, unaware that the man at her side was only a little less unhappy than the one she had left.

When Margot left him he stood for a while clutching the leaflet, the camera slung over his shoulder. He watched as the wicket gate closed behind her and the green she was wearing merged with the green of leaves and mossed boughs. To turn away had the finality of an execution. He glanced unseeing, at the leaflet. There had been awe and rapture in her voice as she spoke of music coming from the air, if one waited.

If only she had stayed away! If only she had not burst in upon him again, bringing a flood of light when he had been almost content to make his way in semi-darkness. Terrible as the past few minutes had been they were only a prelude to the future he faced: a lifetime to be spent with Linden Grey. A glimpse of Margot – it had been no more – had clarified his view of Linden. Knowing that Margot's emotions were not involved, he was puzzled by her reaction. Was it anger – against himself – against Linden? He remembered that Alex had been in love with her and had suddenly gone away. But his own situation was sufficiently grievous to occupy all his thoughts. His head ached; his temples burned; he felt physically ill.

He moved at last – not to go home, he never wanted to go there again – but towards the wicket gate. There was just a possibility that she might come back. But if she did, what good would it do? What could he say to her? What could he say to Linden? He was finding it hard to think clearly or to single out each problem and confront it rationally. Later, perhaps.

He had gone to the gate. Behind him fields lay open to the sky: it was high and clear, with no more than a wisp of white cloud to mar the blue. A perfect day for flying. For leaving it all behind? In sudden weariness he leaned on the gate. It was restful to trace between boughs vistas of green and grey. In all the intricacies of light and shade there was nothing harsh, nothing urgent, nothing clear-cut to rivet the gaze. Not until the woman came.

He was first aware of movement between the trees, the tread of foot on fallen leaves. Then he saw her, a tall woman dressed in brown or black. She was walking steadily and quickly. He undid the latch and opened the gate to let her pass. But she came up to him and stopped. She was bareheaded, her hair done in a coronet of twisted plaits; a gaunt-faced woman, unsmiling. He remembered having seen her at Langland Hall.

200

'Mr Rilston, sir?'

'Yes.'

'I was coming to see you. There's something you ought to know . . . .'

It didn't take long to tell him and when she had done she did not linger but went quickly back the way she had come. Here and there a larch bough quivered and she was gone. The quiet had never been more intense. He turned his back on the wood, on its green depths and voiceless mystery, its capricious changes of light, its endless variations of shape and colour, and looked up with confidence at the day's unclouded blue, its brilliant clarity, its emptiness of people.

So – he had been right after all. For once in his life he had been right, no matter what a mess he had made of things afterwards. He was happy – as if eased of a burden – all the happier for having learned how transient a mood it was, how rare, how fragile. There was only one way to avoid its inevitable decline into misery. There wasn't much time. At any minute doubt, self-hatred and bitter regret would come crawling back.

He smiled, remembering her delight as she came out of the shade into the sunlight – delight at having found him there – and how she had stood, feet among the daisies, head in air, as if waiting to hear the airborne music he had promised. It must end on a high note. The thought pleased him. He went quickly back to the house. There was nothing he needed. He got into his car and without a farewell backward glance drove off to Howlyn.

CHAPTER XXI

The day was warm, a spring day with all the features that poets love: blossom, bird-song and the indescribable sweetness in the air that seems both new and long familiar. Seated on the base of a vanished column in the south transept, Margot had her back to the priory wood. She used to look that way, hoping he would come.

The thrush in the cherry tree stopped singing and presently the blackbird on the gatehouse piped a few tentative notes. They had both preferred blackbirds. Miles said that thrushes were classicists, formal and self-assured, whereas blackbirds were romantic, striving after the unattainable, She had agreed; and now the plaintive phrases of a song left unfinished were as sad as they were sweet.

What had possessed her to leave him like that without a word? He had called after her and she had left him desolate with only a few more hours to live – and then no life at all. There would have been time to go back and find some way – some words – to make things better. It was too late now.

Since she had heard the news two days ago she had been tormented by the thought that in leaving him like that she had driven him too far. They said there had been mist and low cloud over the Cumbrian mountains and although he was more than competent, he was not yet used to sudden changes in visibility. If he had intended never to come back, he had left no sign, no message. Yet, she felt in her heart that he had meant it to happen, that life had been too much for him to manage alone. He was not equal to its awful realities.

She heard the back door of the Hall open and close. Toria was coming through the garden and up the hill to find her. There was no escape. In Toria's movements there was always a relentless quality. She came near and stopped, deliberately, as if the purpose of her entire life had been to arrive at that spot and at that time. She had something in her hand. The post? She must write to Alex. He would be devastated by the news. Being so far away made things worse. When the news of their mother's death had reached him he had gone out into the bush alone and, as he wrote 'got through it somehow'. As he grew older his language was becoming simpler.

Toria sat down on a portion of what was left of the south wall. There was no barrier between them. When Ewan brought the news, Margot was alone in the house and it was Toria who told her. She had little to say but she had supplied a rock-like reliability that was better than sympathy.

'This is for you,' she said, when she had sat for a while without speaking. She indicated the object she held but didn't part with it. 'Mr Rilston asked me to give it to you.'

'Do you mean Miles?' There was no other Mr Rilston. There was now no Mr Rilston at all. The long line had come to a sudden end on the grey screes of the mountain above Wastwater. 'How could that be when he...?'

'I went to see him.'

'When?'

'Just after you saw him.'

She had set off for Bainrigg before Margot did and with the same intention, to see Mr Rilston. The news of his engagement had alarmed her. She had been wrong in waiting instead of speaking to him when Ewan first told her of Miss Grey's intentions. It might now be too late. Hearing Margot at some little distance behind her in the wood, she had diverged to a higher path and waited there – it was not long – until Margot came back and was met by Dr Lance.

'Why did you want to see him?' Margot had listened with growing anger. 'What possible reason could you have?'

'There was something I thought he ought to know.'

'You thought! You don't mean...?' Surely there was only one

thing Toria was in a position to tell. 'You promised not to tell. Didn't you realize that it would distress him? In fact you may have been responsible for . . . .' She stopped just in time. 'I had grieved him enough. If I had behaved differently he might have been happy – it couldn't have been for long.'

'You're wrong about what I had to tell him. I promised not to, didn't I? In any case I don't want those words nor even her name ever to pass my lips again. It's not for me to wreak vengeance on her. That's in higher hands. The truth about her will come out in time without another word from me, and from what I hear it's coming out already.'

Margot's brief anger left her. Toria's interference was preposterous, whatever form it had taken, but she had had good reason to resent Linden who had been responsible for her relapse into vagrancy. Burdons' had been the only home she had: no wonder she bore a grudge. Except that there had always seemed a peculiar intensity in her resentment as if from some other unknown cause.

She herself had now cause for even deeper resentment. Grieving for Miles, she had been mercifully free from thoughts of Linden as if subconsciously avoiding the latest demonstration of her baneful influence, the most cruelly effective of her lies. Now, to be reminded of her was to feel unable to think of her as a normal, if flawed, human being. But what else could she be? With a tremor she recognized as superstitious, Margot turned with relief to Toria whose humanity was not in doubt.

'You had something else to tell him?'

'It was for your sake, to bring you and him together again. I knew he could not love her: I knew her too well for that. She had inveigled him as she nearly did Mr Alex. What I did was for the best but I judged wrong. I grieve for it. The only comfort is that with her there would be only misery for him. But it doesn't do to interfere in people's lives. We're all in higher hands.'

It was a lesson Margot too was beginning to learn.

'What I told him made him happy, I do know that.' Toria's whole aspect had softened. 'But what it may have led to – I don't know. I told him you loved him.'

It was outrageous. No one else in the world would have behaved in such a way. Margot's indignant protest would have been justified but not for the first time Toria's ability to sweep aside the trivial silenced her. Toria dealt only in essentials whether lofty or base.

'It was true, wasn't it?'

'Yes, it was true.'

'When I said it, his face lit up. He was suddenly at peace. "I understood that there was someone else", he said. "No", I told him, "only you". I haven't often seen happiness in a man's face, much less been the one to bring it, but I saw it then. "If only I'd known", he said. "If only I'd been sure". Then when I was leaving him he said, "I have nothing to give her – except this". He took it out of his pocket. "Give her this with my dearest love".' Toria held out the envelope. 'I waited to give it to you. You haven't been wanting to see anyone.'

'It's a roll of film.'

And when, a few days later, Margot opened the packet of photographs, she saw again the gate by the ash tree where they had parted for the first time; the stone-pit full of last year's flowers; the priory ruins taken from the edge of the wood. (He had come as far as that.) She kept them to herself until she felt calm enough to show them to Toria.

'And this one of you, Miss Margot. It's the most beautiful photograph I ever saw in my life.'

'He never saw it.'

'But he saw you looking like that. Looking at him like that.'

Had he understood that it was love for him that made her look like that? In the moment of meeting she had felt the thrill of pure happiness in loving which no other thrill can equal, and had seemed to see it mirrored in his face. And that was all: the recognition of mutual love instantly doomed. Such ecstasy could not have lasted but need it have been so brief, so ruthlessly ended in the absolute finality of death?

She sat for a long time with the photograph in her hand. It told her how she had appeared to him and for the last time. But straining every resource of memory to picture him as he had looked at her, she could only hear his voice calling her name – and remember that she had walked away without answering or looking back.

The spring days crept by. The blackbird practised daily and perfected its song, a threnody for first love. Regret for what might have been was slow to fade. After a time she put the photographs away with his letters. It was to be years before she would look at them again without heart-ache.

CHAPTER XXII

Jane Bondless had grown used to the unpredictability of circumstances and the futility of planning too far ahead. Miss Crane never recovered from the illness which had kept her in Cannes, but lingered month after month, while at Bourton-on-the-Water, Constance Bondless dealt single-handed with the purchase and restoration of the house they had chosen. And the room Margot had painstakingly prepared at Langland Hall remained empty.

Consequently Edward's plan was executed in reverse. Jane could not come to England; instead Margot went to Cannes. Her low spirits and languor after Miles's death had alarmed her father who had not realized the closeness of their attachment. It may have been a word of warning from Toria Link that drove him in sudden panic to take Margot to Cannes himself. They arrived within twenty-four hours of his telegram.

'You're the most sensible woman I know,' he told Jane. 'You'll know what to do.'

She knew there was nothing to be done but wait for the change of scene, fresh company and a share in looking after Miss Crane to have a healing effect. Margot grew fond of the old lady and stayed until she died in the following July – then helped with the sad final arrangements and the closing of the apartment. When she and Jane were free to go home, they were reluctant to part and Jane was persuaded to make a short visit to Langland before joining her sister: a welcome spell of leisure in which she had ample time for letter-writing.

Langland Hall
19 August, 1931

Dear Connie

You were right – up to a point. There is everything here to supply the background of one of Mrs Radcliffe's or Bram Stoker's novels: a ruined priory with at least one hooting owl; an old house, rather dark with rambling passages, cavernous cellars and seven unoccupied bedrooms (there may be more) – situated in open country merging into moorland where heather is in full bloom.

So much for the setting. The characters have strayed from a different milieu. Not a trace of Dracula in Edward Humbert. He is kind, preoccupied – a clever forehead (you know I always notice foreheads) – much saddened since I saw him last – and older. Aren't we all?

My room is charming: a bay overlooking the garden, pale chintzes, a traditional local quilt in white honeycomb; and Margot has converted the dressing-room that opens off it into a tiny sitting-room where I am writing this.

James Pelman met us at Elmdon station and brought us here. He asks to be remembered to you. I told him that you hadn't forgotten those holidays in Cornwall long ago when he was always the one to come to the rescue in emergencies. Remember when you were stuck halfway up – or halfway down Ebb Cliff? I gather that Lance is very like his father.

The two couples who have the smallholdings, the Todds and Amblers, ' produce fresh vegetables, home-grown tomatoes and marrows and we have abundant eggs and goat's milk. Edward was quite touchingly pleased when I told him how much I enjoyed such luxuries. Apparently there were tremendous difficulties when he first took over the Hall, but in the hands of Mrs Beale, the housekeeper, things now run very smoothly. In fact I'm not needed here and thanks to dear Miss Crane's generosity I need never work for my living again. But I have promised to stay on as a guest for a week or two. Margot and I are going to find it hard to part with each other: we have got on so well together.

Has Jobson finished repairing the wall under the bathroom window? There's no point in ordering a carpet for the sitting-room

until he has renewed those floorboards, but you could be looking at
samples. A soft green? Bluish, not yellowish.
  More later.
    My love,

        Jane.

  P.S. I must just add – there is one person here who matches the
setting: a rather daunting woman, in her forties, I should guess,
known as Toria Link. Why did I put it like that? Toria is her name,
short for Victoria, I suppose. Too old to be a tweenie but a sort of
woman of all work. Even Mrs Beale treats her with caution. I
believe she is devoted to Margot. The interesting thing is that she
reminds me of someone – I can't think who. A long pale face, deadly
serious, like one of the awe-stricken onlookers in an oil-painting of
a massacre or a shipwreck. I'm sure she has a history.

Having finished her letter, Miss Bondless found Margot in the
garden and they walked down to Fellside to the post office. The
late August day was warm, their pace leisurely. Although they had
been together for the best part of a year – perhaps because of
that – there was much to talk about.

'If only Mother could have known how well things have turned
out! How comfortably for Father, I mean. Mrs Beale has been a
godsend.'

When in the previous autumn Mrs Rilston left for Cheltenham
and Bainrigg House was closed, Mrs Beale lost no time in trans-
ferring herself to Langland Hall. It was well known that Mr
Humbert was in need of a housekeeper and even before Mr Miles's
tragic death, Mrs Beale had had no intention of remaining at
Bainrigg under the new Mrs Rilston, of whom strange things were
being said in the village. It couldn't possibly be true that Mr Miles's
fiancée had been involved in some way in the death of that girl
whose body was found in the Lucknow Chimney, but neither could
one take orders from the sort of person of whom such things were
said. Her arrival at Langland, bringing with her Jenny and Elsie,
had put Margot's mind at rest. But now—

'I hadn't realized how different it would be. I feel like a guest
in my own home.'

'A pleasant feeling, surely.'

'It doesn't feel right, especially after having been idle for so long.'

'You did think of taking up your studies again. You would have time now.'

Time, but no inclination to retreat into the byways of history. The long holiday had itself been a retreat; the sunshine and palms, the outdoor cafés and well-to-do people with time on their hands already seemed unreal, all the more so in contrast to Fellside with its Co-operative store and the headstock and chimney of its colliery. Men were coming out of the pit gates at the end of a shift, faces blackened with coal dust, eyes and lips black-rimmed and strangely pale.

'Good God! How do they stand it? One has to see them like this to realize what it does to them.'

'It was drummed into us as children. "Never forget that the comfort we enjoy depends on men working a thousand feet underground in seams no higher than this table, for eight hours a day". It used to be longer.'

'That must have curbed your youthful appetites. But your father was right: personally I shall never feel the same about stirring a fire.'

'You're back home then, Miss Margot.'

One of the men had stopped. It was a moment before she recognized him.

'Ewan! How are you? Father told me that you had left us.'

He was thinner, his features taut and more firmly defined.

'It was a good life at the Hall but I was getting soft.' Despite the long shift underground Ewan spoke with energy. 'I told Mr Humbert – I want to get to grips with the workers' struggle against the capitalist exploitation of labour. "You can't do it on your own", he said, "and you need education and experience".'

The upshot was that under Mr Humbert's guidance he had applied for one of the Mineworkers' Training Schemes. It involved work underground and attendance at the Elmdon Technical College.

'I'll have a certificate and maybe get a Union job some day. As I see it now if you want justice in the world you have to fight for it. We want to see these pits nationalized instead of run to fill the pockets of the likes of Laverborne. And we want to get more working men into Parliament.' In his blackened face his eyes shone; his lips, pallid pink, were eloquent.

'Come on, Ewan lad.' A hand was clapped on his shoulder. 'Get off your soap box or you'll miss the bus.'

'I'd better be pushing off.'

'Come and see us, Ewan. And remember me to your mother.' And, when he had gone, 'I've never seen him so happy. I wonder what can have changed him.'

'He's found an aim in life.'

'Toria will miss him.'

'They were friends?'

'In a strange sort of way. I remember her saying that he had a good heart.' At that time there had been little sign of it.

'There's something familiar about her as if I'd seen that face somewhere else.'

They walked home in companionable silence, Jane teased by a resemblance she could not place, Margot dismayed to find herself envying Ewan and wishing that she too could have an aim in life.

'Ewan was right,' she said, as they sat down to lunch. 'Life can be too soft and easy. I don't want it to be like that.'

She had the impression that Jane was not listening. Since there were just the two of them, the meal was informal and it was Toria who brought in the omelette. Her stately manner certainly commanded attention: Jane's eyes never left her until the door closed behind her.

'She's beginning to haunt me. I expected to find a ghost or two at Langland but not the ghost of somebody I've forgotten.'

But the face with its high cheekbones and deep-set eyes was too striking to be that of a ghost – unless the ghost of a martyr perhaps. It was unlikely that in all her varied experience she had seen the woman before. It must be that she was like someone else, or the woe-begone yet forceful countenance, as she had suggested to Connie, was such as an artist might choose as the prototype of suffering womanhood, to include in a painting, the subject a catastrophe of some kind. She could have seen a simi-

211

lar face looking out from a canvas in a gallery or some civic building.

Margot was pleased that Jane found so much to interest her in her father's rather fine collection of volumes on the history of art: Italian, Dutch, English, Spanish, lavishly illustrated.

'You won't mind if I wander round a little – and settle in?'

Jane, lost in contemplation of Hieronymus Bosch's *Hell* had not even heard.

The wandering round and settling in threatened to take longer than Margot intended. There had been changes: the Amblers' goats had multiplied; the kitchen premises had been altered under Mrs Beale's direction; Jenny and Elsie shared one of the empty rooms. Langland without Ewan had not appealed to Bella who had preferred to stay in Ashlaw and was now working at Dr Pelman's (and it was about time the place was cleaned up, as she made no bones about telling him).

Other things had not changed. If the stones of the priory had shed another layer of ancient dust on the level greensward, it was too fine for mortal eye to see. A blackbird, silent on the gatehouse, may not have been the bird that made her weep two Aprils ago. But there was sanctuary still between the ravaged walls such as pilgrims must have found when they came through the bluebell wood. She went a little distance along Beggars' Way but soon turned back in sudden restlessness. There had always been so much to do. She remembered almost with affection the early days at the Hall: the bare boards and uncurtained windows, the howling draughts and improvised meals, the sense of purpose and being needed.

Alex would soon be home. He would not be returning to Kenya. *Africa is too big,* he had written, *and too terrifyingly beautiful. It takes over one's life. One has to keep noticing it. The skies are too wide and too splendid. They diminish me to a pinpoint. And another thing – native life is harsh and primitive but the people are rooted in their natural surroundings. They have dignity and the kind of security that comes with patterns of behaviour centuries old. They haven't suffered – at least not yet – the evils of an industrial revolution. I think they're better off than the victims of the Depression queuing for dole and soup. They're the ones who need help . . . .*

'He's off on another tack,' Lance would say.

But where was Lance? It was surely rather odd that having been home for three days after months of absence she had not yet seen him. She had taken it for granted that he would be at the station or would come on the first evening.

'We don't see much of Lance these days,' Edward remarked that evening at dinner. They were alone: Jane was dining out with Dr Pelman in Elmdon. 'He seems to spend all his spare time in town. I'm beginning to wonder if there's a young lady . . . .'

'Father!' She immediately regretted the protest and added hastily, 'That would be a surprise.' But there had been more than surprise in her reaction to so unwelcome an idea. Other people fell in love and fell out of it again, Alex for instance, or had their hearts broken by it, but not Lance. There would be something incongruous in the concentration of all that single-minded energy on some girl in Elmdon. Which girl? Freda or Phyllis might have known but Phyllis had no sooner been finished than she had become engaged to the nephew of a Swiss banker, and Freda was demonstrating high-class dishes for a commercial photographer. It had always been possible to talk freely to Lance but to ask him about a love affair was out of the question. He would tell her about it when he thought fit.

Absent in the flesh he might be but he cropped up again in the conversation next morning. He had joined his father and Jane for coffee at the Castle Hotel where they had dined.

'Like his father. The same sense of humour but much better looking,' was Jane's verdict, 'and more interesting. He always was as a boy but now – I was really impressed. What he's doing in an out-of-the-way place like Ashlaw' – she gazed dreamily at her breakfast egg – 'I can't imagine. Not wasting his talents, I hope, when he has worlds to conquer. Could it be some sentimental attachment to the old place?'

'Some of us are very fond of Ashlaw.' Margot spoke rather tartly. Lance had never been the sort of person one worried about. Suspecting that she was nevertheless beginning to worry about him, she exerted herself to make the most of the remaining days of Jane's visit. They walked, went for drives and, with Mr Todd's help, resurrected the old pony trap, harnessed the pony,

grown fat in retirement, and ambled along deserted lanes leading eventually to wilder country where the air was heather-
scented and the water pure in peat-brown streams.

'You've done so many things, Jane, and never been bored or
lonely.'

It was their last day. The picnic was over; Margot put the plates
and cups back in the basket and closed the lid.

'Bored? Never.' Jane sat up and brushed purple florets from
her skirt. She was a slim woman, energetic in her movements and
physically strong. Only in the depths of her eyes and in the lines
about them was there evidence of her experience of scenes very
different from this quiet spot under a cloudless sky and of people
very different from her present companion. 'But lonely? Often.
In fact, always. Loneliness is something to tackle or put up with
and get used to. Every human being is lonely: it's a fact of life.
The intervals when one doesn't feel lonely are a sort of bonus,
like this one – and it's time to go home.'

'The tone of that speech was bracing like the ones you made
to homesick soldiers and plaintive orphans and weary old ladies.'

'Don't forget the members of committees, wives of drunken
husbands . . . .'

'And the husbands themselves?'

'Sometimes, though usually it was the wives who drove them to
drink.'

In trying to solve the tantalizing problem of where she had
seen Toria before, Jane had dipped into memories of those
earlier days. She had turned the pages of the Humberts' histories
of art in vain. Some of El Greco's faces were of the right shape
but those were of men; his women were more gentle. Bosch's
Pedlar was not pale enough. She was now less inclined to believe
that Toria had glowered down at her from the wall of an art
gallery. The more she saw of her, though it was never for more
than a minute or two, the more convinced she was that her
memory was of the actual woman. Somewhere, in a hospital or
casualty station, in an orphanage, in a London settlement, in one
of several private houses including a vicarage and an almost
stately home, she had seen Toria Link. It must have been a long
time ago and no more than a glimpse: there had been no close

association and no words had been exchanged. All she remembered was the face. No, there was more: a sense of disaster
connected with it or with the place where she had seen it. That
should not have been surprising: disasters, as Connie often said,
were meat and drink to her sister Jane. And as Jane herself was
to say in telling the story, it was typical of the melodramatic
atmosphere of Langland Hall that clarification should come only
at the eleventh hour, in the very nick of time.

The long journey to the Cotswolds involved a number of
changes and she had to make an early start the next morning.
Margot would come with her as far as Elmdon. Edward had left
even earlier for a consultation in Derbyshire, consequently there
was no car available.

'I thought you'd rather have Polly than a taxi.'

'Much rather! Our last ride!' They waited on the steps as the
trap was brought round. 'It's been perfect, every minute of it.
And you'll come to us as soon as the house is ready, won't you?
After all, Bourton-on-the-Water is a beauty spot. Connie's choice
as you know. I'll get used to it.' Jane looked round. 'I've said
goodbye to everyone but Toria.'

Margot explained that Toria was shopping in Fellside. She
would be waiting at the station and would drive herself and her
packages back to the Hall. Polly was in no hurry and the train was
there when they arrived. There was just time to find an empty
compartment; the door was slammed, the whistle blown and the
train moved. Having settled the hat-box on the rack, Margot
dropped into the corner seat opposite Jane and was addressed in
what she afterwards described as low and thrilling tones.

'Margot! I've got it. I've remembered. It was when she came
out of the waiting-room just now. Toria. That was how I saw her
– in a station rather like this one, with square bay windows opening on to the platform and brass lamps . . . .'

It was during the war. She had been spending a few days at
Oxcote, a small Midland town, with a friend, Eliza Miller, also a
VAD, whose father was a nonconformist minister there. They
were on leave from a spell of duty in a hospital behind the battle
area at Ypres.

'We were both pretty well fagged out. The Germans had

started using gas.' Chlorine and phosgene, she remembered. One minute of exposure to the gas and a man would be fighting for breath, blue in the face. As fluid rose in his lungs, he died of it as if by drowning. The casualties were brought in thick and fast, most of them too late, some blinded; and they were so young, many no more than eighteen or nineteen. Staring out at the quiet countryside between Fellside and Elmdon, she revisited scenes she had at times been able to forget. She had almost forgotten Eliza Miller for that matter.

'And Toria?' They would soon be in Elmdon. There wasn't much time.

'It's all rather vague to me now. Her father was the station master, a highly respected man and an elder of Mr Miller's congregation. The name wasn't Link, by the way. If it had been, I'd have put two and two together without so much mental torture. She must have married.'

'I don't think so.'

'Then she changed her name because of the scandal. I never grasped the details but some money was missing. The station master was held responsible and was dismissed after more than thirty years with the Midland Company. Apparently it was a company rule. What sticks in my memory is that he also lost his home. That's what I remember. I had boarded the train to go home and Eliza was seeing me off. "Look", she said and we saw the two of them, father and daughter, come out of the house at the end of the platform. He locked the door and they went slowly to the gate. As the train pulled out I saw them on the road, two people with nowhere to go. She has kept the sadness I felt in her then.'

Their own train was slowing down. Margot reached for the hat-box and hand luggage: Jane groped for her ticket.

'I never saw Eliza again. We had different postings. But she did mention in a letter that the man had died of a stroke. People said it was of shame and grief. A scoundrel from a neighbouring village was later charged with the theft. There was no news of the daughter. After the funeral she had left without a word to anyone.'

The sad story deserved more sensitive treatment than to be

gasped out as they hurried to change platforms. They parted with regret and with the firm intention of meeting again soon. Margot had planned to stay in town and shop, instead she took the next train to Fellside.

Toria was stacking logs in the woodshed.

'Leave those, Toria. I want to talk – but not here.'

They walked up the hill to the priory, Margot too full of all she had to say to say a word; Toria aloof in her habitual reserve. They sat down, Margot on the base of the fallen column; Toria on the grass with the remains of a buttress to lean on.

'Miss Bondless recognized you, Toria.'

She had been unprepared, but she gave no other sign than a quick intake of breath and then an added stillness.

'You know some of my secrets but you have never told me yours. You never talk about yourself. Miss Bondless thought your father was harshly treated. Would it help to tell me about it? You have nothing to be ashamed of.'

'Miss Bondless doesn't know it all. There's no one living who does know it all, except me. But I owe it to you, Miss Margot, to tell what I wouldn't breathe to anyone else.'

Her natural reticence, intensified by years of solitude, made it hard for her to begin. The story emerged slowly; there were long pauses.

Oxcote had been a sleepy little place before the war when an army camp a mile and a half away brought an increase of trade to the town and an influx of passengers to the station. Among the soldiers who came and went was a sergeant in charge of freight. Waiting for deliveries, he had time to chat to the station-master's daughter. They were drawn to each other, Toria said.

One day in January dense fog had disrupted the timetable; trains had been late all day, including the last train, due at ten minutes past ten. Her friend Steven – she could barely utter the name she had not spoken for sixteen years – had driven over from the camp to make a final enquiry about the consignment he was expecting. By that time the fog had cleared a little. Her father had been called out shortly before ten o'clock to deal with an emergency in the signal box.

As Steven marched up and down the platform she had taken

the unusual step of asking him into the warm kitchen for a cup of tea. Her father would have been agreeable, she assured Margot, but it was unbecoming to be in the house alone with a man late at night and that was one of the reasons why, later on, she had sworn there was no one with her. It was the last time they would be together: his unit was to move out the next day.

The day's takings, sometimes considerable at that busy time, were entered in the ledger and the money with a signed statement of the amount was placed in a black leather bag and padlocked, to be handed to the company collector who came out on the last train. Her father had ventured to complete the paperwork, assuming there would be no more passengers that night and had the bag all ready before he was unexpectedly called out, except – it was his one error in a lifetime of faithful service – he had not locked it.

It lay on the table of the inner room. Toria and Steven were together in the adjoining kitchen. Other couples might have taken the opportunity to draw closer still but Steven always behaved correctly (she had believed) and Toria was on edge, expecting her father's return. Having drunk a cup of tea, Steven was prepared to resume his waiting on the platform. He had promised to come back but the parting might be for a long time and there were so many who never came back. She had gone upstairs to put on her coat, intending to go out with him, and spent a minute or two in tidying her hair.

'That must have been when he did it. It was the only time he was alone. There was no one else who could have taken it.'

By the next morning he was gone before the theft was discovered. He had been clever enough not to take too much from the heavy bag, no more than a few pounds. She had been mistaken in him: he was no better than a common thief. It was partly to conceal her own folly that she had protected him by swearing that she had been alone, not because she forgave him. Disillusionment had been as hard to bear as the loss of home and reputation. There were people in the town who suspected her of taking the money though no charges were brought; disgrace and loss of home were sufficient punishment. She blamed herself for her father's ruin. She accepted the shame of being suspected as her own share of it.

'There can be no worse punishment than to be put to shame and ruin for something you didn't do.'

In telling her story she had kept her voice low: at times it was scarcely audible, but those words were spoken with sudden vehemence and she looked up with a curious defiance at variance with her previously subdued manner. 'Shame, ruin, punishment . . . .' Surely she had used such language before in speaking of some other incident. Margot had been alarmed by the suggestion of total disaster implied by the word 'ruin'. The memory was fleeting: Toria had not quite finished.

She had left Oxcote, had eventually found work on a farm and had stayed there for years until the owner died and the place was sold. The work had been hard but worse hardship followed and she had plumbed the depths. Burdons' had been a palace compared with some of the places where she had worked. There had come a time when, in desperation, she had laid out the few pounds she had kept as a safeguard on haberdashery and a pedlar's tray, to stand in the street and to be taken for a gipsy, until her tray was upset and her goods were trampled on in the dirt of a wet pavement.

Upset! Trampled on!

'Surely you don't mean that it was done deliberately?'

'Perhaps not. But the one who did it cared no more for what she'd done than if I'd been dirt under her feet.'

'A woman! I thought perhaps rough boys . . . .'

'The only rough boy was the one who helped me to pick things up.'

'I can't imagine what sort of woman would behave like that.'

'I swore I'd never speak her name again in hatred.' And as Margot listened in growing amazement, 'It pains me to speak about her at all. But I'll tell you a strange thing: I could hardly believe it, when I came here knowing nothing of what I would find, I found them both here, the two of them. I looked down from the landing and saw her warm by the fire – and the lad who helped me, he was there too.'

Ewan. And Linden! It was almost to be expected that in any calamitous situation she would be involved – she was inescapable – and yet Margot shared Toria's sense of the strangeness. Strange indeed that the three of them should come together again – by chance – in so different a setting! By chance? It would not seem so to Toria who did not believe in chance. The loss of her merchandise must have been the last straw, judging by the suppressed pain in her voice and expression. No wonder she hated Linden – had hated her long before they almost met again at Miss Burdon's. 'It nearly killed me,' she was saying. 'I lost all hope.' It would not have been surprising if she had dreamed – hopelessly one would think – of revenge. The astonishing thing was that she had found a way of achieving it. The instrument had been put into her hand: she had seen Linden steal. That it could only have happened by chance – if one believed in chance – made the complex interweaving of circumstances all the stronger.

'He didn't recognize me.' Her voice had changed. When she had spoken of Linden it was as if her entire personality darkened and she became as she had been when she first came to Langland. On that first night in her bedroom she had been at moments quite frightening. But now Margot was touched by a new softness in her voice. 'At first I didn't recognize him, he was so smartened up – and I hadn't seen his face that time, only his kind hands picking up my things as I knelt on the ground. Then when he told me – told me my own story without knowing who he was telling it to, it gave me a queer feeling. I felt like a stranger to myself.' She hesitated, a trifle embarrassed. 'You won't ever tell him, will you, Miss Margot?' And when Margot assured her earnestly that Ewan should never know from her whom he had helped, 'I don't want him to know how low I once sank.' There was a world of sadness in her dark eyes. 'I wasn't always as I am now.' The incident in the street had indeed been the last straw. From hunger and exhaustion she had collapsed and had been taken to the Elmdon workhouse hospital where she stayed as a patient and then as an indoor worker until she came to Ashlaw.

'And now you know what kind of woman you took in.'

'I know more than you do. You've suffered so much that good news may come as a shock to you.' Margot leaned closer and took Toria's hand in both of hers. 'Listen. You were not mistaken in loving Steven: he didn't take the money. It was a local man. He must have broken in when you and Steven were saying goodbye on the platform. Miss Bondless heard it from her friend Miss Miller, the clergyman's daughter, but by that time you had left and no one knew where to find you.'

Had she been too sudden? So breathtaking a change of fortune coming so unexpectedly might well be too much for Toria to bear. She didn't say a word. There was no outburst; there were no tears of joy. She pulled her hand away, not urgently, struggled to her feet, paused as if to control dizziness and turning her back on the Hall below, walked slowly away, across the cloister green, the roofless nave on her left, and through the gap where fallen stone marked the outline of the chapter house. Watching anxiously, Margot was soothed by the thought that Toria in her dark dress would not have been unfamiliar to those who had walked there when every stone was in place; her dignity would have matched theirs. Her notions of sin and penance and her capacity for suffering would not easily be surpassed.

She had left the level ground of the priory and went on up the hill until her figure was outlined against the sky. On one hand, green pasture, on the other, the deep foliage of the wood; ahead of her the steep drop to the river. And then she was gone.

Was it a final departure? Where could she go? With momentary dread Margot thought of the river. It would be like her to react to good news in some peculiar way. Taut nerves overstretched for years might suddenly snap. With Toria, anything was possible: she was unique, ungovernable by accepted rules of behaviour. Such thoughts were evidence of a certain detachment on her own part. Once perhaps she would have rushed in pursuit, picturing the swift stream and Toria drowning in it. Now she thought it unlikely that Toria would drown herself though there could have been times in the past when she was tempted to put an end to her misery. She had survived one disaster after another and should now in her gloomy fashion survive happiness, assuming that her restored faith in Steven would comfort her for the now strong possibility that he was dead.

The past half-hour had been enlightening, but it had raised new questions and one of them Margot discovered, concerned herself. What had happened to her that she could think of a person – one quite close to her – with such detachment? What had happened to the girl she used to be? Mentally retracing the inward change, she arrived at Ashlaw on a summer day when warm weather had ripened Miss Burdon's strawberries. She had filled a blue bow with rich red fruit . . . .

Naturally there had been changes before that day but the shape of things had been thrown out of joint by the wretched affair of the beads. Strange that its aftermath of suspicion, deceit, disillusion and death should have its counterpart in Toria's story. Perhaps every tragedy has its root in some little act. Such an act had altered the course of her own life. A hopeless longing seized her for the old days at Monk's Dene when there were no dark secrets and one could believe what people said. It was a longing so painful that it drove her back to the house in search of some more productive occupation.

The Hall felt unfamiliar. There emanated from the gleaming furniture, the immaculately draped curtains, the asters in the copper bowl on the hall table and from the absence of any intrusive sound, the air of well-being inseparable from a gentleman's residence in the country. Every item in every room proclaimed with confidence that all was well in the servants' quarters. There was nothing whatever for her to do.

CHAPTER XXIII

Clint Lane was not much changed. Here and there a gutter sagged and another gate had parted from its hinges. The clutter in the back-yards was if possible more dense. From its pram at No 7 came the mournful wail of a resentful baby. But pigeons cooed contentedly in their loft at No 3 and pink willowherb bloomed gallantly over the way.

Margot shared her chicken sandwiches over a pot of tea with Mrs Roper. Ben was now in the Miners' Welfare Nursing Home at Fellside and was as comfortable there as he would ever be.

'Dr Lance arranged it. Nothing's too much trouble for him.'

Ben's removal had left her free to take up baking again: she had been a cook before she married. Wedding, Christmas, christening and birthday cakes were her speciality.

'Likely they'd have asked me to make the wedding cake at the House. Bella Capfield had had a word with the housekeeper and she mentioned it to Mrs Rilston. But it was not to be – and there's the house standing empty with shutters at all the windows. Do you have to go?' Margot had rather abruptly put down her cup. 'It's been a real pleasure to see you after your foreign travels. If only your mother could have seen what a lovely young lady you've turned into.'

Her twice weekly visit to Ben coincided with the change of programme at the Fellside cinema. She was familiar with the idols of the silver screen: Norma Shearer was her favourite but she wasn't much taken with Greta Garbo. A well-bred, well-dressed young lady like Miss Margot took a lot of beating.

'So you've got Mrs Beale.' She was naturally interested in the domestic arrangements at Langland. 'She'd been hankering to go to the Hall ever since that Miss Grey came on the scene at Bainrigg. But I'm forgetting, she's a friend of yours.' She was rather put out at having given offence as Margot now showed firm signs of leaving.

'Ashlaw was always a place for gossip. Do give my best wishes to Mr Roper.' It was an heroic retreat: she would have liked to hear why Mrs Beale disapproved of Miss Grey.

Mrs Judd's clothes-line was empty but she had been ironing when Margot knocked.

'I still do a few – the doctors and Mrs Dobie now that she's not so well – but Rob and Ewan are both giving me a bit of help so I don't need to work so hard. And I've never minded ironing. You can think your own thoughts and sort things out in peace.' She motioned Margot to the rocking chair and sat down, uneasily at first and on the edge of her chair. It seemed hardly right to let the iron cool and sit talking in the middle of the day, but it was pleasant, there was no denying. Her guest was welcome and she had soon relaxed sufficiently to say, 'I found something the other day that reminded me of you, Miss Margot.'

She reached to the top drawer of the dresser and produced a brown paper bag. 'You gave these to Katie once, on her birthday.'

The two white handkerchiefs edged with tatting had been too precious ever to use.

'I'll never get over what happened to her, not as long as I live but' – she was embarrassed – 'I don't know what you'll think, but I've felt better since Nell Bowes told me what she saw. Her that lived in the end house where you can see right across the meadow. They've moved to Fellside .... She saw her, Miss Margot.'

'Her? You mean...?'

'Yes. Katie. Early one morning. She was running across the grass. "As sure as I'm sitting here", Nell said. "She was gone before I fairly took in that it was Katie, fair-haired and in pink, as she was in life. Running, she was". And then, this is the part that brought comfort to my heart, you remember how she ran, sideways like a lapwing trailing one wing? When Nell saw her, she was running straight and free.'

'Oh, Mrs Judd.' Tears sprang to Margot's eyes.

'She was gone in a flash, Nell said, meaning every word of it. Whether it really happened, it's not for me to say. Such a thing would be against all reason. Likely it was a kind of vision Nell had. Be that as it may, it reminded me that Katie has risen above her shortcomings on this earth, as we all do in the end.'

Nell Bowes's story was so engrossing as to exclude other topics. It was some time before Margot looked at her watch and apologized for interrupting the day's work.

'You'll not have heard – Emily's had her second, another boy, the image of Jo. It was Dr Lance that brought her through it. He's a wonder with babies.'

Margot mentioned that she had seen Ewan.

'Fancy him going down the pit. Choosing to, when most of them would do anything to get out of it. He's turned serious.' His mother lowered her voice respectfully. 'It was as if he took himself in hand. "You'll miss the motor bike", I warned him, seeing as it belongs to the Hall. "What's a motor bike", he says, ''in the war against capitalism? They weren't worried about motor bikes in Russia", he says. I'm not sure what he meant.'

Bella, it seemed, was losing heart: Ewan's mind was not on matrimony.

'But she likes it at the doctors'. Anyone would like working for Dr Lance. When he comes along the Lane all the bairns run out to meet him. It's as good as a tonic just to see him at the door. Let's hope he'll stay here and not try to better himself elsewhere . . . .'

Margot's leavetaking had been cordial but brief. Naturally she hoped that he would not try to better himself elsewhere. Such a thing had never occurred to her. Insensibly her brisk nononsense pace grew slower. He had always been there or close at hand, never talking much; yet his empty chair at the table or his absence from a walk had left a noticeable gap. In schooldays he had helped her with geometry and Latin. And earlier still there had been the time when she took one of the chessmen out into the garden and lost it in the long grass beyond the orchard. It was the white knight. She had spoiled the set, they told her; chessmen were not toys to be played with carelessly. The long hopeless search had ended in tears at bed-time.

And then at breakfast there it was – by magic – on her plate. They said he must have got up at first light to look for it. She smiled now, recalling the awe and delight there had been no words for. Her throat tightened at the thought of the young lady in Elmdon.

'Don't do anything silly, like getting married', Alex had said. She would never marry. Miss Crane's nephew, who had prolonged his stay in Cannes indefinitely, might as well have gone home so far as she was concerned. Girls must be self-supporting, her father had insisted (but not for a long time). It was too late for Oxford . . . .

At the far end of the lane she hesitated, wondering whether to go back and call on Mrs Dobie whose cottage was in the main street or to go on to the farm as she had intended. The dilemma was solved by the appearance of Mrs Dobie herself on the path ahead. They had met once before in the same place.

'I was sorry to hear that you haven't been well, Mrs Dobie.'

She had shrunk a little. The long black coat hung on her more loosely. Her hair had thinned and the deep-crowned black hat now touched her eyebrows. The vivid colour of the face beneath had declined into a network of red veins.

'I'm well enough to get about and that's the main thing.' She was a little short of breath. 'I heard tell that you were staying in the south of France. It's very nice there, they say.'

'You mean nicer than here?' Margot was aware of her dry scrutiny. 'I'm glad to be back where I belong.'

'There are worse places. Only' – she drew the collar of her coat more closely to her neck as if feeling cold. They stood near the chimney in the shade of the ash tree – 'there's been something gone wrong here. I've known these fields and paths ever since I could walk. You get a feeling when there's anything amiss.' She moved into the sun and sat down heavily on the grassy bank. 'Dobie and I used to come up here when we were courting. It was different then, just trees, and larks singing, and buttercups and daisies. There wasn't this feeling of death.'

For a chilling moment Margot felt it too. She glanced unwillingly at the chimney in its contortion of barbed wire. The elders and ivy at its base had been uprooted. A single green branch, thin as a wand, pointed outward through a gap in the wire.

'Two young people gone to their graves and not through illness – and the house up there empty. It's no wonder there's talk of ghosts and evil-doing. Idle talk. There's no such things as ghosts. Evil's another matter. There's no stopping that: it's bound to come in one shape or another.' She was silent, recovering her breath and then, 'It's as if Satan chooses some people to do his work. They used to call them witches, but I dare say they were just women who didn't know any better. There'll likely have been a few of them in Ashlaw. My grandmother used to tell of one that lived in a dirty-broken-down place no better than a pig-sty. It was pulled down when they opened the Lucknow Drift.' She looked away, beyond the chimney and into the blue distance. 'Yes, Ashlaw's been here a long time. Close on a thousand years, they say. People come and go – and we're well rid of her, there's no gainsaying. But it shouldn't have happened that sad way. There should have been a better way.'

'You mean the woman your grandmother told you about?'

'Her too, I dare say. She was no good either.'

Had she been rambling a little? She pushed her hat up from her forehead and eased herself upright. Margot lend a helping hand.

'If he'd married her before he died, poor lad, all this would have passed to her. We'd have been in her hands instead of his. From what Ewan Judd says she doesn't look kindly on poorer folk. He saw the way she treated that pedlar woman at the bus-stop in Elmdon, as if she hadn't a drop of pity in her veins . . . . We've had a lucky escape if you can call it that when young Mr Rilston's dead before his time.'

She was not quite steady on her feet. Margot took her arm.

'Let me walk home with you. You're tired.'

'No, love, I'll be all right and there are plenty of doors I can knock on if need be. It's old age, that's all. There's nothing else the matter with me. Keep going, the doctor said.'

'That would be Dr Lance,' Margot supposed, her tone resigned.

'Everybody's taken to him, young and old. He's more than a

good doctor – but I don't need to tell you that: you know him
well enough.'

Margot watched her until she reached the first house in safety.
Talking to Mrs Dobie was always interesting. As she walked slowly
towards the farm, her mood was thoughtful. In a chain of events
uniting all the members of her own small circle, new links were
still emerging. Had everything happened simply at random,
beginning with the freakish descent of a ball into a derelict mine
shaft? She had passed the chimney but she could feel it between
her shoulder blades; impotent now but sinister still; more sinister by far than in the unthinking days of childhood. Suppose
things did not happen at random but were designed to compose
some sort of pattern or to fulfil some purpose, as if, for example,
her entirely voluntary visit to friends in Clint Lane had not been
voluntary at all but was undertaken in obedience to a will not her
own.

Eyes averted, she was aware of Bainrigg House on her right,
secluded among trees, the life gone out of it; and she wished she
had not come this way to hear talk of death and evil-doing.

Bracken grew tall beside the farmyard gate. She pushed it
open and went slowly to the door. It was half open; there was no
one about; even the dog was somewhere else. She raised her
hand to knock and hesitated, unnerved by a stillness so deep that
a blow-fly buzzing in one of the late roses had to be listened to.
Her knock seemed an intrusion. Then feet sounded on the stairs
and slip-slopped along the stone passage. The door opened
wider. She looked down at a girl, a shy eight-year-old, fair-haired,
blue-eyed, and with a look of having come from far away.

'You must be Rosie.'

The child was fantastically dressed in a white lace curtain
covering all but a few inches of her pink cotton frock: an ancient
frilled mob-cap on her head, her mother's shoes on her feet and,
round her neck, hanging down to her waist, a long string of pearl
beads.

CHAPTER XXIV

'Where did you get those beads?'

It's impossible, she told herself. There must be dozens of similar strings of beads. They couldn't be . . . . But she was too startled to be reasonable. For her, in her present mood and in this setting, the sudden appearance of the beads was a reappearance: they had come back: they could come and go according to their own ill will. The thing hanging round Rosie's neck had been the cause of so much distress that in those first agitated moments it seemed a fetish invested with unholy power.

She pulled herself together. They were ordinary beads. The falseness of the pearls was by now only too apparent: the lustre was flaking off and had left here and there a brown blob. They had not worn well.

Her question had been too abrupt. The child backed away, her lips quivering.

'Where did you get the beads, Rosie?' she asked more gently. 'I only asked because someone I know had beads like those.'

'I found them.' The blue eyes upraised were candid like her mother's.

'When? A long time ago?'

Rosie hesitated, pulled down her lower lip with her fore-finger and nodded vaguely. For her the month's holiday from school seemed to last for ever.

'Where did you find them?'

Rosie pointed over the farmyard to the fields beyond.

'Do you know who I am?'

'Miss Humbert.'

'Shall we ask your mother if you can show me where you found the beads?'

'She's out. She's gone down to the village.'

'We'll leave her a note. You go and change your shoes.'

She pencilled a note on a leaf from her pocket diary and put it on the kitchen table. Rosie ran upstairs and came back without the beads, the lace curtain and the mob-cap and in her own shoes. They set off hand in hand, ducked through a gap in the hedge in Lucknow meadow and became friends.

'What did you mother say when you found the beads?'

'I didn't tell her.'

'It was a secret?'

'For my treasure box.' There were other things in it: a ring from a lucky potato, a gold buckle, half a china lady (the top half), the lid of a tin with a ship on it . . . . Margot was interested, remembering a similar hoard.

'You like dressing up?'

'When I'm by myself and there's nobody to play with.'

They skirted the meadow, which sloped in the direction of the village, adjoining on its further side the long back gardens of houses in Ashlaw's main street.

'I was looking for mushrooms. You have to pick them early in the morning. There weren't any but there were some apples. They'd fallen off that tree. I only picked them up, else they'd have been wasted.' She pointed to an apple tree, its branches leaning out over a garden wall. In the unmown grass by the wall there were windfalls, half eaten by rats or pecked by birds. 'And while I was picking them up I saw the beads. Here.' She parted the leaves of a clump of ragwort by a narrow iron gate.

Margot looked over it into an old-fashioned garden and recognized it. The strawberry bed was at the bottom of the slope where it just escaped the shadow of the house and shop.

'It wasn't stealing, was it? They were getting spoilt, lying there. They could have been there a long time, getting rained on.'

'It wasn't stealing. Run home and tell your mother I'll come and see her another day.' A silver sixpence changed hands. Enraptured, Rosie ran off, stopping three times to wave before she disappeared through the hedge. It had been a very special day.

For Margot too. The beads were Miss Burdon's. It was highly unlikely that another identical string could have found its way to the gate at the top of her garden. Whoever stole them had dropped or deliberately left them. On the other hand – she shrank from a discovery so momentous – to imagine that Linden, immaculate in white, would be induced to scramble through a hedge rife with sticky-jacks and nettles into a pathless field, was ludicrous – as ludicrous as to imagine that having stolen the beads, she would make so bizarre and half-hearted an attempt to return them. One could believe that she might steal, and worse – much worse – but she would never risk spoiling her clothes. In any case, Linden, who never strayed from well-trodden paths, not in any sense, would neither know that Miss Burdon had a gate opening on a field nor how to reach it. If it was the thief who left the beads among the ragwort, the thief was not Linden.

Sheer dismay brought Margot literally to her knees. She sank down on the grass, gripping the bars of the gate for support. To her shame, she was disappointed. She wanted it to be Linden. She wanted to blame her for all that had gone awry. With an additional pang she remembered that she had told Alex that Linden had stolen the beads, and it wasn't true. Oh yes, she wanted desperately to see the flaking beads as a symbol of base-ness beneath a glittering surface, to identify their falseness with Linden's.

And sadder still – she had been quick to believe that Katie had not taken the beads. But she must have done. She might have made a confused attempt to return them. Could she in her flight from the shop have hidden them in Church Lane, retrieved them (though dazed with fright), found her way to the back of Miss Burdon's garden and dropped them by her gate? It seemed unlikely that she would associate this gate, if she knew of it, with the shop in the main street. The whole enterprise, weird as it was, seemed too rational to be Katie's.

Her forehead on the iron bars, Margot saw between them the long slope of the garden; at the bottom, beyond the strawberry bed, the flagged path outside the scullery door and, further along, another door giving entry to the back shop. That had been Toria's territory. With relief she remembered that Toria had actually seen Linden take the beads. Her own assumption that Linden was to blame had rested on Toria's word.

Margot turned her face from the warm sun but it could not dispel the shock that set her shivering nor free her from the sensation of being plunged into sudden darkness. Suppose Toria had lied: the lie all the more convincing because part of her story was true? She could have stepped into the shop to rest for a few minutes in the shade and stand motionless among the bales of flannelette sheeting. She could have seen Katie come and go, leaving the shop empty. And then a few long strides would take her to the counter to snatch the beads, take them up the garden, drop them over the gate and come back to clean the scullery window, unnoticed, ignored, despised and rejected – the words would have been familiar to her – having doomed Katie to death and altered several lives.

But why? To incriminate Linden. 'The only comfort I've had is knowing that I could ruin her', she had said; and later, only a few hours ago, 'There's no punishment worse than to be put to shame for something you didn't do'. The similarity between events in Oxcote and in Ashlaw was now more striking. Perhaps in seeking to humiliate Linden for an earlier offence, Toria had drawn on her own experience, cherishing her secret for use when the time came.

To Margot, so intense a hatred seemed as crazy as Katie's fear, or for that matter, though briefly, as Alex's love. There was something about Linden that had a disturbing effect on others. Were there really people who served as instruments of evil like the witches of old, through no choice of their own? Such a person would be distinctive, in some way different. Linden had always been different. It was her difference that had intrigued the girls at school, including, more than most, herself. It was an uncomfortable thought.

Which of the three had taken the beads? Linden because she wanted them: Toria because she wanted to ruin Linden: Katie who wanted nothing in her entire life except to be safe?

Walking home through Priory Wood, Margot came to a decision. For her the incident was closed. Somehow she must put it from her mind. The questions it raised must remain unanswered.

Nothing could be done without reviving unhappiness, and caus-
ing more. The homely fields were now haunted, so that a little
girl gathering mushrooms in the early light became a ghost, and
unimaginably strange things were being said in the village.
People whose lives were drab and dangerous were surely entitled
to enrich them by telling stories of weird happenings in their
own countryside. It had always been so. The stories would last for
a while: they would change in the telling and in time there would
be no one left who knew how they began.

When she closed her curtains that night, Toria had not come
back. The next day brought no sign of her. But on the third day
she was heard in the woodshed, stacking logs as if she had never
left off. She was best left alone. While engaged in so blameless an
occupation, Margot thought with dawning cynicism, even Toria
could do no harm – though with Toria one could never tell. A
quiet woman who came down her crooked stair at dawn to kindle
fire in the cold grate and climbed at nightfall to her narrow
room, she had made the Hall her dwelling place and had
become part of it.

She herself must find something else to think about – something absorbing and of an entirely different kind. In this she was
to be, almost at once, completely successful.

CHAPTER XXV

Her father arrived home the next day. On the morning he left, he had heard news in Elmdon which made him cut short the conference in Derbyshire. His old enemy Bedlow had died.

'Yes, the old blackguard has gone. It's strange, Margot, but I shall miss him. Couldn't stand the man, but his going leaves a gap. He was like no one else – and a good thing too, but he had guts and the tenacity of a bloodhound. The funeral is tomorrow. Could you take a look at my things, black tie and so on?'

'You're going to the funeral?'

'It's the least I can do, not to let enmity go beyond the grave.'

Margot got out and brushed the funeral trappings and saw him off the next morning. Her surprise at his unexpected respect for the old monster was nothing to her amazement at the news he brought back late in the afternoon. She had gone out to meet him as he got out of the car.

'I can't get over it. You won't believe this. All these years and I had absolutely no idea.' He had dropped his hat on the ground and was staring at it absent-mindedly. Margot picked it up. 'Of course there was no reason why we should have known. The situation had existed for years before we came to this district.'

'Father! Tell me what has happened. I command you.'

'Well, wait till you hear. Let's go inside. We'd better sit down. It concerns you too in a way.'

'Then it isn't to do with old Bedlow?' It was disrespectful now that he was dead but she had never heard him spoken of in any other way.

'Oh, but it is. Very much so.'

234

She marched him into the sitting-room and sat him down.

'Now. Tell.'

'I could do with a cup of tea, by the way.'

'Not until . . . .'

'Right. The fact is that Bedlow is – or was – Lance's grandfather.'

'But . . . .'

'Yes. He has a grandfather in Berwick, but people have two grandfathers.'

'His mother's father!'

'He fell out with his daughter when she married. No one knows why. Nothing unusual about that: he fell out with everybody. That's why I'm glad I went to the funeral: considering how well known he was, there weren't many people there. Quinian of course, and Andrews. Laverborne was otherwise engaged, needless to say. It was a surprise to see the Pelmans. We left the cemetery together. Pelman had to go to a case but Lance told me all about it. There had been no contact between his father and grandfather since his mother's funeral, but Lance has been looking after him during his illness. He's coming this evening, by the way.'

The tea was refreshing. He wondered as she refilled his cup why Margot should be so pleased that Bedlow was Lance's grandfather. She seemed quite captivated by the idea – and how like her mother she was. Sarah's eyes had lit up in the same way when he first told her that he loved her. Mother and daughter had the same capacity for unalloyed happiness. It was a long time since he had seen Margot smiling to herself. The months of sunshine with Jane Bondless had done her good.

His own mood was pensive. The funeral had marked the end of an epoch. His contests with Bedlow had been fought with vigour. The antagonists had come from opposite corners of the ring with the glint of battle in their eyes, equal in determination and with the same inability to deal the knock-out blow. Remembering their set-to about the chimney, he saw it in a new light. Bedlow's offensive remarks about 'your lad' were those of a grandfather whose own lad's picture had not appeared in the newspaper. He was entitled to feel annoyed. Well, he was gone;

and he himself was tired, his confidence shaken. Sarah would have understood.

'I'll go up and change,' he said, 'and perhaps have forty winks.'

He had scarcely gone when she heard the car and rushed to the window. Almost at once Lance was in the room. In all the years as they grew up together they had never been alone in this special kind of way, so that she saw him afresh as if for the first time – yet with the familiarity of all that was dear in their shared lives. He was a distinguished-looking man – Jane was right – with an air of summing up situations and knowing how to deal with them, especially this one.

'Lance! I'm so glad ... but sorry to hear about your grandfather.'

'I can see how sorry you are. You're positively beaming.' He came nearer. 'Thank God you haven't changed. You always did blurt things out and then wish you hadn't. Let me look at you.' He took her hands and drew her closer, well pleased with what he saw.

'You've been a long time in coming to look at me .... I was rather hurt. But I didn't know about your grandfather's illness – or even about your grandfather. Father thought you might be in love with a girl in Elmdon when you spent so much time there. Oh, I'm sorry!' Dreadful thought: the existence of an ailing grandfather need not preclude that of an attractive girl.

'Are there any girls in Elmdon?' His voice was tender. He drew her closer still and stroked her hair. 'Dearest Meg.' He gently touched her cheek. 'You must know, there's no one but you.'

'I didn't know. How could I?'

'You've had long enough to find out. I've loved you since you were six – or earlier – since long before I knew the meaning of the word.'

'You never said ....'

'I'm saying it now. I've always loved you. The condition is serious, incurable, life-long, terminal.'

'It's such a comfort to be loved by a doctor. In that grisly kind of way.'

'Being without you is certainly like an illness. This last year has been the worst I've lived through, though the year before that was pretty bad.'

'I'm glad you didn't bring this up when I was six. I wouldn't have felt so marvellously happy now if I'd known for years.' To be held close in his arms was like the homecoming after a difficult journey. 'I've been rather slow in realizing how much I need you, now more than ever.'

'You've got over Miles?'

'It was a sad dream.' She moved away. 'A strange sad interval, never quite real. It could never have been like this. But how blessed I've been. Both of you so good.'

'It seemed only too real to me.' He joined her on the window-seat. 'He had all the qualities I haven't got. Most important, charm. Miles had it, and Alex. You'd better face up to it: I have no charm.'

'You don't need it, whatever it is.' He seemed to her almost – in fact, quite perfect. She must have been blind all these years. 'What is it exactly?'

'How should I know? Charm is indescribable.'

'If you did know, you'd take it up seriously and make a thorough study of it. I wouldn't see you for months, perhaps years. I couldn't bear it. As a matter of fact' – she became serious herself – 'being charmed and spellbound can actually happen to people, not only in fairy tales.'

'You've experienced it?'

'I'll tell you sometime. I have so much to tell you.'

There would be plenty of time. She was no longer restless. Her love, the natural flowering of an early affection into delight in his tenderness, his kiss, his understanding, had already distanced the distress of recent years. They went out into the garden. All very well to be wary of witchcraft but the evening was enchanted; in its softened light the Hall resumed its rightful air of picturesque antiquity. The garden was flower-scented. The whole world had changed.

'I've waited for this so long,' he said. 'I couldn't tell you sooner, that you're all the world to me, I mean. When your family came to Monk's Dene it was as if a new life began. I can just about remember how my father and I grubbed along before that. Your people were so good to me that I was always scared stiff of doing anything to upset them. It would have been overstepping the mark to try to monopolize their daughter. But it was tough – having to watch you fall in love with someone else.'

'I promise never to do it again.'

Would she have been so happy now in Lance's arms, so deeply content, if she had not known the anguish of the earlier love? There seemed nothing more to wish for in the present hour, their first together, as the flush of sunset faded and the harvest moon appeared. They talked, were silent, talked again.

'Tell me about your unknown grandfather.'

'It was an odd business. I soon cottoned on to the fact that he was the enemy in your father's battles with the company. I couldn't remember ever having seen him so it was easy to keep quiet about him. No need to warn my father to do the same: he never mentioned him.'

'But you became friends?'

'He suddenly surfaced at the time of Katie's death. He'd read about it in the *Gazette* and seen my name – and came up with the offer to pay all my medical fees, board and lodgings. Naturally I went to see him. We got on rather well. My mother was barely mentioned. Heaven knows what had gone wrong. I think he felt more than he was capable of expressing. Communication was one of the things he hadn't learned.'

In the old man's last days they had become closer.

'I have something to confess,' Lance said. 'But first, can you give me your solemn word that you love me for my own sake and *for no other reason?*'

'No matter what the confession is about?'

'That's the whole point. No matter what.'

'It's a fearful risk but you have my solemn word.'

'It's embarrassing. I haven't yet got used to the idea. The fact is – I'm going to be alarmingly rich. The old man has left me everything: stocks and shares, investments in coal, iron, steel, railways, shipping, rows of houses. I may be exaggerating but there's an awful lot of it. You're laughing at me but it's been a shock, I can tell you.'

'Never mind.' Margot kissed him again. 'It's a disability you can't help. We must put up with it. For some women your wealth might even make up for your lack of charm.'

'You're taking it well – and it certainly will transform the practice. We'll be able to take on an assistant – and a dispenser – and make life easier for the district nurse. And that's just a start. I've been lucky,' he added solemnly. 'If my grandfather had died sooner I might have attracted the attention of Linden. Even now I don't feel safe.'

But the Greys, he thought, had left Gordon Street and possibly the district. The only intruder was Edward who came quietly down the path to the alcove in the balustrade where they sat.

'When I see a man with his arm round my only daughter, I am bound to ask his intentions.' Lance blushed and got to his feet. Margot drew her father to the empty place: his voice had been husky. 'Your mother would have been overjoyed. It was her dearest wish, years and years ago. You were like a son to her, Lance, and to me.' He cleared his throat. 'And even if I'd known who your grandfather was, it wouldn't have made a ha'porth of difference. If you stick to your guns as well as he did, you'll not do too badly. At any rate, I'm glad you've both come to your senses at last.'

'I came to mine when I heard that all the bairns in Clint Lane rush out to meet him. There must be some reason, I thought. Something I've overlooked.'

'They also rush out to meet the refuse cart and the fresh-herring woman,' Lance reminded her.

No plans could be made until Alex came home. Both were content to prolong the serenely happy days of their engagement until the spring. Margot became a familiar passenger in the doctor's car and claimed that there were some children who rushed out to see the lady whom the doctor was going to marry. In more than one stricken household she made herself useful by nursing the baby or minding the toddlers while Lance saw the invalid. On one special occasion she took charge of four while their mother was delivered of twins. When she was called in and saw Lance triumphant with a baby in each arm, it seemed to her so touching that she burst into tears.

'I'm getting soft,' she said, 'like Ewan.'

'And for once I'm not in a position to give you a handkerchief.'

On the way home they talked as usual about their own future home. Several houses in the district might be suitable or could be adapted to their needs, money (it had become a refrain) being no object. The most desirable was tacitly eliminated. Only much later when they had found the house they wanted, did Lance mention that Bainrigg House would make an ideal convalescent home for miners and their families.

'I think the old man would be pleased to be remembered in that way. Towards the end he talked about his earlier days as a trapper in the pit at the age of seven, a frightened child sitting hour after hour in the dark. His job was to open and close the trapdoor to control the current of air in order to sweep off gas from the coal face. From then on he never stopped working until almost the end. He can't have spent more than a pittance on himself and never forgot the early hardships.'

It was agreed that he would have approved of a Bedlow Convalescent Home.

Meanwhile they continued house-hunting with enthusiasm gradually yielding to despair and as months passed, to panic.

The Cedars, a well-built Edwardian house on the Elmdon road faced the wrong way. Kitchen premises were flooded with afternoon sunshine while the living-rooms languished in shade. A converted inn between Ashlaw and Fellside was suitably situated. Originally a cruck house, it had a wealth of oak beams and stone corbels but no electricity, and septic tanks were anathema to Lance, while to Margot, still smarting from the early days at Langland, the prospect of reconstruction and extension was a fearsome one. A villa for sale in Ashlaw, a blatantly new structure of red brick, was unappealing and deserved to be pulled down for defacing the village.

'It isn't going to be easy.' Lance stated the obvious. 'Perhaps we should build.'

'It will take ages.'

A highly desirable site could be purchased on farmland and near the church. They would have to make up their minds quickly as the farmer was anxious to sell. But they hesitated.

Despite her reluctance to repeat the Langland ordeal, Margot would have preferred an old house to one visibly taking shape and offering daily opportunities to regret wrong decisions.

'In a few months,' Lance said, 'we shall be married and home-less. And on no account—'

'... Will we seek or accept accommodation at Langland Hall.' It was not the first time he had said it and Margot's endorsement was heartfelt.

But when winter set in with heavy rain and early snowfall, every house looked drab and uninviting except – perversely – the Hall with its splendid fires, thick carpets and heavy curtains. The search must be postponed to the spring.

The mayor's charity ball in November was as glittering an occasion as Elmdon could produce. It was held in the banqueting hall of the castle and as Alex liked to say, all Elmdon's youth and chivalry were generally there. He would miss it this year and so avoid an encounter he would not have enjoyed.

Margot had given thought to her dress. Evening gowns were long again. From her experience in Cannes she had learned the effectiveness of simplicity and her unadorned midnight blue had a slim and youthful elegance. She and Lance had no sooner sat down at one of the small tables encircling the dance floor than Lance was drawn into a group of medical men and she was left alone, free for a few minutes to look round for old friends.

The announcement of Mr and Mrs Barford riveted her attention on the couple who were shaking hands with the mayor and mayoress. As if by fateful magnetism they were drawn to her side of the hall and to a table just beyond hers. Impossible to avoid a greeting.

'Linden!'

'Margot!'

Each achieved the feminine feat of taking in the other's appearance at a glance; nor did Margot fail also to take in that of Mr Barford, a highly polished and well-groomed young man with dark hair and with a tendency to look round the room and especially at the dancers in an exploratory way.

'I heard that you had left Elmdon.'

'We're living in London. I've been spending a few days here with Mother.' There could not be awkwardness in Linden's presence, not at least on such an occasion as this: her manners were so beautiful. Now, conscious of a touch of impatience on his part, she introduced her companion.

'You haven't met my stepson, Godfrey. This is Margot Humbert, Godfrey. You remember – from Langland Hall.'

'How do you do?' Margot succeeded in concealing her bewilderment.

'How do you do, Miss Humbert?' Godfrey made no attempt to conceal his admiration.

'I'll sit with Margot for a minute, if I may. Do go and dance.'

'You'll want to talk. Until later perhaps?' He made a little bow and left them.

'They ought to have announced us as Mrs Barford and Mr Godfrey Barford.' The lack of correctness was provoking but not to be dwelt on.

For once Linden was the more talkative. In the three years since they had last met, Margot's thoughts of her had become so hopelessly complex that no single thread suitable for conversation could be disentangled: she simply didn't know what to say. 'So you married Godfrey's father', was too obvious as was the reason for so prudent a choice.

'You are still at Langland? It must have been a relief to get away from Ashlaw.'

'You didn't like Ashlaw?'

Linden's long lashes veiled her eyes for an instant as if she might swoon with distaste.

'I hadn't been used to such a place or such people.' Safely established in Belgravia and with the support of millions of cinema-goers, she need not hesitate to deplore so uncongenial a district and its coarse inhabitants. 'We knew, the very first day we came to lunch with your parents, that the place was impossible socially. Oh, you know I don't mean Monk's Dene: one felt perfectly safe there.'

'The very first day? I'm surprised that you ever came again.'

'You mustn't think me unappreciative of the very pleasant times we had with you.' But later there had been objectionable incidents, typical, she supposed of a district where there were so many ignorant working people. 'I don't know why but I felt a hostility. Perhaps the people there are always resentful of strangers. Once when I walked down from Bainrigg to send a telegram for Mrs Rilston, women were gossiping on their doorsteps. When they saw me they called to their children and went in and shut the doors. It seemed deliberate. I felt them looking at me as I passed the windows. So rude.'

She fingered a bracelet and looked at her rings. They included a handsome emerald. Margot thought her appearance just a little overdone, especially as to jewellery. Necklaces were not then fashionable and Linden's flashed rather too blatantly.

She murmured something about the people of Ashlaw meaning no harm.

'I'm not so sure.' She marvelled at the change in Margot: she had been such a quaint little thing, such a chatterbox too. 'You may not have heard; I didn't want it known but it doesn't matter now: I was attacked one night, at Bainrigg, by two ruffians.'

Margot, silently hazarding a guess as to their identity, looked suitably concerned though judging by Linden's sedate manner, little harm had been done. Whatever the Judds had intended, their intention had evidently misfired like every other attempt to put things right in a situation without precedent where there were no rules for guidance.

'Fortunately Miles was there to look after me. In fact it brought us together . . . .'

'I wonder' – Margot's attitude had hardened – 'if you had become associated in people's minds with Katie.'

'Katie? That crazy girl. But why should they?'

'You were known to be the last person to see her alive that day when you walked down from Bainrigg towards the chimney.' She had looked at Linden repeatedly in the past, with pleasure, admiration, doubt, suspicion and with unacknowledged dread. But she had never looked at her as she did now: directly, deliberately, straight in the eyes. They were beautiful eyes, of shape and size perfectly proportionate to a beautiful face, in colour, between blue and grey, overhung by long dark lashes under delicately arched brows. Whether from some quality of the light or lack of

it – from the golden lanterns, or from some slight change in the
configuration of the face, she saw them as not merely heavy-
lidded but curiously hooded. It occurred to her that she had
never seen them brighten or soften or kindle with anger or fun.
They reflected nothing: responded to nothing. With Linden the
act of seeing was little more than physical: she saw what was there
but only as it concerned herself. So that in any real sense she had
not seen Katie at all, ever.

'You said you hadn't seen her by the chimney. Remember? But
I think you must have done.'

Linden's raised eyebrows and the faintest possible suggestion
of a shrug, no more than a movement of the shoulders, implied
that about an incident so remote as to be almost beyond recol-
lection, she had nothing to say. Margot persisted.

'What a dreadful thing it would have been if you had actually
seen her die when you might have been able to save her.'

The devious remark brought a swift response.

'How could I save her when she was already . . . .' They both
started, Margot quite violently, as with a blare of saxophones the
band burst into a jaunty rendering of 'Here we go gathering nuts
in May'. The dancers were changing partners in a Paul Jones.
The rest of the sentence was lost, but Linden's lips continued to
move. Perhaps she too was changing her tune. The dancers
regrouped to the tune of a waltz.

'Whenever she saw me she ran away.'

The music was softer now but Margot wasn't listening. It didn't
matter what Linden said. She had seen Katie in her last desperate moments and had done nothing, said nothing. Linden never
did anything: she simply existed as she was. What lay beneath the
smooth surface Margot would never know, only suspect the
absence of anything but a squalid self-interest. It was Katie who
had sensed cruel indifference and had known what it signified; it
was as if she knew that where heart and soul were lacking the
void they left might harbour a malign spirit which, finding an
emptiness, occupied it. Katie alone had felt its presence from the
beginning, from the first instant of their meeting under the pear
tree; had recognized it and fled from it.

'She always behaved so strangely. One didn't know what she

would do next. I had never come into contact with half-wits and such people. You didn't mind: you were such a good little girl. Do you remember how shocked you were about my not saying my prayers? So quaint.' She smiled. Her smile no longer charmed. 'You were so earnest that I tried it – and kept on trying. It was no trouble – and it worked.'

'How do you know?'

'I prayed for one particular thing. Nothing else. That was all I wanted.'

'And you got it.' It sparkled in the necklace, gleamed in the heavy ivory satin of her dress and bolstered her superb confidence.

'Arthur is very generous – and to Mother too. She has a delightful flat in Canon's Walk. You know, those Queen Anne houses overlooking the park.'

A dancing couple turned their heads and smiled: Godfrey and his partner. Margot's heart warmed to him as to a condemned man granted a merciful reprieve.

'And I see you are engaged.'

'To Lance.'

'I'm not surprised. And you won't mind the rigours of a doctor's life' – and, mindful of the correct thing, to say – 'I hope you will be very happy.'

Judging that the conversation had been of the required length, she rose to go: a beautiful, successful woman whom Margot, that quaint child, had so ardently admired. She watched her as she joined Godfrey at their table. Presently to the tune of 'They didn't believe me', they glided into a slow foxtrot. Linden was smiling. It seemed to Margot that nothing could save her from the desolation of remaining always as she was then: lacking sympathy and imagination, she also lacked the ability to change.

In the ladies' room later in the evening, Linden studied her reflection in a mirror, carefully removed a soupçon of lipstick and decided to sell the necklace.

Margot never saw her again.

CHAPTER XXVI

Margot pushed open the window so as to be sure of hearing Lance's arrival and settled down to wait. He had telephoned that he must see her: it was important. The other two went on talking. They had been talking ever since Alex came home in December and it was now May. His skin had lost its putty-coloured colonial pallor, he had shaved off his assistant district officer's moustache, had become very friendly with Angela Bavistock and was in every way his old self, only more so, as Lance said.

There had been a good deal to talk about, including the news in January that Mr Ainsley, agent for the Fellside Coal Company, had resigned in order to take up an appointment in Australia. As it happened, the Humberts had not heard the news when Lance arrived at the Hall one morning, hustled Margot into the sitting-room and closed the door.

'Now listen carefully. This is going to interest you.'

'Lance! You've heard of a house.'

'I have heard of a house. I don't know how you will feel about it. It has certain features that you like . . . .'

'You're being very cautious. Old or new?'

'Not new.'

'I have a feeling you're holding something back. Go on. What are the features I might like?'

'Spacious – a family home – drawing-dining-morning rooms – two kitchens. Five bedrooms – an old dairy . . . .'

'It does sound promising.'

'A large garden – an orchard . . . .'

'Exactly right. Rather like our beloved Monk's Dene. Where...?'

'It is our beloved Monk's Dene, my darling. The Ainsleys will be moving out – in April or May at the latest. I say.' He had been too blunt: she was pale and speechless. 'It is what you want, isn't it?'

'More than anything in the world. I never even dreamed that it was possible. And you?'

'Sixty seconds from breakfast-table to surgery – or less. What more could I ask? But seriously, Meg, it does seem like an answer to prayer. Monk's Dene has been home to both of us. Where else could we live?'

It was harder than ever to part. Not until every conceivable advantage had been aired and every resource of language expressive of satisfaction deployed, did Lance reluctantly tear himself away, leaving Margot to pass on the news.

The repercussions of Mr Ainsley's resignation were so favourable that according to Alex they should all be grateful to him for having married an Australian. The board of directors had no hesitation as to whom they wanted as his successor.

'I shall have to think it over.' Edward's air of giving careful thought to the offer was a dismal failure: he was plainly delighted and in time heard to admit that he had been hasty in leaving. He was to take up the appointment on the first of June. The wedding was to be in the same month.

Alex, fresh from Kenya, had made an immediate impact upon the Hall. He approved: the former morgue was now not only a home giving a man the space he needed, its potential usefulness had scarcely been tapped. -Tapping would make possible an extension of land use, more cultivation, a small pedigree herd. There would be no problem about extending the lease: as a substantial shareholder in the coal company, Lance would be given a seat on the board and would scotch any attempt to buy the Langland estate or, at the very least, see that it was not put to unsuitable use. In any case they were safe until 1938 and after that could reasonably count on another ten or twenty years without change. The older mines would eventually be worked out: slag heaps would give way to green pastures and there would be a return to agriculture and a revival of rural life.

Meanwhile, (Edward breathed again; gratified though he was

by Alex's change of heart, he needed time to adjust to it) there would be divers cultural activities at the Hall: music, exhibitions of local artists' work.

On this May morning they were discussing a series of lectures on local features. Mining for example. His father would open the course with a lecture on the legacy of ancient forests, black diamond, coal: source of all wealth; most precious of all minerals, the power on which all industry depended. In mining there existed both tragedy and poetry as in great works of art.

It soon became apparent, again to his father's relief, that it would be Alex who would be giving the lectures on coal.

'And I'd tone it down a bit,' he advised, mindful of the possible audience.

'Don't worry, Dad. I'll underpin it with statistics and stark facts.'

They were outlining the first paragraph and hadn't heard the car.

Knowing that Lance would not want to get involved, Margot went out to join him.

'Alex is amazing,' Lance said as they drove into town. 'Imagine his persuading the Bavistocks to take him on after fobbing them off for more than three years – and at a higher salary because he is now more experienced.'

'Angela is the apple of her father's eye, remember.' Not that Alex's persuasive powers were in need of support.

'He'll come down to earth: she'll see to that.'

'Scarcely any of it will happen. Dreams aren't meant to take shape.' It was surely a gift to bring colour and light to mundane reality even if the glow could not last. Clouds had lifted in the past few months. After the long silence everyone was talking again. 'Is it because we are so happy that other people seem happier too? Everything rose-coloured for a change?'

'Not everybody. That's one of the things I have to tell you. But first, prepare for a pleasant surprise.'

The Ainsleys had collected the last of their things and the house was now empty. He would collect the keys from the house-agent in Elmdon and they would take possession that very afternoon and explore the house, every inch of which they knew and could find blindfold. As he had patients to see in Hope Carr, Margot said that she would make her own way back to Ashlaw.

'You had something else to tell,' Margot reminded him as they were about to part in Elmdon. 'You know of someone who isn't happy?'

'An old friend I came across in the Masonic Nursing Home. She asked after you and is anxious to see you. She hasn't much time left . . . .'

'Miss Burdon?'

The meagre figure in the narrow white bed was barely recognizable as the buxom woman who had once loomed so large.

'Only a few minutes.' The nurse placed a chair. 'It's Miss Humbert, dear.'

'Margot.' The voice had not changed. Still deep, it emanated from the wasted body as if it didn't belong there.

'Lance told me that you were here. I'm sorry you've been so poorly.'

The fleshless cheeks and sunken red-rimmed eyes, together with the falsely bright manner of the nurse, were ominous.

'You and Lance. So suitable. I should give you a wedding present but I'm not in a position . . . .' She paused for breath. 'Only best wishes. I made a boudoir cap for your mother when she married.'

'I still have it, Miss Burdon.' The monstrous creation of lawn, lace and satin ribbons had been a problem when she dealt with her mother's things. It fitted none of the categories of disposable objects – was too grand, too well preserved in its original tissue paper to be consigned to the dustbin. 'And it's as good as new.'

'Happier days!' Her eyes wandered as if in search of something she had forgotten, to the door, the edge of the screen, to Margot. She stirred uneasily on her rampart of pillows. Against their insistent whiteness her face was grey, her nose thin and sharp. 'Such a surprise to see Lance again and I thought, there's Margot. I'll tell Margot. Now that your mother is gone, there's no one else to tell. I've thought of it so much. For years.'

'You want me to do something for you?'

'Not now. Not until I'm gone, too. I can't face any more . . . .
If anything could be done about it, I should be the one ... but I
can't.' Her mouth drooped. She whispered. 'It's no good. I
can't.'

'There's no need for you to do anything except try to get well.'

'After I'm dead, it won't matter then. If I tell you, Margot, you
can decide what to do. They've been on my mind so long.'

Some inkling of what they might be filled Margot with alarm.
Was Miss Burdon by virtue of her feebleness and distress about to
trap her once more in the maze she had wandered through, left
behind and for the past few months forgotten?

'Do you remember the beads that were missing – and all the
fuss? It made me ill, you know. I had to stay indoors, a prisoner
in my own house, but I could hear what they were shouting
outside – and my windows were broken . . . .'

'It isn't good for you to talk. The nurse said—'

'I think I suffered a slight stroke and should have called in the
doctor but I soldiered on. After they went away it was quiet and
dark with the shutters closed.' She had had ample time to go
through her stock which was to be sold to a travelling agent for a
cut-price firm in Manchester. 'All good quality. And that was how
I found them.'

The silence was long enough to penetrate even Miss Burdon's
limited awareness. Margot was aware of her growing uneasiness
but could feel no sympathy.

'You found the beads and didn't tell?' she said at last.

'I dared not tell. Not after what happened.'

After what had happened to Katie? Was she thinking of that or
of saving her own thick skin? At the sight of her, a poor sick creature near her end, Margot's anger cooled. She forced herself to
speak quietly.

'What did you do with them?'

'I didn't know what to do. There they were in their box on the
shelf. I must have put them away and forgotten, then looked for
them on the counter.' She dared not harbour them in the house
or shop and in her panic had wanted only to be rid of them and
escape the consequences of having made 'all the fuss' for nothing. 'I took them up the garden and dropped them over the gate.

No one ever goes there but if they were found it would look as if . . . .' Her eyelids drooped.

'As if the person who stole them had dropped them there? You wanted us to go on thinking that Katie had taken them?'

'What else could I do?' Slow tears found their way down her grey cheeks. 'I was so frightened and I've been afraid ever since in case it was somehow found out that I had made a mistake. But now that I've told you, it's a weight off my mind. You will know what to do.' However sluggish her conscience, however shallow her remorse, her distress at least was genuine. 'After all, that's what it was, wasn't it? Just a mistake. A simple mistake.'

With an effort Margot took her hand.

'Yes,' she said as gently as she could. 'It was a mistake and you have suffered for it.'

She was not the only one to have suffered. It should have been heartening to know that neither Katie, Toria nor Linden had stolen the beads. No one had stolen the beads. But as she left the nursing home, Margot was too deeply absorbed in the implications of Miss Burdon's confession to be other than disheartened, however perversely. It was small comfort to know that untimely deaths, sad partings and bitter misunderstandings had resulted, not from a theft, but from the mere suspicion of a theft, to feel that she had been lured into a wild-goose-chase of a particularly painful, indeed tragic kind, and that all her thinking had been based on error.

At the station she bought a ticket and having remembered nothing of the journey, left the train at Ashlaw. She was the only person to alight and the road to the village a quarter of a mile away was deserted. Hawthorns were in bloom, hedges adrift in white cow-parsley. She walked slowly, still in the abstraction of a sleep-walker.

And then – was it the air, fresh and fragrant – or the change of scene – or the movement? She could not have told at what point or by what mingling of memory, deduction and intuition it dawned on her that in confessing her mistake, Miss Burdon had confessed to the wrong mistake. Enlightenment came with a mental picture of pearl beads draped on black velvet. Miss

Burdon had forgotten, as she herself had forgotten, that there had been two strings of beads.

'Shall we try the effect?' She remembered the rather pathetic girlishness in Miss Burdon's voice as she opened the cabinet. Linden had arranged the beads inside. But they were not to be kept there on display, not until the new stock had been rearranged. Afterwards, having put them away, Miss Burdon would look for the other string on the counter and fail to find it. And then – it could have been weeks later – alone in the dim light behind the shutters, taking stock, she would find the beads in their case on the shelf. 'A slight stroke', a gap in consciousness, solitude, worry over the loss of her business would account for much more than a lapse of memory.

The beads in Rosie's treasure box were not the stolen beads. The pieces slipped back into place; the puzzle was once more as nearly complete as it could ever be with one important piece still missing. It was wrong to think of it as a return to normality. All the same, Margot's spirits rose. Knowing full well that it would mean concealing half of the truth and misrepresenting the other half with the duplicity she had so strongly condemned in Linden, she also knew what must be done.

When Miss Burdon died (poor Miss Burdon, her mistake was pardonable though her treatment of Katie was not) the Judds must be told that the beads had been found. Katie's name would be cleared. It would be known throughout Ashlaw and beyond that Miss Margot had heard it from old Sally Burdon's own lips as she passed away. The Judds and their neighbours would appreciate a death-bed confession. Its aura of drama would be similar to that of ghosts and evil-doing. Evil had been done, as Mrs Dobie had perceived, though it might never be known by whom.

In exonerating Katie, she would also be exonerating two others, one of whom would know that the beads had not been found. It would be interesting to see Toria's reaction to Miss Burdon's confession. Linden had slipped gracefully out of earshot. Should the news ever reach her, it would be received with composure – and politely, of course. Which of them was guilty? In her unique role of judge and jury, in the absence of evidence, knowing them both, Margot was almost sure that it was not Linden, who had other ways of acquiring personal adornments – and of a more expensive kind.

It was Toria whom she simultaneously condemned and pardoned. In her most wretched state she had seemed to find a means of retribution. Her thinking had been tortuous and incomplete: she had not foreseen – how could she? – that whoever suffered from her action it would not be Linden. Toria on the other hand had doomed herself to pangs of conscience it would be hard to assuage, even though night after night she climbed the crooked stair to her narrow room and prayed for forgiveness – which very likely she did. Yet she had not started the landslide. The first pebble had been dislodged when Linden brought her to her knees on a muddy pavement in Elmdon years ago.

And Katie? There came the rustle of wings in the hedge, the distant clang of the church bell. Margot half-turned as she had often done to find Katie just behind her, frail and light as one of the flowering stems that trembled as she passed. For an instant she was almost there again, her lips parting in a cautious smile; her eyes frightened: a changeling in the wicked mortal world. But as long as Ashlaw folk told stories by the fire it was Katie who would be remembered with regret by those who mourned the death of innocence. Long after Rosie Larson grew up and left the farm, the ghost of a girl who went to her death wrongly accused would haunt Lucknow Meadow.

In its long history Ashlaw had no doubt acquired its share of shameful secrets. She herself held one minute morsel of secret knowledge, a tiny fragment to add to the sum of wrongs as numerous as the grains of sand on all the sea-shores of the world. The notion intrigued her. It confirmed her sense of belonging.

And after all it was a village where the most active life went on under the surface. A hundred fathoms beneath her feet men were toiling in the dark while she stood waist-deep in flowers. A lark was singing; lilac in Larsons' garden would be coming into bloom. The contrasts could never be reconciled, nor ever forgotten, but perhaps they could be shared. There was so much to do. There was nowhere else in the world where she wanted to be.

Margot drew a deep breath and discovered the enchantment

of maytime in a country lane, hedges white with blossom and Queen Anne's lace. The effect was bridal. She remembered that she was gloriously happy; knew that Lance would not be far away.

In the garden at Monk's Dene, the pear tree had shed its petals on the path. Wild roses would soon be flowering on the high wall. It was as if the years of exile had never been: as if there had been no interruption in the familiar cycle of seasons, no threat to the secure sequence of days. That was an illusion, but absence had served to intensify the happiness of coming back. She remembered with yearning how her mother had loved the place. To the memories it held they would add more, with a blessed sense of continuity in a world of change.

From the gateway where there had once been a rustic arch, she looked across the lane towards the War Memorial.

'You're shivering.'

He had come quietly. She felt his arm around her without surprise. He was always there when she needed him.

'I was remembering.'

In its hollow between trees the memorial, once large and awe-inspiring, was unexpectedly slender and vulnerable.

'That faint line.' Margot peered and pointed. 'Can you see? It isn't a crack?'

'Not yet.'

In time it would come. Like the Quaker schoolroom and the old rectory, the column would tilt, sink and crumble, taking the names of all the dead soldiers with it into oblivion. Katie was right. Nothing on earth was safe, not even the earth itself.

And yet, in recompense, how beautiful it was – with sunlight shimmering on young leaves in the sheltered garden and the old house awaiting their return.